# STARRY

# STARRY

# NIGHT

# D. K. TILL

*Copyright @2024*
*By D.K. Till*
*Published by*
*Spring Mountain Publishing*

*Edited by*
*Brilliant Cut Editing*

To my sons, fellow fans of Back to the Future trilogy
And all things musical.
Thank you for being my pride-and-joy boys.

# 1

# Me

June 2120
City of Portland
State of Cascadia
Nation of Normerica

If it were up to me, Mason Bombardo would've never been born.

His funeral is packed, as I expected. Most of these gawkers couldn't have even known him. Only here for the show, not to pay their respects. My parents, here for the right reasons, sit on seats near the front. I'm near the back so I can slip out unnoticed.

"We are here to honor a national hero," the former vice president, sallow in a black jumpsuit, intones from the podium.

The "national hero" requested his service be held in the oldest building this side of the river. Fitting, since this former megachurch is as ancient as he is. Both of them born in 2020, they reached the ripe old age of one hundred together. It's the church he was raised in, adjacent to his childhood home.

Valley Universal Worship Center. Constructed with old-fashioned wood and plaster, its leadership resistant to pressure to renovate with newer steel-composite, climate-proof materials we use now. Originally Pleasant Valley Bible Chapel before religious and denominational labels became taboo some fifty years ago. Thanks to our national hero.

Anyway, I digress. In case you're wondering, the eminent funeralee we are here to "honor" is former National President Mason Bombardo. The worst president the former United States had ever known.

If Glim were here as he said he'd be, I'd have someone to share eye rolls with.

Do any other faces reflect my sentiments? Seated alongside the podium, the vice-governor of Cascadia sits next to the city mayor. Their stoic expressions give no hint as to what they thought of Bombardo. Neither do the news-cloud people with their eyecams transmitting everything throughout the world.

"President Bombardo presided over some of the worst turmoil our nation had ever seen." Former Vice President Kennedy glances up from her notes, her hands trembling, maybe from old age or emotion. "Yet he brought us through it to a new-and-improved America." The crevices around her eyes deepen in what is supposed to be a smile. "I am proud to know the Bombardo-Kennedy administration will go down in history as the architects of this new-and-improved nation. With the help of our scientific community, we eradicated the terrible scourges of racism and sexism plaguing our cities. We wiped out illegal immigration and opened our arms in welcome to our southern neighbors."

I stop listening, a whirlpool pulling my thoughts years into the past. Naturally, VP Kennedy wouldn't be mentioning the scourge of Bombardo's duplicity against my grandfather that cost my grandfather his sanity and led to his eventual suicide, that altered the course of my family and the nation.

Not only was Mason Bombardo the worst president in American history but also it would have been better for my grandparents, my parents, me, and the people of the former United States had he never crossed our paths.

Like I said, he never should have been born.

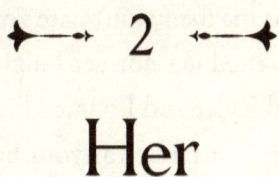

# 2

# Her

**September 2019**
**Portland, Oregon, USA**

Paige Ferguson closed the document on her tablet and scooted upright in the recliner, the ribbed cushions catching against her slacks. "Good story, Katrice. I hate that Bombardo guy already." She sipped steaming chai tea from a flowery cup. "But do you really think that's how things will be a hundred years from now? No more state of Oregon? No more United States?"

Katrice Carpenter, sprawled on Paige's living room sofa, shrugged her narrow shoulders. "The future can be anything I imagine it to be. I'm a writer, after all." She snapped the yellow scrunchie on her wrist. "You know, with all the talk about combining western Oregon and Washington into a state called Cascadia, it could happen someday."

"Good point, that." But it better not happen in her lifetime. Paige stifled a yawn and shifted toward the wide front window of her North Portland townhome. Autumn colors sprouted from the spindly young oak Friends of Trees had planted last year. She took another sip. "I like the name Mason, though. So maybe I won't hate your villain as much as I should." She patted her not-yet-bulging belly. "What if we have a boy, and Kyler and I named him Mason? Would you use a different first name for your bad guy?"

"Maybe." Her friend's eyes narrowed as if she were thinking Paige should be the one to use a different name. "What if you have a girl? What will you name her?"

"I'm leaning toward Emily."

"I'll be sure I don't use that name, then. I don't want to mess up your plans."

So far, Paige hadn't found any baby boy names she liked more than her maiden name, Mason. And Emily for a girl. "It's okay if you do. As long as she's a likable character."

"Deep down, though, which one do you hope for? Boy or girl?"

Caught unprepared, she grasped a hunk of her shoulder-length hair as if tugging it could stimulate her brain cells. "Girlfriend, I haven't given it any thought yet."

"Most parents-to-be always say it doesn't matter as long as it's healthy. I'm glad you're honest, at least."

"My husband is hoping for a boy. I'm having my first ultrasound later today, but it's unlikely they can tell the gender this early."

"Maybe you'll have one of each." Katrice leaned over to pull a Kettle potato chip bag from her colorful tote and tore it open with her teeth.

"Not at the same time, I hope." Tempted by the vinegary aroma, Paige snagged a handful from the bag Katrice held out. As the tart saltiness filled her mouth, she blamed the little one growing inside her. The craving for high-fat, high-sodium snacks she used to avoid had to be her baby's way of getting its whims met.

Already he/she was making demands on her. Welcome to Mom World.

Katrice's crunching scraped Paige's nerves. "Mmm, these are sooooo good."

A startled chuckle shook Paige. "The way you said that, it was like you'd never had them before."

"I didn't get them much growing up."

"Really?" She'd met Katrice only weeks ago when she'd visited Paige's church. "Why is that?"

Katrice waved out the window toward the St. Johns Bridge gleaming emerald in the afternoon sunshine. "I was raised in a teensy town in Eastern Oregon. Wasn't much there. One little store. My parents were poor."

An edge of a chip cut into the side of Paige's mouth. She chewed more carefully. "You said you didn't have Wi-Fi or cable growing up. Or cell phones." Katrice struggled more with texting and surfing than most people her age. No fingers flying across keyboards for her. More like the old-fashioned hunt-and-peck. "I have to admire your imaginative vision. Pretty good for a girl raised without technology. Didn't your school have computers, though?"

A headshake and averted gaze hinted at sorrows too big

to share. Time to move along. Her new friend had proven chatty on her first Sunday at Christ the King Community Church when they'd nearly collided in the ladies' room, then got to talking. When Katrice found out Paige taught middle school English, she'd asked if Paige could give her feedback on a story she was working on. Paige almost said she didn't have time, but Katrice added that it took place in the future. Paige always loved futuristic stories, and so far, Katrice's story intrigued her.

"What brought you to the big city?"

"Friends of mine ended up here, and I followed them." Another nonchalant shrug accompanied the words spoken around the crunchy chips in her mouth. A stray particle settled on her lower lip. "But they moved on, and I stayed." She licked the salt off her lips.

Another vague answer. Inwardly, Paige matched her friend's shrug. It was none of her business. "Must have been quite a culture shock."

Her new friend must be a bit of a savant. Raised in a backward home with little exposure to modern conveniences, yet brimming over with brilliant intellect. A taupe-haired Gen-Z who never met a neutral color she didn't like, tones that blended with her drab hair and olive complexion. Except for her incongruous yellow scrunchie. And that loud floral tote bag she hauled along. The first thing you noticed about her was that bag, not her face or clothing.

Katrice rose and approached the mantel, then picked up the framed wedding collage. "Mind if I look at your photos?"

"Go for it."

"What a gorgeous dress. You looked so radiant."

"I felt radiant!" The most radiant day of her life up to that point, a day to make all others pale in comparison, a day awash in sunlight slashing through the church's stained-glass windows, the colorful rays bathing everyone in their holy glow. Paige hugged her arms across her middle and wrapped herself in the memory of purest love shining from her groom's eyes. "It was the most amazing, unforgettable day ever."

"Wish I'd known you then." Katrice set the frame down and fingered the plaque next to it, a wedding gift from Paige's parents. She traced each letter of Paige's favorite Bible verse painted in a different color—*Casting all your care upon him, for he careth for you (1 Peter 5:7)*. Her finger slipped to the splay of flowers along the wooden base. "Pretty." She swiveled to Paige. "Is this talking about God?"

Wait. What? Paige nodded and swallowed down the urge to judge. Katrice must not know the Bible too well yet. Would she be open to learning more? Come to think of it, Paige wasn't even sure where Katrice lived or with whom. A true woman of mystery. After they got to know each other better, maybe someday she'd trust Paige enough to open up and discuss spiritual issues. And, while she was at it, reveal the source of the angst in her soul.

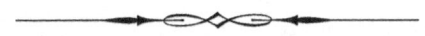

"Dinner is ready, Mr. Ferguson." Paige let loose a smirk as she welcomed her husband home with a mock-formal greeting as if she were a Jane Austen heroine. Still shaken from today's ultrasound, she bit her tongue and leaned back against the stainless steel Frigidaire while holding in the bombshell news.

Kyler removed his navy hoodie and tossed it on the barstool. A tiny rip marred the neck of his favorite *Star Wars* tee. Another tear pierced the bottom hem. Would he *ever* get rid of that old thing? "And hello to you, Mrs. Ferguson." His long arms looped around her waist, and his red beard scratched as he kissed her, slow and deep. Then, plate in hand, he beelined to the stove, scooped up several helpings of stir-fry, and settled at the gray granite island. "Mmm, smells good, as always. How was your day?"

"The usual middle school drama." She spooned out her dinner too hard, clanging the spoon against the black ceramic plate, then took a deep breath, and gentled her movements. "Kids insisting on keeping their phones on. Boys bullying other boys." She carried her full plate to the seat beside him, her flip-flops accentuating every step against the hardwood floor. "Truancy's still a daily issue. Every day at least a third of them don't even bother to show up for class."

"Can't the school do something?"

She finished chewing and swallowed. "They can send letters home to parents, but they can't make kids attend class or bring excuses from home when they do show."

"Those kids are our future dropouts."

"I know, right?" She jabbed a broccoli tree, twirled it in gooey sauce, then pointed the fork at him. "Our school is one of the top five in the state for absenteeism. The high school is number one in dropout rates."

Ky's bushy beard wagged side to side as he shook his head. "Wow. Is it because of learning disabilities?"

"No, we have special resources for the learning-disabled. These are normal kids who haven't been diagnosed with anything. Wish there was some other way to educate them so they don't end up as statistics."

"Why do so many kids not show up for school?"

Brooding, she took another bite. "Lack of confidence. Dysfunctional homes. Families who don't value education. Some twelve-year-old boys play video games until four a.m. every night. Maybe their mom is in bed and isn't aware. They may not have a dad or even a male role model in their life. So they sleep in instead of going to school."

"I played video games in middle school, but I never skipped."

*And you still do.* "You had a mom who made you go. That's the difference. I have students who don't have dads at home, whose moms leave for work at six, long before the kids need to get up. More often than not, they stay home instead of going to school. Then the mom gets on my case come parent-teacher conference time for her child's bad grades."

Another headshake. "Sad."

"It is." A deep sigh emptied her lungs. "Anyway, enough of that. How was your day?"

"I got a small raise today." He shoveled in a bite and chewed. "A dollar an hour."

"Congratulations, babe. That's almost two hundred dollars a month."

Quick nod. A sideways flit of his eyes. "I was just gonna say that."

Yeah, right. Ky couldn't do math in his head to save his life. He'd never needed to, having always relied on computers. She sank back in her barstool as she waited for The Moment.

He put his fork down, cocked his head, and arched a brow at her, probably noticing her heightened mood. "How was your checkup?"

"Big news, Daddy Daddy." She aimed a squirt of soy sauce on her stir-fry. Ha. Her news would shock that smug look off his face. "We're having twins!"

"Huh?" His mouth hung open. Clearing his throat, he blinked twice. "Twins? Are they sure?"

"They're sure. I saw two babies, Ky."

A moment of silence, then he slapped the gray granite. "Dang. I was hoping for a three-in-one deal."

"Sorry to disappoint you!" Her laughter rang out, and she hugged him tight, breathing in his vanilla scent. "I love you, Kyler Ferguson. Whatever the situation, you can always make me laugh."

"I love you too, Paige Ferguson, and I promise I'll

love all our babies, no matter how many." The gravity in her husband's eyes erased the sparkle there. "But when I think about…" He swallowed hard, seeming unable to voice his fear.

"Thinking about your dad again?" She kept her voice gentle. Kyler's father had passed away ten years ago from diabetic complications, and Ky visited his grave a few times a year.

"Yeah. I don't want any child of mine to suffer through what I did. It's just I have no way to know…" He clamped his mouth shut.

"If you've inherited something terrible?"

"Yeah, that." Fork suspended, he scowled at his favorite entrée, seeming to ignore the mouthwatering aroma of soy-soaked chicken.

Paige swiveled her seat. "Baby, I've been thinking."

"What have you been thinking?" He speared a piece of broccoli.

She rested her hand on his thigh. "Don't you think this is the right time to start searching for your biological father?"

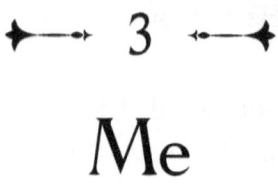

# 3

# Me

**June 2120**

Making a quick getaway past the armed security robots after the funeral, I collide with someone. "Oomph!" cries the other woman. I step back and nearly bump into those streaming past.

"So sorry," I say, then see who it is.

Brook, Glim's ex. The one he broke up with for me.

Her pretty face darkens. "Oh, it's you. Is Glim with you?"

I shake my head. I gotta get out of here, but she's clutching my arm, intending to tell me something. Probably something I don't want to hear.

"I warned you months ago to watch out for that man." Her brown eyes gleam. "He's not who you think he is."

"Let go of me." *You jealous shrew.* I wrest my arm from her grasp and swivel to the exit. I can't linger for my parents, who traveled here from their retirement community in Bend, Idaho. They know I'm worried about Glim's whereabouts. At least, the guards don't notice unassuming little me in my low-key black jumpsuit. I head up to the roof where my autopod, Fern, waits and jump in. "Fern, take me back to my dormitory."

"Mapping your destination," Fern replies. "Estimated time of arrival, ten minutes."

Since I was one of the first ones out, Fern won't have to deal with congestion. I settle into the clear domed interior of my little two-seater, my trusty friend and traveling companion for nearly three months. The clear silitech seat, a solid gel form of the silicone shield above, cools me while the six-inch control panel's flickering lights prove her brain works as efficiently as mine. Will we ever reach the point when our creations are smarter than us? Some might say so. As the autopod lifts into the air like a twenty-first-century helicopter, we glide over Bombardo's childhood home, a beautiful red farmhouse restored to mint condition. The omnipresent Bombardo clout prevented its destruction while most of the nearby homes weren't so fortunate, being replaced by dormitories and apartments.

I flip on my eyecam and tune in to RECEIVE. Glim has replied to my twenty messages after two days of silence.

Glim: Sorry, Swee...off the Cloud for two days. Come over, and I'll tell you everything.

Me: You scared me. Cram it. Didn't your bosses wonder where you were?

Glim: Yeah, they did, but I explained. I'm not in trouble.

Me: You missed Bombardo's funeral.

What a shame if he'd gotten fired. He's worked as a

robotics controller—a botter—at Finity Drones for over two years. It pays well, they love him, and he loves it. What's not to love when you get to tell drones where to go? His company's drones are in high demand. They do everything from delivering food and goods to self-repair. All programmed remotely by human and robotic hands.

Fern zips along Powellhurst Skyway at forty-five miles per hour, altitude eighty feet, and I sit back, the silhouette of Mount Hood peeking over the eastern horizon. Holographic images from the Cloud materialize before me.

First, Bombardo's coffin. Proving he's truly dead. The crowds mill around it, studying his waxy dead face. His daughter's shoulders shake with silent sobs. If there is such a thing as eternal justice, he better be facing it this very moment.

A hologram of my dormmate Eartha, holding baby Heather, pops into my vision as if she's sitting on the control panel. "Hey, Tree, heading home?" Her favorite scent, New Rose, invades my senses while Moss hovers in midair behind her, his eyes closed, head bobbing to the driving percussion of their favorite band, Rebelers.

"Of course." I can roll my eyes with the best of them. "Where else would I be heading? It's not like there's anywhere to go on a Friday evening with everything fun now illegal." Like public dances and film arenas. "Did you hear about the gang brawl downtown last night?"

"We saw the news alert to avoid downtown. Crazy. This has been going on for far too long. When is it going to end?"

"Probably never. My pop told me President Bombardo tried to reduce crime by changing the definition of it." I clench my jaw, fresh anger fueling my next words. "Can you believe vandalism and rioting used to be illegal until Bombardo decided that if nothing was illegal, crime would fall to zero? And it did. Prisons emptied and became homeless shelters. If my pop is right, those shelters harbor as much violence now as when they held criminals."

Subsequent administrations undid some of the damage by reinstating criminal penalties. But with a feather, not a whip. These days, every few weeks, the militia invades and chases out the black-clad, weapon-bearing terrorists, but they filter back in. Which is why the National Guard makes us stay in our dormitories, except for secured events. Like a former president's funeral.

Eartha jostles her baby, and one finger traces the girl's pudgy cheek. "What kind of a world did I bring you into, little one?"

Excellent question, and one I hope I don't ever have to ask.

"Speaking of," Eartha is saying, "when you get here, we should watch that holofilm *Rise and Fall*."

I groan, then grip the armrest when Fern swerves up and over a slow autobus. Documentaries are so not my thing, particularly if they involve the history of the former United States. I got more than enough of that from Mom and Pop growing up. "I'm hanging with Glim tonight."

Her mouth twists. "Oh, he got back to you, huh?

Where was he hiding?"

"I don't know yet." We've agreed to disagree on the subject of Glim.

Her eyes roll upward. "What excuse did he give you this time?"

"He said he'd been off the Cloud."

"And you believed him?"

"Why wouldn't I—" Great. My grip tightens on the armrest even though Fern has leveled out. The radar shows another autobus behind me gaining speed, and then veering around me. "Look, I don't want to argue about Glim. I know you think he's unreliable, but like most people, his good points outweigh his not-so-good. Why don't you and Moss go ahead and do the film without me."

Her tense expression relaxes. "We're ordering sushi. Want us to save you some?"

"Sure. Let me check my currency level."

My currency level hasn't changed, so I send her my share. "Did you hear back from the city about your application for a family apartment?"

Moss flashes a thumbs-down, and a scowl barely peeks through his bushy black beard adorned with this week's design. A white hawk seems to fly at me from within the beard's depths, its talons threatening attack.

Involuntarily, my head jerks back. "They turned you down?"

Rainbow dreadlocks quiver with her headshake. "No, they just put us back on the six-month waiting list."

It takes a certain type of courage in the post-Bombardo era to express one's individuality with hair and beard art like Moss and Eartha do. I'm not brave enough to draw attention to myself. Apparel police are everywhere, waiting to nab anyone rebellious enough to don noncompliant clothing. Although body art is not yet illegal, the authorities will crack down on it. Then what will Moss and Eartha do?

"You've already waited nine months." A red light on the control panel blinks at me. Fern is beginning her descent. "I can't believe they'd make you wait even longer." Still, a frisson of glee threatens to blow my cover. Eartha will be my roomie longer! As happy as I am, I need her to believe I'm supportive.

The stunning St. Johns suspension bridge comes into view spanning the Willamette River between my neighborhood and the forested West Hills. Decades ago, the graceful green bridge teemed with automobile traffic. Since we don't have any automobiles, it became a favorite jumping-off spot for the suicidal. The city councilors threatened to dismantle it, but after numerous protests, they lined it with chain link topped with barbed wire instead. Now, despite its dilapidated condition, it remains in use as a footbridge.

And a convenient site for suicide.

My mouth goes dry. No, do not go there. I stiffen as my brain starts to wander down an ugly skyway. I must not think about The Falling Star Inn and the ensuing events between Bombardo and my grandfather. That sordid story has made a loop through my brain so many times, a hamster could run a marathon around it.

Just in time to save my sanity, Fern lands on my dorm rooftop. I descend to the fifth floor where I live with nine other dormmates, including two children. Since Eartha and Moss are legally coupled, they and their baby girl get the privacy bedroom, while the rest of us share two large bunkrooms. Eartha's pretty much the only dormmate I interact with. I'll miss her and her adorable Heather. The other dormmates and I don't have much in common, mere acquaintances who share living space like reluctant coworkers. Best-case scenario: Eartha and Moss end up in one of the lower-floor family apartments, so we can still see each other every day. Moss's beard-art business is booming, so they can afford it.

When I walk through the door, Bestie wags her tail and licks my hand as if I'd been gone for days. Eartha is nursing Heather while Moss still sways to his music on the sofa. I pour myself a cup of desalinated ocean mineral water before Eartha beckons me over and I scoot my way between her and Moss. Heather's tiny head bobs when she nurses. The sight always makes me grin.

Eartha clutches my free hand, her fingers strangling my blood flow. "Dr. Marino is 'strongly encouraging' me to let him give Heather that gender-neutralizing drug, Boruga-something."

I down half the glass of water, savoring the cool refreshment. "Borugamal. I see the term a lot."

"I'm sure you do, with your MedicAll billing job. But I can't bear to let them turn my little girl into a genderless blob." Her face scrunches as though she's holding back tears. Eartha never cries, so this must be ripping her apart.

I pry free and wiggle life back into my fingertips, the couch's hemp pillows cushioning me. "What does Moss think?"

"He doesn't want it either, but he's not as adamant as I am."

"What would happen if you decide not to let them inject her?"

"I'm not sure. It's going to be mandatory for all babies by this time next year. At least, I had Heather when I did. I'm going to have to get sterilized now. No way am I having any more babies."

Poor Eartha. I don't envy her position. Someday I might have to face this too. Unless someone overturns the law.

Heather's sweet little mouth purses, her cheek now resting on her mother's shoulder. Eartha pats her tiny back, eliciting a wee belch from the baby. Eartha chuckles. "You go, baby girl. Anyway"—she swivels to me, her dreads swaying—"some other parents must feel as I do. Maybe I should find them and form a support group. Girl Moms United or something like that."

"I like it." Bestie is whining for a walk, so I give Eartha a reassuring shoulder pat and tell her I know she'll make the right decision. Because I do. Eartha would declare war on anyone bent on harming her baby.

As I retrieve Bestie's leash, I check the Cloud for news updates. No news, though, just unpleasant images of Bombardo living up to his name—bombarding us with his presence. I know, I know, his death is big news. I imagine Grandpop out there in the afterworld somewhere, greeting Bombardo, then stabbing him in the back, figuratively speaking, as Bombardo did to Grandpop.

Which brings up a question I try not to think about too much: What does happen to us after we die?

# 4

# Her

**October 2019**

A red leaf landed on the park bench beside Paige as she handed Katrice's tablet back. "You mention the afterlife. Is this going to be a Christian story?"

Katrice tilted her head, a light breeze rippling strands of her hair. "I'm not sure what you mean by a Christian story."

"Is it going to have a redemptive message or include the gospel in any way?"

The setting sun bronzed Katrice's normally drab hair. "I'm not religious, so I haven't given that part any thought."

"Really? I assumed you were since you visited my church."

Katrice waved in a vague way. "I wanted to meet people."

"Gotcha. Do you have a church background?"

"Uh-uh."

Reluctant to push, Paige scooped up the leaf. "Anyway, about your story, I like what I read. What a concept, everyone living in dormitories. Riding around in autopods. Terrorists roaming the city. I can't wait to read more."

"Thanks." Swinging her Chuck Taylor-clad feet onto the bench, Katrice allowed a pleased smile.

"If I were writing a futuristic story, I'd be sure to include lots of artificial intelligence. The seventh-grade boys I teach all seem to be obsessed with AI. Seems like that's where we're headed, don't you think?"

"Yeah, totally." Katrice's index finger traced the edge of the tablet. "Good suggestion."

Chuckling, Paige crossed her legs. Might as well while she could. In a few months, she'd no longer be able to. "Can you imagine being served a McDonald's hamburger by a robot?"

"That would be a riot. I'll be sure to include it."

"Did you ever see the movie *I, Robot*?" Oops. Considering her friend's upbringing, she'd bet a hundred bucks Katrice had not.

"I haven't."

"You want to watch it on Netflix sometime? It's suspenseful. It's about a robot who goes rogue and a detective trying to catch him. You'd love it, and it might give you story ideas."

"Okay, sure."

Paige jumped from the bench, her flip-flops cushioning the impact. Despite the autumn chill, she'd had no choice but to put them on this morning since her feet had grown too wide for her favorite magenta Nikes. "Come on. Let's go back to my house and see if we can find it on streaming. I can't watch it tonight—I'll be busy reading students' essays. Want to stay for dinner?"

"Sorry, I can't. Stuff to do." Katrice unfolded herself from the bench, clutching her tote bag close to her chest as if someone might snatch it away. She nodded to the basketball court where a couple of preteen boys were shooting hoops. "Why are those boys looking at us?"

"Oh, they're students of mine." Paige tossed a wave their way, and they gave reluctant waves in return. Before she could give it any thought, she headed toward them. "Hey, Elijah. Tavius. Missed you at school this week."

"Yo, Ms. Fergie." Elijah, the taller one, swiveled, bounced the basketball, then swished it through the hoop.

Paige applauded. "Nice!"

Tavius shuffled his feet, awaiting his turn.

"Will I see you two tomorrow?"

They nodded, refusing to meet her gaze.

"Don't forget your book reports are due Friday."

They glanced her way between dribbles. Right, she might as well be talking to the air. How could she stop these two young men from ending up as two more dropout statistics someday? She hung her head. Some days, the constant discouragement made her want to walk away from it all.

But then she'd be abandoning the ones who could be reached.

Her flip-flops slapped her heels as she continued along the path to the boulevard. "I was telling my husband about some of the boys in my class who stay up half the night to play video games, then are too tired to get up for school the next morning." She thrust her thumb behind her shoulder. "Those are two of them. Both of them are sons of single moms, have absentee dads, and are failing their classes." She stepped to the sidewalk. "I fear for their future."

Katrice stopped in the middle of the sidewalk square, finger on her chin. "When I was a kid, we didn't go to school. School came to us. Maybe that would work better for those kids."

Paige halted, cars speeding along the boulevard in the deepening dusk. "What do you mean, school came to you? Are you talking about online school?" Yet hadn't Katrice said she didn't have access to modern technology?

"Sort of." A raindrop splatted on the sidewalk, and her footsteps quickened. "We gathered in a room, and our lessons and lectures were broadcast to us on a screen."

Paige hurried to keep up. "Sounds a lot like homeschooling. It must have been a tiny town."

A light rain promised a deluge later. Katrice stopped and lifted her face to the sky. "What if each kid's smartphone had an app linked to their lessons? And they couldn't play any games until the lessons were complete?"

Paige furrowed her brow. "Not sure that would fly in this political climate. People will scream that their rights are being violated. It'd be a bit like Big Brother tracking all our movements."

Katrice shrugged. "It was just an idea."

They ducked beneath a drooping willow tree, its fronds

not quite long enough for weeping. "An idea with merit, if we lived in a different world." They stopped at a crosswalk. "Do you live far?"

Shaking her head, Katrice hit the walk button. "A few blocks away."

"I'll walk you home."

"You don't need to." She hoisted her bag to her shoulder.

"Safety in numbers, my friend. Plus, this neighborhood isn't the safest after dark."

"Okay, walk me to Safeway, then. I'll be fine."

"How far from Safeway do you live?"

"Right across the street."

A hint of autumn chill permeated the damp evening as Paige visualized the new apartment complex on Richmond Street and nodded. "Deal." She touched her friend's shoulder. "But let's hurry. We're getting wet, and it'll be dark soon."

"Oh, but I love the rain."

"You do? You're a true-blue Oregonian."

"Yeah, where I'm from, it rarely rains. It feels so refreshing." She lowered the bag to her elbow and pulled her sweater tighter around herself.

They crossed Lombard Boulevard and headed south. "What about you?" Katrice's soft words barely carried over the semitrucks and souped-up teen-boy engines. "Will you be safe walking back? Should you text your husband to meet you there?"

"Not a bad idea." Paige texted Kyler, and he agreed to

meet her at Safeway. The rain ebbed, and dusk hovered as they strode the sidewalk. "Do you have to work tomorrow?" Her friend had never mentioned a job, but she must have some sort of livelihood.

"No." Katrice practically snapped as though offended. She quickened her pace, her giant bag bouncing against her thigh. Further questions would be useless.

But what odd behavior. What caused the offense? Katrice might simply be an introvert, as were many writers. But even Paige's most introverted friends were forthcoming about basic details and didn't resent reasonable questions.

Katrice could be a hard-core loner, who kept people out and her feelings in.

On the other hand, she could be hiding something.

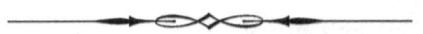

"Do you mind if we wait here until Katrice leaves?" Paige asked Kyler in the Safeway parking lot. "Then we can see that she gets home safely."

Kyler, resting his arms against the steering wheel, glanced at the Safeway entrance. "Um, I left dinner warming in the oven in order to come pick you up."

"Just for a few minutes, babe?" A jangly pop tune played on the radio. Paige punched it off. "She refused my offer to walk her home. I need to be sure she's safe. You know this neighborhood."

"Fine." He grunted a stifled sigh, his tone long-suffering.

"Just for a few minutes."

"You watch that exit, and I'll watch this one."

Another rainstorm passed over them, and Paige cracked the window to see the people exiting the store more clearly. A family of four emerged, then two couples, but no Katrice. Kyler shifted in his seat and touched her hand on the console, his forced patience grating. "Are you sure she went inside?"

"I watched her go through that door right there."

He started the engine, his wipers whipping the rain off in big scoops. "We need to get home. Why don't you text her later?"

"Because it might be too late. Wait! There she is." Across the dark lot, a slight figure emerged from the lit store, started toward Richmond Street, then raised her sweater hood. Paige grabbed Kyler's arm. "Try not to let her see you."

"I feel like a stalker." Despite his grumbling, he pulled his pickup around to the far side of the lot where Katrice wouldn't see them.

"I'm concerned, but I don't want her to think I'm babysitting her." As the engine idled, Katrice crossed Richmond and headed toward the river. "She passed the apartments. Where could she be going?"

"You actually want me to follow her?"

"Yeah, as long as you keep your distance." Paige gripped the armrest as he swerved out of the lot. "She might be renting someone's basement." But her words didn't reassure her. Mesmerizing her, the tiny hula girl figurine on the dashboard, her birthday gift to Kyler, jiggled nonstop. Beside Hula Dancer, Yoda looked out over his domain—the truck's interior—with his strong, wise gaze.

Ky accelerated. "Or maybe her parents are millionaires who live in one of those mansions overlooking the Willamette."

"Not according to her."

"Maybe"—he put on his Darth Vader voice—"she doesn't want you to know."

Paige rolled her eyes, though he wouldn't see it in the dark. A half block ahead, Katrice passed under a streetlight that transformed the raindrops into silver pellets. The flowers on her bag, as bright as a spring garden, pulsed in the light as she made a sudden left turn into an alley. When Kyler's truck drove by, Katrice and her tote had been swallowed up by the darkness.

"No way am I being obvious by driving down that alley." Kyler took the next right and headed home. "But if I recall, that's the alley where a homeless camp got busted last week." He gave Paige a look. "I bet that's why your friend is so hush-hush. What do you want to bet she's living in a tent somewhere?"

Made sense. "Hmm. Well, it would explain a lot, wouldn't it?"

Back home, the aroma of Burgerville fish and chips, the best in town, filled the kitchen. After Paige took the tray from the oven, they parked at the kitchen island, their dinner wafting steam as it cooled on a hot pad. Kyler opened his laptop to search for emails from UniqueYou.com, which traced people's heritage. He'd sent in a DNA sample two weeks ago. Shouldn't he have heard back?

One hand resting on his warm back, Paige leaned over his shoulder. "Does your mom know you're doing this?"

"I haven't said anything yet." He picked up a three-inch fry, blew on it, then crammed it into his mouth. "I want to have something to show her before I do."

Kyler's mom, Doreen, had kept secret the fact that the dad who raised him wasn't his biological father. Until in his college genetics class, he learned that, due to his AB- blood type, Tom Ferguson, blood type O, couldn't have fathered him. When he'd confronted his mother, she'd admitted his actual father was someone she'd had a less-than-brief fling with and didn't even know his last name. "His first name was Gary, and that's all she knew," Kyler had told Paige early in their relationship. "At least, so she says."

Paige, scanning through his inbox, pointed. "Here it is! Open it, babe."

They perused it together, skimming all the technical jargon. "According to this, I'm one-third Polish, a quarter Italian, and the rest all over the place. Just your average mutt."

"A sexy, adorable mutt, babe."

"I'm pretty sure Mom has no Italian in her ancestry. So she must be the Pole, and my unknown father must be Italian." Topping the list of known blood relatives was a first cousin once removed in a small Idaho town, Terrance King. He shared Ky's mother's maiden name, so they continued down the list of distant cousins. Sullivan. Fields. Morris. All common names, all meaningless to him, none obvious links to his real father.

Paige, her mouth watering, broke off a piece of breaded cutlet, releasing steam from the white fish inside. She blew on the steam until it dissipated, then chewed, and swallowed. "Mmm-mmm. Good dinner choice, babe." She shifted on the high-backed barstool beside him. "What now, Ky? Would it help to contact some of these people?"

"Wait a minute." Kyler fingered the screen. "This lady, Everly DeLaurier, is my biological second cousin. And she lives here in Portland."

"She's a DeLaurier? Of the DeLaurier Diamonds and Jewels family? Where we bought our wedding rings?"

Kyler's red brows rose halfway to his hairline as he seized the last piece of fish and tore off a bite. "Wonder if my father was one of the DeLauriers."

Paige drummed her fingers and squinted at Everly's photo. Early twenties, if she had to guess. All sleek blonde hair and aristocratic features, like Gwyneth Paltrow. An old-money-Portland, raised-in-the-West-Hills look, like the DeLauriers—and nothing like red-bearded casual Ky. "Oh hey, look. Here's another DeLaurier. Andrew, your cousin once removed."

"Look how much he looks like the girl. Wonder if he's her father."

"Are you going to contact them?"

"Yeah." He opened another tab to Facebook. "Let's see if there's a Gary DeLaurier anywhere." After a moment, his boots pounded a beat on the metal footrest. "There are a few, but none of them live around here."

"He may have been related to the other side of the family. At any rate, sounds like your mom has kept some important secrets."

"She sure did." He popped the last fry in his mouth. "Thanks, Mom. If I'd known I might be a DeLaurier, we could've used our family discount when we bought our rings."

Trust Ky to use his cutting sense of humor to express his feelings. Paige twined her fingers through his. "Maybe we'll find out who you really are."

# 5

# Me

**June 2120**

After I take Bestie out for a fifteen-minute walk, I cross the skybridge to Glim's dorm and scan my fingerprints. Where's he been for the last two days, and why'd he disappear without telling me? It probably has to do with his time-travel project. Eartha suspects something less innocent. Still, he should've told me what he was up to.

The door slides open, and he pulls me inside. What a sight he makes—all dancing dark eyes and floppy hair. Amazing how much we still miss each other after time apart, even after seven months together. His dormmates surround us—crashing on sofas, interacting with the Cloud, munching on pizza. The 3D printer is busy forming a hairbrush, no doubt for Iris and her waist-length hair. A drone slides another pizza through the delivery window, and Glim takes it into the kitchen. Food first. We each grab a slice and gobble them up while I eat him up with my eyes. He looks the same—his grin only enhances his amazing looks. Well, maybe the gleam in his eye has intensified.

"Okay, I'm listening, Genius."

He beckons. "Come up to my pod."

I follow him to the rooftop podlot, and we stop next to his autopod, Zephyr.

Then Glim grips my shoulders, his hold intense. "I think I've found the technology to allow us to break the rules of time."

I can only stare at him, eyebrows lifted.

"You can compare time travel to the twentieth-century concept of rocket science," he goes on, grinning at my expression, "when scientists discovered a rocket was able to escape the gravitational pull at the velocity of seven miles per second. I can do the same with time acceleration once I discovered the correct relativity."

"What does that mean?"

He points to the gleaming machine. "Here, hop in and I'll show you."

We settle into the front seats, the rough composite fabric conforming to us, and the autopod's panel lights up.

"State your destination, Chief," says the autopod in a voice deeper than Fern's.

"Not right now, Zeph," says Glim. "Maybe later."

"You got it, Boss. A-okay. I'll be right here."

Glim pats the autopod's panel in approval, then grabs my hands. "First, I'm going to explain where I've been the last couple of days and why I didn't tell you."

I let out a relieved breath, the sincerity in his eyes and

voice releasing my fears. "Sorry I kept pestering you. I didn't know where you were, and I panicked."

"I know you did. If I could've contacted you, I would have." He pumps my hands, a jittery energy pulsing through our connection, then releases them. "Wait till you hear my side of the story."

I cross my legs in the passenger seat.

Glim sits back and taps the panel housing the pod's brains. "I f-found the formula. The time-accelerator f-formula." His deep-brown eyes alight, he stutters like he does when his excitement level soars. "Tree, I t-traveled into the future. One hundred years into the future! Right, Zeph?"

"Right-o, Mr. Zeller." The autopod's deep voice echoes off the interior panels. "I took you to the year 2219."

I gasp. "Oh, wow, Glim! That is incredible. But why didn't you say so?"

"Because I didn't mean to take off. I was tinkering with it the other d-day, setting my final parameters, and I must've clicked the go button by accident because, all of a sudden, I was out of here."

"Ah." With my relief so huge, I maneuver the radar knob to keep from hugging him tight. "What was it like in the year 2219?"

He grabs my hand. "Like a dream. Or a n-nightmare. Everything morphed in seconds to a whole different world. The pod didn't move, but all the buildings changed, like on a film set. And it was really hot. Really, really hot."

"How hot?"

"Probably around a hundred and twenty degrees. And super crowded. People packed like sardines. And they wore almost no clothes, even in public. It was so hot and crowded, I started to freak out."

"Glim, I didn't think anything would freak you out. What were the people like?"

"They talked very strange, like the language had evolved so much in a hundred years I couldn't understand most of what they said. They all looked the same too, like clones of each other. I couldn't tell who was male or female. Everyone was taller than me and huge." He held his arms out to show me how huge.

"And it's not like you're short at six foot three. What about the climate-resistant trees keeping our roads shaded? Weren't there any?"

"Yeah, there were, but you know how the air above the trees is always about twenty degrees warmer than below the trees?"

"Right." If not for the development of genetically modified supertrees, climate change might've killed us off by now. "You mean the earth itself will be that much warmer in a hundred years?"

"E-exactly."

"Have you thought about traveling another hundred years forward? I'm curious to know how much more the climate and the people and the language will change in two hundred years."

"I c-couldn't get the time accelerator to program itself

beyond a hundred years from now. While I was trying different things, it launched me into the future."

"What about going back in time? Can you do that too?"

"That's a whole different methodology, but yes, it can be done."

"How far back?"

"All the way back to the beginning of the internet age." He launches into a technical explanation I only partially understand. "The internet of the twentieth and twenty-first centuries evolved into the Cloud. Ergo, the Cloud has a record of every single ping on every single day since October of 1969, when the first electronic communication successfully transmitted. As long as there are electronic pings on a particular date, Zephyr's brain can find it and–and launch him back to that date."

"But not prior to 1969?"

"C-correct. As far as the Cloud is concerned, time prior to October 1969 doesn't exist."

"But it wouldn't recognize future dates either, then. So how were you able to make Zephyr go forward in time?"

"Like I said, another methodology. I-I programmed Zeph to extrapolate forward by the number of days in a year. For instance, there are roughly 36,524 days in a hundred years. The program can jump forward a maximum of 36,000 days—"

"Why 36,000?"

"It happens to be the limit of his brainpower. No offense, Zep-adee."

The little green light on Zephyr's panel pulses as he speaks. "No prob, Mr. Z."

"With some more tweaking, I'll be able to…"

I tune out his technical explanation. Strange how the panel looks the same as it always has. "So when you went into the future, it wasn't exactly one hundred years?"

"I wasn't able to go further than 98.63 years. Close enough."

I lean against his shoulder. "I want to go. Let's go together next time."

"We can't, Swee. I can send you there in Zeph, but he can only transport one person at a time."

"How come?"

"When Zeph senses someone in one of the other seats, he thinks he needs to wait for confirmation from the passengers, just like when he's transporting us. But I omitted the confirmation piece for time travel. Would've made it way more complex than it needed to be."

I grip his hand, the idea of going alone into the future terrifying. "I won't go without you."

"I p-promise you, Tree, someday I'll find the secret to unlimited time travel. I'm applying for a patent, and once it's approved, I'm going to be the r-richest guy in Portland."

"What good will all that wealth do you? It's not like you're allowed to own more than two autopods, or buy a mansion."

"But I can b-buy my parents and my brother the nicest condos around."

"You won't be allowed to flaunt all that wealth. They'll make you put most of it in the common fund."

Glim's head drooped, but my pessimistic words wouldn't discourage him. Sure enough, his head lifted, and a smile played around his mouth. "There're ways to get around that. Plus, a-all of history and everything that lies ahead will be at our fingertips."

He's right. I'm visualizing traveling back in time to exact justice on the man who has it coming. I'm picturing a happy reversal of fate for my family—a family free of the regrets that hounded them for decades. In my imaginary world, the innocent are spared and the guilty convicted.

Could I get so forch?

What if my imaginary world were ever to come true? What if I were the catalyst for righting old wrongs? How many lifetimes would it take? I eye the panel hiding Zephyr's brains, and I can't help but hope.

# 6

# Her

**October 2019**

"I love it." Paige set Katrice's iPad on the kitchen island. Contemporary Christian music wafted through the speakers. "It makes me want to jump in Zeph and do some time traveling."

"I know what you mean."

"Good name for a dog. Bestie. And what a cute term of endearment you thought of."

"You mean Swee?"

Paige chuckled. "Yeah. Can't wait to use it on my husband. How did you come up with it?"

Katrice, her mouth quirking as she fought off an appreciative smile, said, "If we can say Bae for Baby, we can say Swee for Sweetie."

Amazing how her friend's mind worked. "You ought to have your character travel back to our time." A cold autumn rain pounded on Paige's kitchen window and seeped through invisible cracks. She shivered. She needed a sweater. And hot coffee. "Imagine the adjustments your heroine would have to make and the challenges she'd face."

"I was thinking the same thing." Katrice scooped her tablet into her bulging flowered bag.

What all did her friend keep in that huge thing? Biting her lip, Paige lowered the volume on the counter's built-in speaker. No way could she ask. If the last week proved anything, it proved Katrice wouldn't share anything personal unless and until she chose to.

At least Katrice had answered the text that night after Paige and Kyler got home, assuring Paige she'd made it home safely. Katrice might not share where home was, so exercising patience, Paige must build Katrice's faith in her friendship and trust her friend would open up.

Paige popped a pod of decaf in the Keurig, even though it would make her run to the bathroom before long. "Want some coffee? Water, juice?"

"Just water, thanks."

"You got it." She poured them each filtered water and set the glasses down, then reached for her sweater from the coat hooks by the back door. "Are you cold? I have sweaters and jackets if you need one."

"Yeah, it's a little chilly."

Paige handed her a navy hoodie, adjusted the thermostat, then braced against the counter before the Keurig. "I enjoyed that chapter—especially the way you described the technology behind time travel. You made it sound real. Makes me wish it were possible."

Katrice offered one of her half smiles. "So if it were, where would you go?"

"Hmm, great question!" She drummed her fingers on the granite counter. "Assuming I could travel further back than 1969, the first place I'd go would be first-century Palestine. I'd love to meet all those New Testament characters in real life. How about you?"

"Oh, easy. I'd go two hundred years into the future to see how close my story is to reality."

"And I'd go with you." Paige retrieved the full cup of coffee, then slid onto the padded barstool beside her friend. "I, too, want to see how close to reality you got. How did you come up with your ideas?"

"You only have to look around at what's happening. I looked at the current trends and projected them forward several decades, then let my imagination take over."

"Let's hope we find better solutions before then." Silence fell as the topic on Paige's mind and heart urged her on. The MercyMe song "Even If" competed with the soft buzz of the refrigerator. Humming along to the band, she breathed in the rich coffee scent, the smell alone energizing her and pushing her on, but she'd better broach it in a manner that didn't push Katrice away. She snugged the warm mug against the hollows of her palms, conquering the lingering chill. "I've missed you at church. It hasn't been the same without you."

"I've missed you too." Sipping her water, Katrice furrowed her brow. "I decided to visit another church for a while." When Paige opened her mouth, Katrice held out her hand. "Not that I don't like your church. Honestly. I wanted to try others to see what else is out there."

"Got it. You don't want to limit your options."

"Right."

"I understand. I do." Paige twisted the mug in her hands. On its side, primary colors in crayon-style lettering wrote the words—*Teachers plant seeds that grow forever*. "My husband said as much to me last night when he wanted to talk about house hunting."

"You're moving?"

"Well, not right away. We're checking the market right now." She pointed behind her at the window overlooking a tiny backyard. "I mean, look at the size of this lot. 'Cozy' is how the listing described it. Typical Portland townhouse. Two years ago, it was perfect for a couple of newlyweds like us, but I can't see us raising a family here. Especially twins."

"You're having twins?"

"Yeah, I must've forgotten to mention it." The coffee warmed Paige's throat on its way down. "So maybe I will have one of each, like you predicted."

Katrice pressed her lips together and raised her brows as if to say, "Told ya so."

"Anyway"—Paige clattered the mug onto the counter—"Kyler's been checking out some real estate websites. Lord willing, he wants some acreage."

"You've never told me how you met your husband." Katrice rested her elbows on the counter, her fingers tapping together. "Was it a meet-cute?"

Paige's heart swelled. "It was a total meet-cute. We met at a Blazer game."

"I can totally see you two as a meet-cute."

"He was there with a couple of friends, and I was there with my parents, who were visiting me from Missoula, Montana, where I was raised."

"When was this?"

She tapped her toes as the music segued into an upbeat Toby Mac song.

"Four years ago." Bouncing her knees, she sipped her coffee. "I'd graduated from University of Montana and found my first teaching job here at St. Johns Middle School. I ended up seated next to a supercute guy with this sort of nerdy energy, and during the first time-out, he gave me the corniest pickup line ever. But his tone and his expression made me crack up."

"What was it?"

"He said, 'What's a nice girl like you doing in a raunchy place like this?'" She twisted her face in imitation.

Laughing, Katrice clapped. "I can picture him saying that. Then what?"

Paige shook her head, smirking, and then sobered. "I think I fell halfway in love with him that night. After we'd dated for a few months, he broke my heart one day and told me he couldn't keep going out with me unless we were walking with the Lord together. He was a believer in Christ, and I wasn't. I spent an agonizing month without him, trying to figure out what he meant by 'walking with the Lord.' Finally, I broke down and called him and asked if I could start going to church with him."

"What'd he say?"

"He said yes. And here we are."

"Sweet."

"Four months later, I got what he meant by 'walking with the Lord.'" She smudged a cross fingerprint on the granite counter. "I sometimes marvel at how we almost missed each other. The timing was that precise."

Katrice tucked her bland hair behind her ears. "How so?"

"I almost didn't go to that game. It was my dad's last-minute decision. Their trip had been delayed by two days due to snow, so on the day they arrived, the Blazers happened to have a home game that night. And voilà, there were a few tickets available." Warmed by the memory, she unbuttoned her sweater. "What if the snowstorm in Montana hadn't happened? What if my dad hadn't insisted on taking us to that game? What if…what if…I'm still in awe of God's timing."

"Amazing story." Katrice plunked her cheek on her palm, her Chuck Taylors kicking at the island. "If you guys move, will you still go to that church?"

"I guess it would depend on how far away we are."

"I hope, wherever you end up, it's not too far. It'll be hard to get together since I don't have a car."

"Oh, don't worry about the transportation piece. I don't mind driving." Paige looped her feet around the stool bars.

"Kyler says he found a promising place out east, off Foster, toward Damascus. It's a good price for the size. That's when *I* reminded *him* not to limit our options."

"That's pretty far from here."

"I know. We're just looking for now. The Lord only knows where we'll settle."

After their dinner of burritos smothered in cheese sauce, Kyler showed Paige the property on the real estate website. A pretty white farmhouse-style home rose from a spread of emerald-green lawn. "Wow, a whole acre." She traced her finger along the data section of the home's listing. "Two thousand square feet, four beds, two baths. Babe, this is a winner."

"Plus, it's closer to my job." He often griped about his stressful commute to an electronics plant in Gresham. "But further from yours."

"True."

"Still, much better than this place."

"I thought you liked our little cottage."

"This house is like a supermodel. Tall and skinny, looks great on the outside, but on the inside, there's not much personality."

A laugh snorted out despite her best efforts. "Now, Ky, our friend Olga would be extremely offended."

His bushy beard spread out as his sparkly-eyed grin said

he saw through her fake outrage. She gave him a fist bump, then returned to the site, and zoomed out to get a better look at the area. "It's fairly rural. The nearest neighbors are quite a ways apart."

"And it's in Pleasant Valley. So it's got to be a pleasant place to raise kids."

"Ha ha. Can we go see it?"

"Of course. I'll set it up with the Realtor tomorrow."

Where had she seen the name Pleasant Valley recently? It was an obscure, semirural area in outer southeast Portland with scant commercial activity. The question nagged at her—wait! Three weeks ago. Katrice's story. The first chapter mentioned a church in Pleasant Valley where a former president's funeral was held.

She could ask Katrice if she could reread that chapter to confirm her recollection. What an interesting coincidence. But maybe not. Maybe Katrice had spent time in that area before she moved to the St. John's neighborhood.

Too bad Paige couldn't simply ask. But her friend would only bristle and clam up. She couldn't bear to part with anything personal.

Kyler set his phone down with a clank. "I got another message from Everly DeLaurier."

"Really?" Saturday morning, she and Ky were meeting Everly for coffee. She'd promised to bring some photos. Ky's hunch was confirmed—she was Andrew DeLaurier's daughter. If Everly proved as forthcoming as she seemed, they could be getting long-awaited answers on Kyler's true heritage. "What'd she say?"

He slid the phone closer to her. "Her great-grandparents happened to be the brother and sister-in-law of the founder of the family jewelry business, Charles DeLaurier. 'They had eight kids,'" he read aloud, "'so it's possible one of them was your grandparent. I'm excited to help you find your biological father, and I'll try to come up with as many names as I can remember. But my dad doesn't know of any cousins named Gary.'"

"Okay, help me understand." She breathed deep, a cheesy chili-powder scent lingering. "If you two are second cousins, then her parent and your parent are first cousins?"

"Right, and our grandparents would be siblings."

"But you might be descended from Andrew's mother and not the DeLaurier side."

"True. I'm hoping Everly can tell me."

"Considering all the offspring from both sides of the family, you could be looking at dozens of cousins."

Kyler grinned at her rhyme. "Dozens of cousins. Sounds like a movie title." He swiped the screen as his beard drooped. "Anyway, don't you think it's odd they don't know of any Garys? I wonder if Mom didn't give me my father's real name."

"Or, you and Everly could be cousins on your mother's side, not on your dad's at all."

Ky shook his head. "If Mom were a DeLaurier, she definitely would've said something by now. Especially when we shopped for rings. She totally would've encouraged us to get the family discount."

"Good point."

"Think what it would mean if I were a DeLaurier. It would sure make up for a lot."

# 7

# Me

**June 2120**

Glim and I continue to sit there, staring out at nothing as I mentally chew on possibilities. "You were there for two days, though. What did you do all that time? And how did you get back? What do the people ride in?"

I have at least ten more questions for him. But his eyes are glazing over already, so I clamp my lips and give him a chance to reply.

"In actual time, I was there for a few hours. I wandered around," he says, "dumbstruck at all—all the changes. I thought to myself this is a result of the policies we are pushing. Like the—the law passed last year that all babies have to be injected with the new gender-neutralizing drug."

"Eartha and I were talking about that." A sneer pushes my lip sideways. "Another of Bombardo's brilliant ideas. It's taken this long for the technology to catch up."

"I know. He th-thought it would eliminate male dominance, like making us all the same light-brown skin tone was supposed to eliminate racial tensions."

"Speaking of Bombardo, I have a lot more to say about that. But I'll let you finish first. What was this building like?"

Glim straightens his shoulders. "It was forch—this building was intact, though much, much older. I don't think it was used as a dorm anymore. Strange machinery I didn't recognize filled the rooms."

"What kind of machinery?"

His dark gaze probes mine. "My best guess? Small rockets. I believe the autopod evolves into personal rocket ships and maybe individuals travel to outer space in a hundred years."

"Cool! So in a hundred years, the population will explode, the earth will heat up like an oven, and people will be forced to seek new homes in outer space. Gender distinctions will be eliminated, and everyone will be a Goliath. Anything else we need to warn our future children about?"

When he doesn't reply—what can he say?—I throw out my next question. "Was it hard getting back?"

He nodded. "Sort of. I had to reverse the original specs several times before"—with a wary glance at the panel, he drops his voice to a whisper—"Zeph figured out what I wanted him to do."

Flashing green light, faster this time. "I heard that, Boss. Next time maybe know what you're doing before you start messing with my brain."

I grin.

But Glim gives the panel a dark look. He doesn't take well to pushback. "It took a while, and I was starting to wonder if I would ever get back."

"Glim, that would've been terrible!" The idea sets my heart shuddering. To never know what had become of him—what an unthinkable fate.

He's still staring at the panel. "And then when I did get back, the return date was two days off." His speech slows the way it does when he's trying to keep from stammering. "That's why you haven't seen me since Wednesday."

"You just wanted to skip Bombardo's funeral, didn't you?" Maybe teasing him will wrest the truth out of him. "You promised you'd go, but you disappeared."

"I told you I didn't mean to." Instead of meeting my eyes, his gaze follows a man and woman striding the lot to their pod. His hands knead in his lap.

He's made that twisted-fingers gesture before, accompanied by careful speech. Could he be fabricating? Is Eartha right about him?

Would a smart guy like him miscalculate by two days? Did he do it to avoid Brook? But he couldn't have known she'd be there, could he? I open my mouth to tell him I ran into her, but something stops me.

And her warning haunts me. I haven't known him long, and I've seen how other girls look at him. Sometimes he looks back.

Maybe I should've lingered at the funeral and let her explain.

Finally, he turns to me, cute grin intact, his gaze steady on mine, and my tension lets loose with a whoosh.

"At least you're back safe and sound." I place my hand on his. "Can you take us on a short trip across town? I have something to show you."

"Sure. Where to?"

I speak to the autopod's panel. "Take us to Southeast Seventh and Burnside."

A confused Zephyr asks, "Boss?"

Once Glim confirms the instruction, Zephyr comes alive with a hum and a jolt, and we lift off. My heart climbs to my throat and lodges there at the sudden altitude shift, even though I should be used to it by now. I tell Glim all about Bombardo's funeral, omitting the encounter with Brook. Glim nods along. Below us, supertrees form a canopy over the roads and buildings, keeping us cool in summer and warm in winter. About thirty years ago, a few years before I was born, most of the paved roads were torn up and planted with these trees engineered to grow faster, taller, wider than natural trees, and boy, do they work. Our city was one of the first to implement them.

Zeph runs into some congestion, so up and over he goes to get around the pods blocking his way. Of course, their radars are telling them to do the same thing, so soon we have a mile-high vertical lineup of pods, all jockeying for position while moving forward in sync, but never colliding.

I look up and laugh at them.

Technology is a wonderful thing.

"Have you told your brother or parents about your amazing invention?"

"I told my brother, and he wants me to take him for a ride next time he's in town."

Glim's fraternal twin lives two hundred miles south, near the California border. I've never met him, but I've seen images. Glim is cuter by far.

"Your parents would be proud of you. All that money they spent on private tutoring paid off. You should tell them."

"Helix must've told them. He couldn't keep this sort of thing to himself. I call him my evil twin."

I laugh, picturing Helix, his nose too sharp for handsome, his piercing eyes not quite symmetrical, giving him the visage of an eager elf. Amazing how perfectly symmetrical Glim's features are. All it takes is some random wrenches DNA throws into human genetics.

We sail over our city framed by soaring brown mountains and reach our destination in about ten minutes. Zephyr lowers himself through the supertrees to street level, and I point to a crumbling two-story building missing most of its brick façade. An ancient wooden sign with a faded-but-still-cute blue meteor logo adorns the beveled front door. With its ornate windows, it must have been stunning in its glory days. "My grandpop worked here for Bombardo."

"So this is it." Glim eyes the building through the dimming light. Darkness will fall soon, so I need to hurry. The gangs love nighttime, and the robots know it. We need to be out of here and on our way back by sunset.

"Yes, the old Falling Star Inn." I swallow hard, half regretting this decision and not sure why I came. Curiosity? An attempt to impress Glim?

An impossible desire to redeem the past?

I white-knuckle the armrest. "One of the most notorious buildings in Portland, with one of the most infamous histories."

"I've heard rumors."

"They are largely true. For instance, did you know there was a murder here way back in 1995?" I smirk at him, enjoying the look on his face. "The place was popular with tourists, as I understand. Then one night in February, a man entered the building and shot one of the employees to death." I lower my voice to an eerie whisper. "But they never found the guy. He disappeared that night, and to this day, no one knows who it was."

I wait for any sign of waning interest, but he still watches me, his eyes agleam. Encouraged, I go on. "Fast forward to 2065, when it goes up for sale again. My grandpop's uncle Mason Bombardo—this was a few years before he ran for the Senate, by the way—decided to buy it, turn it into an upscale boutique hotel, and rename it with the original name Falling Star Inn."

"And you're telling me all this, why?"

"Because. How would you feel about traveling back in time?"

# 8

# Her

**October 2019**

Over coffee on Saturday, Everly DeLaurier proved more laid-back than her online photo suggested. Her genuine smile and friendly direct gaze put Paige at ease. Only her russet Columbia Sportswear pullover and matching joggers hinted at her high-tier economic status. If she noticed Paige's ancient gray hoodie and Ky's faded tee, no judgment shaded her eyes. Paige squelched a pang of envy at Everly's effortless polish, a look Paige had to spend hours of primping, hair-straightening, and calisthenics to achieve.

Across the booth at Pearly Gates Coffee Place in the Pearl District, owned by their church friend Norma Daily, Everly's cell phone beeped on the maple table. A young man's photo flashed on the screen. She glanced at it, rolled her eyes, and then silenced it.

Everly's smile disappeared, and the first hint of judgment flashed when she noticed the Bible verse printed on her cup: John 3:16. "Oh, interesting," she commented before testing Norma's popular pumpkin-spice cocoa.

"Yeah, the owner is a Christian," Ky explained. "She considers this place her ministry."

Behind the register, Norma greeted each customer with a smile and sometimes a hug.

Everly raised her brows. "Does she give out free food to the poor homeless folks around here?"

A slight challenge lingered in Everly's voice—*Do you give out food to the needy?*

"As a matter of fact, she does." Paige breathed in deep, using effort to keep down her defensiveness. Norma didn't need defending. "Every chance she gets."

"Well, that's good, then." Everly waved away her concern as easily as brushing rain off her face. "Now, let's get down to business—your birth father." She tapped the folder Paige had been eyeing. "Great news! My dad did some more brainstorming and remembered his dad's youngest sister, my great-aunt Ingrid, had a son named Gary. Unfortunately, he didn't remember Ingrid's first husband's name. Gary's father."

"Can you ask Ingrid?"

"She died about twenty years ago. Car accident. She lived in Southern California since my dad was a boy. Which is why he doesn't know much about her. But I'll ask around. One of my great-aunts or uncles must remember who she married."

"And can hopefully contact Gary." Ky nodded at the folder. "Whatcha got there?"

"Some old photos of Dad's family. I thought you might

like looking through them. Maybe you'll see some family resemblance."

As they thumbed through old photographs, Everly's phone beeped throughout, which she'd glance at, then ignore. The same three guys kept trying to contact her. Why wouldn't she put the phone away?

Maybe the constant attention fed a need. Like the super-popular, effortlessly beautiful high school girls who could afford to ignore most boys, knowing it made them try all the harder. Knowing the best catches would be theirs.

And what was with how Everly's manicured hand lingered on Ky's fingers when she'd pass him a photo?

Many of the photos were faded, filled with strangers, only one of whom showed any resemblance to Ky. Paige held up the photo. "Who's this?"

"That's Frank DeLaurier Jr, my cousin once removed. My great-uncle Franklin's son." Everly studied Ky, grinning. "And, if I'm right, your cousin as well. He's as handsome as you, like most of the men in the family."

Her guileless smile widened at Ky's blush.

Was Everly flirting with her own cousin?

"This is incredible." Ky's mouth puckered as he stared at the photo of his look-alike cousin. "To think I have blood relatives who look like me." A hint of moisture sheened his green eyes. "And never even knew about all those years. Does he live around here?"

"Mm-hmm, he lives in North Portland."

As Kyler's eyes gleamed, Paige could predict what he

would say next. "What if our paths had crossed? Would we have seen the resemblance, I wonder? If we were coworkers, would people ask us if we were related? Of course, we'd have said no, no relation."

They ended with a promise from Everly to continue searching for Gary. On the way home, Kyler couldn't stop grinning. "Wow, I'm a DeLaurier. Not a Ferguson."

Covering his hand with hers, Paige forced a grin, squelching the words she wanted to say about flirtatious relatives. "It's cool, but it doesn't change who you are in my heart, babe."

"Let's go tell Mom. I want to see her face."

Twenty-eight minutes later, they pulled up a cramped driveway. As soon as Doreen opened the door, her two Irish setters bounded up to Ky and Paige, licking and jumping. As usual, Doreen Ferguson's Southeast Portland bungalow, vintage 1952, smelled of coffee and wet dogs.

"Down, girls," Ky ordered while petting their shiny heads.

Bending, Paige scratched behind Caitlyn's ears, and the dog's deep-brown eyes glowed at her. "How's my sweet girly-girl?"

Siobhan gave Ky a welcoming bark as both dogs' tails whipped back and forth.

"You'd think it had been years since they'd seen you." Doreen adjusted the baseball cap on her short-cropped blonde hair. A coffee stain marred the hem of her kiss-me-I'm-Irish sweatshirt like a mud puddle. Assuming Kyler's DNA results were accurate, Doreen had more coffee in her blood than Irish. Kyler kissed her cheek anyway.

Doreen gestured at the messy sofa. "Now, come sit down. I'm dying to know your news. Couldn't think of anything bigger than twin grandbabies, so you got me curious."

Paige brushed at the forest-green sofa cushion but couldn't make a dent in the dog fur. Forced to sit anyway, she perched on the edge. Caitlyn laid her snout in Paige's lap, drooling as Paige patted her beautiful coat. She always had to run a lint roller over her clothes after visiting Doreen—fair collateral damage. The two dogs were such a beloved part of the family, and she couldn't hold it against them.

Doreen set two mugs of fresh hot coffee on the cocktail table, regular for Ky and decaf for Paige, and then sat across from them in the recliner, searching her son's face.

Ky cleared his throat, wasting no time getting to the point. "Mom, I did a DNA test, and guess what? I'm part Italian and part Polish. Which one did I get from you and which from my father?"

Doreen lifted her brows. "Hmm. Well, my maternal grandfather immigrated here from Eastern Europe as a boy, but he always claimed he was Prussian."

Paige leaned forward. "Which is now Poland."

"Right." Doreen gave a nod, her eyes flitting, just as her son did when he pretended to know something already. "Kyler, your biological father was a handsome, charismatic type. It wouldn't surprise me if he was of good Italian stock."

"Yet I found out my father was a DeLaurier, Mom.

Sounds more French than Italian to me."

"Whoa." Doreen clapped a hand over her heart. "Whatever I was hoping for, I was not expecting that. A DeLaurier? You mean the family who owns the jewelry stores?"

"Yes." When Siobhan whined for attention, Ky stroked the dog's fur. "But he's not a direct descendant. He's a distant cousin of the jewelers. Did you know?"

"Of course not. The night I met Gary, he told me his last name—no way was it DeLaurier."

"No, it wouldn't be. His mom was a DeLaurier. What was his last name?"

"I don't remember. It was kind of an odd name. It made me think of a major street in Portland." She tugged at her Nike cap, her eyes glazed over with long-ago memories. "But I can't recall which one."

"Powell?" Ky ventured. "Halsey? Stark?"

"Lovejoy?" Paige picked up her mug, inked paw prints stamped on its surface. "Burnside?"

Doreen shook her head, then shrugged. "If it comes to me, I'll let you know. Are you hoping to connect with your biological father after all these years?"

"I'm not sure. It would be cool to meet him, see how much of me I see in him."

"I can tell you for sure you resemble Gary."

Ky beamed. "Him and his cousin Frank, apparently."

Paige scooted closer to him, stretching her arm across his wide back.

Doreen crossed her legs and swiveled the recliner back and forth. "Can you tell me how you learned all this?"

"Sure." Kyler, his hand resting on Siobhan's curled-up body, launched into the story.

Doreen's expression grew more grave. When he finished, she let out a pent-up breath. "Wow. You'll have to let me know what you find out about him."

"Mom, did Dad know he wasn't my father?"

"He did. Of course. I was a few months pregnant when I met him, but we fell in love. I was running from God at the time." She reached for her Mrs. Doubtfire glasses and held them by one end, sending them swaying. The hypnotic movement mesmerized Paige. "One Sunday, before I started showing, I felt this urge to visit my old church. I missed all my friends. So glad I did, because, in walks this handsome man, and he wasn't wearing a ring." Her voice rose in pitch as she put her glasses on, magnifying her clear green eyes, so like Ky's. "I introduced myself, and soon we were dating. I was ecstatic. For the first time ever, a quality Christian man wanted to be with me. It wasn't long before I repented of my wayward ways and got right with God. I couldn't keep my pregnancy a secret for long, but he was cool with it." She slapped her palm over her heart as if the memory were too big to contain. "He felt God must have orchestrated it so my baby could have a godly father. But as you grew, we both thought it would be easier not to tell you. I wanted you to have a normal father-son relationship, and telling you would have just gotten in the way of that, we believed." She stilled. "And now you know. Maybe we were wrong. I don't know. I hope you're not angry with your father and me."

"No, not angry." The struggle blotched Ky's neck and knotted up his hands as he kneaded Siobhan's coat. "Dad was a good man. You guys meant well. I get it."

"And you're old enough to decide what you're going to do with this information. I can't say I blame you for wanting to know. I would too."

# 9

# Me

**June 2120**

We have a lot of preparation to do, Glim and I, before we send him off into the past. He'll need to know how people dressed and talked back in the 1990s. How did people communicate prior to the Cloud? What kinds of food were typically eaten? What did they wear?

Such a different world from the one I grew up in. "When my pop's father was a boy," I tell Glim, "everyone drove their automobiles to stores when they needed anything. They didn't have the convenience of drone delivery."

"Books," he says, when I ask him how he's going to immerse himself in twentieth-century culture. "The Librarium!"

Of course, he's right. The former county library, now a museum, is filled with books made of paper from all eras until the last ones were printed sixty years ago. We hop in Zeph again and make our way downtown. Soaking in the sight of the soaring wooded hills bisecting the city, I crane over at the five thousand acres of Forest Park, high and remote, its network of trails secreted in a wilderness of shadowy evergreens. I've traveled to several metropolises up and down the West Coast on the Intercontinental Train and have yet to see a more beautiful metropolis than the Rose City. All this aggressively green scenery hitting on you all the time. Seducing you. Nothing like it exists anywhere I've been.

Ten minutes later, we enter the two-hundred-year-old building and approach the fiction section on the top floor. With all the books and historical artifacts locked up behind glass cabinets, actual volunteers only occasionally staff the museum. No drones or delivery here. It's strictly old school.

I gravitate toward the glass cases displaying antique US money, while Glim examines a shelf of ancient books—tall ones, thick ones, ragged ones. "There are so many to choose from," he says.

He flags down a volunteer and tells him what he's looking for. The man opens one of the fiction cabinets and pulls out an inch-thick red book. "I recommend the twentieth-century author Stephen King. You'll get a good feel for the culture."

Glim studies the book, flipping its pages carefully, holding the old volume like a fragile thing, like it might break apart in his slender hands. But how will he be able to read it? Not that Glim can't read printed text. But we're slow readers, having been raised on audio text and among the last batch of students to be taught the obsolete arts of reading and writing. After all, why bother to learn something the Cloud does for you?

As if reading my mind, he asks the man, "Is there a way to read this in the Cloud?"

The man nods. Apparently, a Cloud site can scan old texts and read them into his ear chip. Good to know. Glim tucks the book under his arm and heads toward the exit.

"Hey, you can't leave with that," the man calls. "You have to keep it here."

Glim and I swivel like robots getting ordered around. "Seriously?"

"This is a museum. All items must remain here." The man gestures to a table. We sit, and he helps Glim find the Cloud reader he needs. Since we're going to be here awhile, I might as well get myself a book to read also. The volunteer helps me pick out a book from sixty years ago, and Glim and I settle in.

Then on the way home, a rare rain shower slashes across Zeph in the darkening afternoon, draping the scenery below in a shimmery wet veil, and I rest my head against the dome as if I could absorb the weather by osmosis. "Okay, are you ready to visit the twentieth century?"

"Not even close," he says. "I'm going to need more time to finish that book. It's a great story. Way better than anything I've read recently."

"Was it hard to understand?"

"I understood probably eighty-five percent of the words,

enough to follow the story. But those people back then used some words I've never heard of."

"Like what?"

"Like vinyl. Not sure what that is. Also motley and hot rod and dude. But I did learn about automobiles. People called them cars. They were a primitive forerunner of autopods. And much less safe."

True, autopods are about as safe as it's possible to get. Yet sometimes a malfunction causes one to fall from the sky and crash. It happened to Lux, a former dormmate of Glim's. Last month, his autopod dropped to the ground with no warning, killing him, his girlfriend, and their two-month-old baby. The city was in shock for a week with outraged cries to the autopod industry to "make autopods safer."

But overall, autopods are far safer and cleaner than cars were.

Beyond rain-spattered windows, the supertrees undulate in the winds below. "Cars and their fossil fuels are the reason we needed these climate-resistant trees." Or so says the doctrine we've been taught all our lives.

He nods, his faraway gaze telling me he's not listening. "Let's go back tomorrow so I can finish the book. If I still don't feel ready, I'll get another."

"However long it takes. There's no rush."

"Right. The past isn't going anywhere."

I nod. Next question. "What about food? What did they eat back then?"

"Not that much different from what we eat. The food

all had the same names, but I suspect it wasn't made in labs like ours is. Their food came from factories."

"Clothing?"

"I didn't hear a single mention of a jumpsuit." We both look down at ours, mine navy blue, his black—the only clothing anyone is allowed to purchase. The idea is, if we all dress the same, class conflicts will disappear.

I voice my fear. "Do you think you'll stand out in a jumpsuit?"

"I don't know. Guess I'll find out."

Over the next days, he works his job from the museum so he can get that book read. He ends up reading two more Stephen King novels.

And then, a week later, he summons me via hologram. "Okay, I'm ready."

# 10

# Her

**October 2019**

Paige drooped as the familiar lethargy sapped her. The little ones inside her were changing her body in so many unexpected ways. In twenty-pound increments. No wonder she craved enormous quantities of Mexican and Chinese food. At the rate she had gained weight, she might approach the two-hundred-pound mark by their March due date. Not to mention, the frequent bathroom trips. Those babies might as well be aliens hijacking her basic bodily functions. Too bad she and Ky had packed an excess of activities into their Saturday like they did prebabies when she had boundless youthful energy.

After lunching with talkative Doreen, she was happy to have an excuse to leave, despite her fondness for her amiable mother-in-law. By midafternoon, Ky drove them away in Paige's little white Versa, this time to meet the Realtor for a tour of the Pleasant Valley house. "This is even more exciting than when we bought our townhouse," Paige said as the houses grew further apart while the trees grew denser and closer together, her weariness already fading. "A big house on one whole acre. I have a good feeling about this one, babe."

"Didn't you wonder, though, why it was so far below market?"

"The thought did cross my mind."

"It could mean it needs some serious rehab."

"Oh, please don't say that." And she'd been on such an optimistic high. Sometimes Ky could be a real wet blanket.

"Just being realistic." He made a right turn into a long driveway, and there it was. "We're here."

After he parked behind a red Ford Escort sporting the realty company logo, Paige got out. Across the road, a vacant field rimmed by trees beckoned her to explore. On this side, evergreens as tall as skyscrapers framed the property. Oh, she could live here in a heartbeat. So peaceful. No cars roaring by, no kids shouting, greenery everywhere. She gripped Ky's hand and grinned at him. "I love it here. What a great place this would be to raise kids."

He merely nodded. With his brows so furrowed, he must be deep in thought. They picked their way along the rutted drive to where Lucy Jarvis, the Realtor, waited for them. Her smile, as bright as her glossy honey-brown ponytail, gave no hint that the house had any glitches. "Here come the new mommy and daddy. Of twins, no less!" She made it sound like the most exciting news of the century. Then she led them inside.

Paige gaped at the high coved ceilings and vintage architectural features. She'd bet it boasted many a nook and cranny. "What year was this house built?"

"In 1935," Lucy said, still in that celebratory tone.

"I gotta know," Ky ventured. "Why the low asking price?"

Lucy nodded, her smile never faltering. "Of course! Ask me anything. There are a couple of reasons for the below-market price." She removed her black puffer jacket and draped it over a wooden rocking chair Paige hoped came with the house. "It's a rush sale due to some unfortunate financial circumstances the owners experienced. Plus, there's the pending construction across the street."

The field she'd noticed earlier? Paige strode to the front picture window. It showed no sign of activity. "What are they building over there?"

"I believe it's going to be a church, but I don't have any details yet. Full disclosure—whoever buys this place will need to put up with the noise and mess for a while."

Paige nudged Ky, seeking a clue on what he was thinking. Could she put up with machinery and congestion if they were to buy this house? Particularly while pregnant? She'd enjoyed the peaceful serenity from the start. How would she feel when it was shattered? And could they find such a good deal anywhere else?

At least with a church across the street, Sundays would be the worst of the chaos after it was built. It wouldn't be as bad as an apartment building or a school causing constant traffic and commotion.

It might not be too bad. She slid her arm through Kyler's. "I don't know about you, but I'm ready for the grand tour."

By the time they drove home, Paige had fallen in love. Ky reminded her not to get carried away. "If there are serious problems with the house, we wouldn't be the first couple to get stuck with a money pit."

*Oh, shush, and let me enjoy the high of finding the perfect home.* "But it's such a great fit for us, Ky," she said instead, twisting in her seat to brace against the door, scooting further from his oddly irritating vanilla scent. "In so many ways. And I agree with Lucy. It'll get snapped up at that price. I didn't see any obvious issues. Did you?"

"No." His fingers drummed the steering wheel, his brow furrowed, and his beard jutted out with his stubborn expression. "It's well-built, solid, surrounded by old-growth evergreens."

"It's got some cool features, like a claw-foot tub. And did you notice that laundry chute?"

"They've done a lot of updating too."

"So how can we turn down such an opportunity?"

"We need to think this through. We don't know how good the roof is. Or the foundation. Or…"

"You want the house to go to someone else?"

"You want to make an offer right now?" He didn't bother to hide his sarcasm.

"Yes, Ky." Her breathing quickened. "Yes, I do."

"We haven't even prayed about it yet."

Paige rested her hand on his thigh. "Dear Lord, if this house is Your will for us, please let our offer be accepted and let there not be any major problems." She opened her eyes. "There. We prayed."

He sighed. "Okay. Would it make you happy if we make an offer contingent on the official inspection?"

"Meaning?"

"If the inspection reveals the house needs any expensive repairs, we withdraw the offer."

This was as close to victory as she'd get. "Okay." Praying she wouldn't regret the agreement, she squeezed her hands together. "Let's do this, Swee."

"What did you call me?"

"You mean you've never heard the term Swee before?"

"Um, no." Ky swerved to avoid a pothole. "Is that an actual word?"

She patted his thigh, his denim jeans coarse beneath her fingers. "Just giving you a hard time, babe. I mean, Swee. I got the term from Katrice's story. The main character and her boyfriend call each other Swee. And I kind of like it."

"I can't see me calling you that."

"Well, cram it."

# 11

# Me

**June 2120**

I kiss Glim goodbye, and he and Zeph sail away to the old Falling Star Inn building. He promises not to be gone long. Zeph is timed to return to the present fifteen minutes from now. Adding to that the ten-minute return ride, I have twenty-five minutes to pace and worry.

My brain dares to ask the unthinkable: Is it possible to have timed his return to five minutes ago? But that is too freaky to wrap my thoughts around.

I might as well go back to my dorm to wait. This podlot, inhabited by glass-and-metallic entities but no humanity, screams isolation. As I cross the skybridge, the June sun dapples through the trees and casts sun-puddles on the buildings. On the packed-dirt road, a lady walks her dog, and a couple pushes a stroller along the sidewalk. People meander in and out of the Commons on the ground floor, our central gathering place for socializing. Inside, robots serve beverages and snacks, and a human manager oversees everything. Glim and I hang out there every couple of weeks or so.

I enter my dorm where Bestie will offer companionship while I stew and fret, even while my dormmates ignore me as they do whatever they're doing in the Cloud. Sure enough, either they stare into space or their fingers poke and manipulate their invisible portals like old-fashioned mimes trapped in a box. Nobody's paying any attention to the humming 3D printer spitting out shoes for someone, probably Moss. The lunch someone ordered drops through the delivery window. "Whose sandwich is this?" I yell, and Eartha gets up from one of the sofas.

"Where've you been?"

"Time traveling with Glim." I grin at her widened eyes. "Just kidding."

"Cram, you. Don't mess with me. You got me going there."

Bestie and I tromp to the bedroom where my bunk bed beckons. I tune my ear chip to Glim but hear nothing. So I lie there snuggled beside my contented dog—and wait. No point trying to distract myself with my Cloudsite, cram it. Neither my favorite band nor holoshows nor local news gets my mind and heart off Glim. Bestie's serenity can't penetrate my angst. My uncooperative brain follows one what-if rabbit trail after another.

This is merely an experimental run. If Glim succeeds in landing at the scene of a 1995 murder, we'll know traveling back to the scene of a crime in 2070 will also work. I smirk. How ironic that both crimes originated in the same building.

But what if Zephyr malfunctions?

Or what if something goes wrong when Glim arrives in 1995 and he's delayed?

Well, the length of time he stays there is meaningless in the present, right? He's coming back in five minutes, whether he stays in the past for ten years or ten minutes.

I grip that fact with both hands and get up. Time to go meet him and welcome him back to 2120.

I stomp across the bridge and peek in the podlot, my breath coming hard and fast. I can barely stand to look at Zeph's still empty spot.

Until it materializes like a ghost come to life, Glim grinning inside the dome. If I were the fainting type, I'd be on the floor. Steadying myself against the wall, I wait until the swoons ebb, then rush to Glim. I'd have knocked him over if Zeph wasn't there. "Oh, Swee. So glad you made it back. Tell me everything!"

He grabs my hand and pulls me inside. I scramble over him and land in the passenger seat. "I went back to the night of the shooting." He pumps my hands. "February 4, 1995. It was probably close to ten p.m. It was surreal, Tree. The b-building changed before my eyes. All the crumbled brick—replaced. Imagine watching a sped-up film of a building reconstruction. That's what it was like."

My eyes widen. My breath hitches as the scenario plays out in my mind.

"You can't imagine the intense cold. It was s-so freezing. I've never experienced the like. I wondered how people could live in it. It was weird to look up and see a s-starry night sky."

"You mean because there were no supertrees?"

"And no clouds either. The place was deserted except for automobiles going along the street, and the only person I saw was a guy standing by the front door. He was tough-looking and wore lots of clothing—apparently much better prepared for the cold than I was."

"You didn't see any signs of the murder?"

"Well"—his speech slows—"the guy standing outside seemed to be keeping an eye out. I got out of Z-Zeph, and that drew his attention. He couldn't see Zeph because it was in a different time dimension, but he saw me since I'm human and we transcend time. I stood there, looking up at the building. Then he came toward me, this mean look on his face, and asked if he could help me with something. I made some excuse like, just looking for a bathroom. He sneered, obviously not believing it, and told me there was a gas station around the corner."

"What's a gas station?"

"A place where automobiles refueled."

I try to picture it but can't quite make it work.

"The guy seemed aggressive, so I thought it best to head back. Plus, it was so cold. I felt like I was in a fridgerator. So sorry. I don't have much to report."

"That's okay. You may have seen the murderer without

realizing it. Why else would that guy have been trying to intimidate you into staying away? He must've gone into the building as soon as you left."

"I didn't stick around to see. But when I go back, I need to remember to wear ex-extra clothing."

"You want to go back to 1995?"

"Yeah." He breathes the word as if hardly believing it.

"You don't mean going back to the same night, I hope?"

"No, no…"

"What will you do, then? When you return?"

"Spy on my ancestors. Among other things."

What other things? "That would be so fun. I know who mine are. Do you know yours?"

"Yeah, the ones on the Zeller side." He beams his ginormous grin at me. "I need some currency like they used back then so I can buy clothes like they w-wore." He gazes out the window, his thoughts obviously miles—no, years—away. "Also, it was before the days of hologram technology. Everyone used devices called cell phones, and they had computers to access the Cloud. I mean, the internet. I'm sure they cost money. How am I supposed to get my hands on some old-fashioned US money?"

A vision arises in my mind's eye. I give him a love-punch on his right biceps. "I know how to acquire some currency."

# ✦— ➤ 12 ◂— ✦

# Her

**October 2019**

Pepper's Hot Brews on North Lombard buzzed with coffee-fueled energy, the din of conversations echoing from its turquoise walls. "How did you hear about the Falling Star Inn Murder?" Paige, seated across a picnic table from Katrice, scanned the manuscript on the tablet screen. "And why did you decide to focus on it in your story?"

Katrice talked through a bite of muffin, tilting her head. "Don't you find local murders fascinating? I do. And I have a good reason for including it, but I don't want to ruin the story for you by telling you. You'll have to find out."

"Fair enough." Where was this going? Had Katrice been connected to any of the players somehow? Paige resumed reading. She'd read up on the murder details to see how accurate Katrice's account was. Paige had been a toddler in Montana when the hotel employee's murder made headlines, and by the time she relocated here, the city had moved on and the Falling Star was no more.

"Oh, and did you intend to spell 'refrigerator' wrong?"

"Yeah, that was on purpose."

"Your future readers may not realize—"

"It's just that people don't always speak perfectly, right?"

"I get your point." Paige sank back on her cushioned picnic bench. Across the way, pink-haired hipsters and baby boomers shared coffee together. Only at Pepper's on a Saturday morning, a place where, like the TV Cheers, everybody knows your name. And where you knew theirs, particularly the three regular baristas. Chaz with their hardware-studded face and gauged earlobes. Jenna, all rainbow hair and tatted arms. And nerdy Clarke, as Portland as a rainy day. How must she and Katrice look to others? Such a study in contrasts—herself clad in Ky's comfy old denim jacket and her artfully holey maternity jeans, vis-à-vis Katrice's plain black sweats. And her teal-green-streaked bob and pale skin versus Katrice's monochromatic coloring. Ky razzed her about her streak sometimes, but come on, he fell in love with her edgy look, remember?

"Hey, how is your health these days? Any pregnancy complications?" Katrice startled her, her words accompanied by a pair of pink cheeks as though she felt awkward asking. "Any morning sickness?"

"So far, no. Isn't that amazing? I feel so fortunate. I've heard horror stories of moms-to-be being sick for months."

Katrice, her color returning to normal, leaned inches closer. "How are your doctor checkups? Any issues with your health or the babies' yet?"

The Katrice she knew didn't ask—or answer—questions. Yet here she was, peering at Paige like this was the most important conversation she'd have all day.

Best not to scare her friend by acting surprised. "So far, everything looks great." Paige met her friend's steady stare with an optimistic grin. "It's early days yet, but my ob-gyn hasn't found any issues. I've already gained forty pounds, can you believe it?" She grimaced at the rich éclair in front of her, beckoning her to indulge in a most irresistible way. "Probably because I can't stop eating."

Her frown deepened at a vision of slim, attractive Everly. If Everly ever married and had kids, she'd sail through pregnancy, her trim figure intact. "Hey, Katrice, have you ever traced your ancestry?"

"Sure. Of course."

Whoa. What a definitive response. "Really?" A girl at the next table wearing a Portland State hoodie glanced over, then returned her focus to her textbook and whipped-cream-covered shake. Paige lowered her voice. "What did you find?"

"I was able to trace it all the way back to my great-grandparents on my father's side."

"Oh, cool." *Finally, we're getting somewhere.* "What were their names?"

"Matthew and Emmeline Carpenter."

Her breath caught. What a beautiful name. "Emmeline? Not Emily?"

"Correct. Emme*leen*, not Emi*ly*."

"I love that name. So I hope one of my babies is a girl. It has a nice retro sound, don't you think?"

Katrice snapped the yellow scrunchie on her wrist twice. Was she nervous? But why would she be? "It sounds more retro than Emily does. It's a great baby name. I think you should use it."

Emmeline Ferguson. Yep, that was a keeper.

"Were your great-grandparents from around here?"

"Yeah." Katrice took a long sip of cocoa, wiped her mouth, and sighed. "Have you?"

"Traced my ancestry? No, but Ky did." Paige filled Katrice in on their progress thus far. "We're waiting to hear back from Everly whether she tracked down Gary, his presumed father. She's texted a couple of times since we met with her. Seems the holdup is her great-aunt Ingrid died a while back and the other great-aunts and uncles are either passed on or ill. Her dad remembers Ingrid's first husband but doesn't remember his name. Apparently, their brief marriage produced a son."

"So this son could be anywhere. I wonder why none of her father's cousins remember their cousin Gary."

Judging by their loud laughter, three guys by the window were trying to win a noise competition. Paige rolled her eyes, waiting for them to declare a winner. "A few remember him, but they lost touch long ago."

Katrice's already serious expression turned somber. "It's like he dropped off the face of the earth."

"Lord willing, he's still alive. Kyler could have some

half-siblings he doesn't know about."

"But the site would've told him so, wouldn't it?"

Paige swirled her coffee, forming a muddy whirlpool. "Well, only if the person is a member of that site. With so many ancestry sites out there, it's pure chance if one of your close blood relatives happens to have joined the same site as you. We used UniqueYou. Which site did you use?"

Katrice's gaze slid to the window. "The main one." Her voice scraped with tension as she watched something outside.

Paige's wooden bench grated against tile flooring as she craned past the loud boomers by the window. A good-looking young guy stood outside, peering in. "Do you know that guy?"

A split-second of emotion sparked in Katrice's eyes, and her monochrome coloring blotched. "I've seen him around."

"He's hot like Ashton Kutcher. Go for it, girl." Paige stood and patted Katrice's arm. "I need to get home, anyway. You go do what you need to do. Hopefully, he's single and available." She grabbed her purse and, talking over her shoulder, scooted around a chair the pink-haired hipster had pushed too far into the aisle. "Keep me posted if you get your meet-cute, will you?"

# 13

# Me

**June 2120**

"I'll tell you my idea for obtaining twentieth-century paper currency." I cross my legs and lean in. "But only if you figure out a way to take me with you."

We're back at my dorm, sitting in Fern, and his eyes darken. But he gives my arm a playful poke. "I already told you why I can't."

"Yeah, but what about Fern?" I pat her control panel. "How much time would it take for you to install the time traveler in her?"

He gawks as if the idea never occurred to him.

Fern's yellow light blinks, indicating her confusion, and I tell her I'll explain it all later. "Thank you," she replies.

As I wait, my imagination runs wild. What a life, traveling through time with my man, fixing broken lives. How many shattered pasts need fixing, after all? *If I can do it for my own, I can do it for you. Just call me the Traveling Vigilantess.*

But I'm getting ahead of myself.

"Fine." Is that reluctance in his tone? "I'll turn Fern into a mean, lean, time-travelin' machine. Now, tell me your scheme for the currency." His dark eyes bore holes into my head as if he wants to reach inside and steal the idea for himself.

But dare I give it to him so easily? I bite my lip, hard. I haven't known him long. Would he make an idle promise to appease me? He needs to earn it. "After you've modified Fern, I'll tell you my idea."

"You're trying to drive me crazy, aren't you?" he mutters, rolling his eyes, but a tiny grin escapes out the corners of his sexy mouth.

Then, for two nail-biting, jumping-out-of-my-skin weeks, Glim works to add the time traveler to Fern. He only has time outside of his work shifts, and I endure my gut clenching, worried he'll find some excuse to abandon the project. Sometimes he lets me watch, giving me access to his Cloud site where he's recalibrating Fern's control panel. None of it makes sense, but at least, I don't have to comprehend this part. As long as it works when it's time to use it.

I'm crossing the skybridge to check on his progress when he steps into Zephyr, then fiddles with the control panel as though he's preparing to leave. His autopod is easy to spot, having been manufactured by HondaFord as a family pod with five back seats. Which is why our group uses Glim's pod whenever we go anywhere.

I'm about to wave, but he gets right back out again.

I suck in a sharp breath. Whoa. Talk about a transformation in his expression. From neutral to skyrocket in one second. I rush toward him. "Hey, what's up?"

A shutter drops over his eyes. "Not much. How about you?"

I stop, grinning like an idiot at the face I adore. "I saw you get in like you were going somewhere. Did you forget something?"

"Oh, y-yeah, I d-did." He halts and takes a deep breath. He slows his speech. "I'll let you know when I'm done with Fern, okay?"

I can only nod. I don't like when he talks to me like I'm old or feeble or an idiot. Sure, it's a coping mechanism for his stuttering, but I still feel small and insignificant.

So I square my shoulders and widen my stance. "Almost done?"

He grins back and drops a quick kiss on my lips. "One more day should do it."

As I recross the skybridge, it dawns on me.

He'd gone time traveling.

And didn't say a word about it.

His secretive time traveling has my dander up, but what can I say? I won't be one of those nagging girlfriends I can't stand. So I'll bide my time. Maybe he'll let something slip.

"Fern's good to go," he tells me the next day. "Time for you to keep your end. Tell me how to get some twentieth-century currency." He tilts his head, scrutinizing me. Despite myself, a delicious shiver runs up my spine at the look in his eyes. "Do you have a relative with an old stash?"

I shake my head. "Can we test it first to make sure it works?"

"I already did. It w-works."

"Show me."

"You could drive a guy crazy," he mutters, but beckons me inside. He must've figured out he's not going to get any information from me until I'm confident he's come through. From the passenger seat, I memorize his movements as he brings the control hologram alive. Light surges through the interior. "I'll p-program it for one day in the past. Yesterday. You'll spend one minute there, then I-I'll be waiting right here when you return." On the hologram display, he shows me an icon of a boomerang. Huh, that wasn't there before. "This is your emergency return button, in case you ever need it."

I chew my lips. In case I ever need it? For instance, getting stranded in the past or the future?

Glim gets out and shuts me inside, indifferent to the fear his words wrought.

Fern beeps. "Destination: one day ago."

This is happening! My muscles tense all over. It's really happening.

Glim vanishes. Subtle changes around me spike my

awe. Autopods previously there have shifted or vanished. Like during my first roller-coaster ride as a child, that same onslaught of wonder thrills and terrifies me.

Suddenly, all is calm. I'm sitting in Fern, her date display noting yesterday, and I breathe deep. Someone is walking in my direction.

It's me. Heading toward Fern.

Pulse stuttering, I jab the boomerang.

Glim materializes outside the window, and I throw open the door and collapse into his arms, my throat raspy from gasping.

"Back so soon?" he says.

"I saw myself," I mumble against his sturdy chest.

"Ha. Freaked you out, did it?"

"Yeah." Yet I'm ready for more. "I have an idea." I rest my palms on his shoulders, put on my most imploring expression. "Send me to tomorrow, and I'll be sure and wave at myself."

He laughs and obliges. Fern takes me one day in the future. And there I am, waving and smiling at me. I wave and smile back, then laugh at the unreality of the scene. Knowing I'll be there at that exact moment and spot tomorrow.

Back in the present, he gives me a quick tutorial, then high-fives me, and congratulates me on graduating from Time Travel 101. With honors. Then he sets me at arm's length, his palm outstretched. "Pay up, my Swee." He rubs his fingers together. "Currency, man. Currency."

Jittering in my seat, I nod and grin. "Okay. Ready? The Librarium!" I punch the air as if I'd just won the Nobel Prize in physics. "Did you notice that cabinet full of old paper money? Stacks and stacks of one-hundred-dollar bills. They're worthless now, but they were worth a lot a hundred years ago."

Glim closes his eyes as if visualizing the scene. "I didn't notice a currency display. But don't they have everything locked up? How do you propose getting it out of there? Bash the glass cabinet with an ax?"

"Sure, Glim! Let's do that. Not," I add in case my sarcasm is lost on him. "We shouldn't have to do that. Since the currency isn't worth anything other than as a historical display, maybe the museum would let us buy some from them. We might even be able to persuade them to let us 'borrow' some as long as we promise to bring it back."

"They'll want to know why."

"We'll think of something. Between the two of us, we have one great brain."

# 14

# Her

**October 2019**

The trees on West Burnside sported autumnal hues. Dead leaves lined the shoulders of the steep boulevard and dropped onto the Versa's windshield as Paige craned around while Ky climbed higher into the West Hills.

He jerked a thumb right then left when they reached the turnoff. "Which way?"

She checked her phone, her gut clenching in dread and thrills. "Take a right here. Everly's house is about a quarter mile from Pittock Mansion."

His eyes gleamed. Did he feel as intimidated by meeting Everly's parents as Paige did? "They'd love to meet you," Everly had assured them. "You're family now!"

He swerved onto Barnes Road, even steeper than the road they'd left. Massive homes set back from the hilly wooded street painted an accurate picture of the DeLaurier economic status. A shiver crept up Paige's spine. She, a country-raised Montana girl, was out of her element.

"We're in Old Portland Money Land," he said. "I bet Everly's family has their own personal chef who's cooking up a prime rib dinner as we speak."

Paige's mouth watered. "Here's Primrose Lane. To the left, my love." She grinned when Ky braked hard at the narrow lane barely visible in the dim light. He proceeded to the left, and the car crawled along a ribbon of pavement. "Look at these houses, Ky. Don't you feel a little overwhelmed? Aren't you afraid of bumbling like a bumpkin around these people?"

"Well, if I'm thinking about coming across unsophisticated, it's more likely I'll come across that way. So I plan to focus on getting to know my new family, not on myself."

Easy for him to say. But good advice. Good thing he'd worn his nicest Macy's dress shirt, sans tie. "Here we are." She pointed to a sprawling flawless lawn. Through a grove of old oaks appeared an equally sprawling brick edifice. She checked her phone map again. "This is number 698, but it reminds me of a small college campus. Not a private residence."

Ky turned into the drive and parked behind a Mercedes SUV with the dealer tags still on it. An imposing covered porch burst with an assortment of colorful potted plants. Even in the dimming light of the setting sun, the landscaped yard could qualify as a showcase piece in *Sunset Magazine*.

The DeLaurier home was everything Paige imagined it would be, and then some.

Everly must've been watching for them because she

emerged from the front door nearly at a run a moment after Paige and Ky got out. Everly's skinny jeans, topped with a Nike sweatshirt, showed off her slim figure. Rushing to their car, she greeted Paige with an excited hug, then likewise to Ky. Whoa. Since when did her husband's face light up like that?

"Oh, I'm so glad you guys made it!" Everly clasped one of their hands in each of hers, towing them behind her. "Come on in and meet the fam."

Her puppy-dog enthusiasm put Paige at ease. At least for now. But what would the rest of the evening be like?

As if in answer to Paige's unspoken fear, Everly cast a wink at Ky over her shoulder. "My dad is excited to meet you. I told him you're a true DeLaurier man. They're all handsome devils, and they know it."

Ky's blush accentuated his goofy grin. Dropping Everly's hand, Paige elbowed him hard and leaned toward his ear. "You do realize she's your cousin, right?"

The grin vanished as she slipped her hand through his arm and out of Everly's grasp, glaring at the back of Everly's perfectly coifed head. Everly, unaware of the drama she'd sown, ushered them into a vast foyer studded with European-style artworks framed in bronze and chrome. Paige resisted the temptation to touch a marble sculpture of a woman kneeling in the corner as if in prayer.

"Come on, you two," Everly beckoned. "They're in the living room."

Paige shuffled behind, grinding her teeth and eyeing

the escape route to drag Ky out the door and back to the car. Ky, however, dogged his cousin's steps, lapping up every starstruck moment.

In another art-studded room with a high cove ceiling and luxurious furnishings, a woman with a tanned, freckled face stood and held out both hands. "I'm Charlene, Everly's mom." She clasped Paige's hand, then leaned in and kissed her cheek, her chin-length blonde hair tickling Paige's neck before she drew back. "And this is my husband, Andrew."

The man sporting a Ralph Lauren polo could've stepped from the tasting room of a Yamhill Valley winery. He slapped Ky on the back. "Welcome to the family. Kyler, is it?"

"Yes, sir." Ky's voice cracked and he harrumphed. Was he battling butterflies after all? "Kyler Ferguson. My wife, Paige."

"I understand you're the son of my long-lost first cousin, Gary."

"I believe so, sir."

"Everly's told us so much about you!" Charlene's smile gleamed as white as her home's pristine walls. Obvious where Everly's friendly manner came from.

Paige released her hand and gestured to the room. "You have a lovely home, Mrs. DeLaurier."

"Thank you. We enjoy it. And please, call me Charlene."

Charlene DeLaurier. What a perfect rich-lady name. Paige had ventured into downtown's Saks Fifth Avenue once, the Christmas before it closed. The price tags on clothing like Charlene wore—tailored bolero jackets, flawless linen trousers—had sent her scurrying right back out.

"Would you like a drink?" Charlene's gold and silver bangles clanged on her tanned wrist, exactly like the ones Everly wore last weekend. "I have wine or soft drinks."

"Sprite?"

"Absolutely. Kyler?"

"Same."

"Let's go into the dining room." Charlene led them into a room as large as the first floor of Paige and Ky's townhouse, then went to a wet bar to prepare their drinks. Charlene's unlined face reflected her status—untroubled by need, unlimited access to anything her heart desired. She didn't struggle to pay bills or put food on the table. She didn't wonder how she would fill her gas tank. And Everly, as an only child, had attended pricey Northwest Academy, wore Nordstrom fashions, and did ski camp at Mount Bachelor every winter.

*Put on your big girl pants, Paige.* If the DeLauriers weren't so personable and welcoming, Paige might battle ugly envy. But who could resent such nice people?

They seated Ky between Paige and Everly, across the shiny mahogany table from the parents. Over the dinner of prime rib and new potatoes served by a maid—Kyler's nudge said, "see, I told you so"—and a fresh tossed salad, Andrew and Charlene queried how they met and what instigated Kyler's search for his father. "We all lost touch with Gary when his mother remarried and moved to Southern Cal." Andrew snapped his fingers. "I've got another photo album somewhere. I'll look for it. If I find it, I'll loan it to you."

Paige only half listened as she forked a tender bite of medium-rare meat into her mouth. Polished silverware clinked on delicate floral china. Polite smiles all around. She forced a plastic smile—most likely, the only plastic in the room—as Everly touched Ky's hand every time a dish was passed and his abashed pleasure at Everly's admiring glances pierced her heart. Had the stars in his eyes blinded him to his dumpy, pregnant wife?

Unfortunately, Paige couldn't make a scene. At least, not here. Fortunately, Charlene distracted her with questions about her pregnancy to which Paige gave rote answers as she swallowed back tears. Longing to slap Everly. And Ky. All of the above. Paige gulped down Sprite on ice in a futile effort to shrink the tear-lump in her throat.

Still, Charlene's warmth drew Paige in. "I understand you two are buying a house."

Paige jumped into the home-buying topic. One subject led to another, and soon, she began regaling her hostess on the trials of teaching middle school.

Charlene gave a sympathetic nod. "Yes, public schools have changed a lot since I was a student. It's why Andrew and I decided to send Everly to private school."

If only all kids could afford such a privilege. "It's sad, how many kids' hearts aren't in it. If more of them had access to one-on-one mentoring, they'd have a better chance to succeed, but we don't have the resources."

"Online schooling is becoming more popular."

Before Paige could reply, a movement from Everly's place caught her attention. She was elbowing Ky. And Ky, grinning, elbowed her back.

Paige had had enough. She thrust her shoulder at his arm, with which he had lifted his Sprite. Soda and ice spilled down his hand and splattered his slacks. "Yikes!" He glared. "What was that for?"

"So sorry, honey." Paige's cheeks burned. Tactful Charlene told them not to worry, got up, and brought over a damp rag.

Laughing, Everly piled it on. "Hey, you got the DeLaurier klutz gene."

Ky, his face as red as Paige's, dabbed the moisture from his chair and clothing. Paige wrestled two bites of fresh berry tartlet down her throat, and the meal ended. No one mentioned the mishap, and Andrew invited them into the den to watch the final quarter of the Blazers vs. Lakers game. "Blazers up by ten," he said.

Paige willed Ky to read her mind—*I want to go home*—but he tailed Andrew into the den and got comfortable on the plush black-leather sofa. But where was Everly? Had she grown tired of flirting?

Paige settled beside him, resigned. Ky needed this bonding time with his new family. And she needed some "me" time. After getting directions to the restroom from Andrew, she ambled along a wide, dim hallway, her canvas slip-on shoes silent on the slick hardwood floor.

Female voices floated from nearby. "Leave that poor man alone," Charlene insisted. "He's not one of your prospects.

He's a married man. And a relative."

"Seriously, Mom, I don't know why you're making such a big deal out of it." Everly huffed. "He's one of those types of guys that's fun to mess with. You know it doesn't mean anything."

"But do he and his wife know that?"

Good thing Paige hadn't worn her noisy flip-flops. She darted into the dark bathroom, not even taking time to find the light switch. Enclosed inside, she locked the door and leaned against it. Deep breaths calmed her pulse and cooled her cheeks. Then the tears fell.

# 15

# Me

**July 2120**

We wait until the next afternoon when Glim is done with his work shift—10:00 a.m. to 3:00 p.m. Friday through Wednesday, which overlaps my work shift four of the six days.

Wednesday at three, I sign out of my work cloud and head to the kitchen for coffee. Eartha wants to chat, but I blow her off. I already know what it's about. She and Moss aren't doing well, and she wants him to move out. She's thinking he and Glim could swap dorms. Because of the possible impact on Heather if her parents uncouple, I grit my teeth.

And I don't have time right now to discuss the implications—whether Glim and I could live together without it changing our relationship dynamic. Whether we should be legally coupled. All it takes is to share a living space, and we get all the legal perks of coupledom. One great bonus for him: Prairie, my dorm's proprietor, is a good-natured, reasonable woman who lets us be, whereas Gertrud, his nosy European immigrant proprietor, knocks on their door at least once a week to "check in."

We've never discussed it, but he and I need to have "the talk."

Eartha grabs my shoulders and turns me to face her. "Hey, Tree, did you by chance borrow any of my medications?"

Huh? Nearly dropping my coffee cup, I shake my head, in a hurry to join Glim.

"Well, that's just funny. 'Cause someone's been messing around in my medicine cabinet, and the security history indicates it was you."

Now she has my attention. I abandon the coffee. "Me? No way. Why would I mess with your meds?"

"Why would your fingerprints show up on my cabinet?"

"I don't know. What was the day and time?"

"Last weekend. The day you were supposedly in Bend visiting your parents."

"I *was* in Bend! You saw the images. Feel free to call my parents and ask. They'll vouch for me."

"How do I know you didn't zip here and back?"

"Why would I? I'm not interested in your meds. It must've been a glitch." I snap my fingers. "Hey, what about Breeze? Maybe she needed to borrow something for her nursing job."

"I already asked her. She said she didn't."

I notch up my chin, refusing to be intimidated by Eartha's glare. Our friendship better survive this. "Look, I swear I didn't go anywhere near your meds. I don't know why it would show I did. Is something missing?"

"Yeah, but it's that medication I used while I was pregnant. The Predsomaril. I don't need it for anything anymore, but I don't like the idea of someone 'borrowing' it without telling me. Makes me feel violated." She tilts her head at me, mouth hung open. "Are you pregnant?"

"Me? No way! I told you it wasn't me. Maybe Breeze did it and hacked the system to make it look like me. I can't think of any other explanation. But it sounds like no harm done?"

Her reluctant nod lets me go. "I guess."

"I have to go now." I hug her to show no hard feelings and then run out and join Glim in Zeph. It had to be Breezy. Of all my dormmates, she keeps the most to herself. If she needed the medicine quickly, she'd do the most expedient thing. But why not ask Eartha? But then, Eartha could be intimidating with her deep voice and towering frame. Little Breezy might've been scared of her.

I shrug. Better things to focus on. Glim and I zip off to the Librarium. I haven't told him yet of Eartha's dorm-swap idea. He likes things—that is, our relationship—the way they are. We've never discussed our future other than in the context of time traveling.

Whoa. Whenever we travel to the future, we'll have a future together by default.

With that settled, I relax and enjoy the view on the seven-minute trip to the city center. We glide into the museum roof podlot and park Zephyr, then descend to the ground-floor currency displays and offices. Glim must plan to charm the museum management out of their cash, but I ask him anyway.

He takes my hand. "You just watch. Watch and be impressed, S-swee."

His confident smirk reassures me. Our mission will succeed.

Inside, we find a volunteer near the currency display. "Hi." Glim's jaunty wave catches the man's attention. "Can I ask you about this cabinet?" His slowed-down speech prevents stuttering, which might raise suspicion.

"Of course." The man's long nose twitches as if he's battling allergies.

Glim puts on his big, friendly grin as he leans on the glass, despite the sign warning us against it. "We're in need of some currency from the twentieth century and wondered if there's a way we could buy or borrow some of this."

The man, Oakley, per his name tag, tilts his head. "That's the first time anyone's ever made that request. Can I ask what you need it for?"

"Sure!" Glim's smile broadens. "We're planning to travel a hundred years back in time and will need some cash once we get there. You know, for food, shelter, all that."

Oakley chuckles good-naturedly, but his nostrils flare. The story sounds preposterous. "Am I supposed to believe that?"

Laughing, Glim holds up a palm. "Sorry, just messing around. We need it for a scavenger hunt."

"I see." Oakley's face clears. "How soon do you need it?"

"By Turkey Day for my family get-together."

"That's over a month away."

"Yeah, we want to get an early start." Glim points inside the glass. "See that stack of fifties? A small bag of those would work great, if you don't mind."

"For a scavenger hunt?"

"Yeah. I mean, it's not worth anything. But a bag of antique US currency"—he slips his arm over my shoulder—"would practically guarantee my swee and me a win. My family's supercompetitive, you see."

"What'll you get if you win?"

"Lifelong respect and tickets to a Portland Tigers game."

Judging by his vigorous nod, Oakley gets it. He tells us he has to consult with his manager, so we wait and pace, glancing at each other repeatedly, unable to focus on anything. One thought nags me: If this mission fails, we might as well not bother to travel to the past.

A tall woman in an ivory linen jumpsuit, tailed by Oakley, approaches, and the old-fashioned LED lighting catches her name badge—Hawaii Ingram, Museum Director. "Are you the couple asking about the currency?"

Glim nods and gives her outstretched hand a businesslike shake. "Yes, ma'am."

"You'd like to borrow it for a scavenger hunt?" Her mouth quirks.

Yes! Let her believe we're a couple of harmless fun-seekers.

"Yes," I say. "We promise to bring it back after Turkey

Day."

"We don't often do this," she says. "But every once in a while, we allow patrons to borrow materials as long as they document their return date and sign it out."

"No problem at all, ma'am." Glim is so smooth. I'm probably the only one picking up the tiny crack—the desperate relief—in his tone.

"Come on into my office." She gestures to a closed door. "The forms are in the Cloud."

Ten minutes later, we walk out with two thousand US dollars each. How forch!

# 16

# Her

**October 2019**

Yes! The official inspection proved the Pleasant Valley house had a solid foundation and roof. Paige gave a victory punch in the burnt-coffee-scented teacher's lounge after she'd downloaded and read the inspection report. She forwarded the report to Kyler, then dropped onto the lumpy couch to wait for him to read it and react.

She didn't have to wait long before he texted that the inspection looked good. Deep down, he'd probably been hoping to be proven right. Would he rather have a problematic house than be wrong?

"We're moving!" she told Olga, who stood near the sink helping herself to a cup of coffee.

Olga tossed her silky hair over a shoulder and propelled her giraffe legs to Paige. "Yay, you!"

"The inspection report listed minor things we'll have to fix. But the plumbing is in good working order, and the roof was replaced about five years ago."

"Seems odd they'd let such a great house go so cheap."

"I know. But we'll take it. You won't hear any complaint from me."

"Unless it's haunted." Olga turned her wide violet eyes to Paige, an amused twinkle there.

A couple of teachers sitting nearby snickered. "Hey, it happened to some friends of ours," PE teacher Jeff Douglas said. "Better check that report for 'evidence of paranormal activity.'"

Paige laughed along to cover up a twinge of her heart. She hadn't once thought of that possibility. What if...

But no. As believers in Christ, she and Kyler were protected under His blood. Ghosts, spirits, demons... none of them could harm her or Kyler. Or their little ones.

To shut her colleagues up, she skimmed the report again. "The inspector didn't find any ghosts."

"That's because they only come out at night."

Olga laughed at Jeff's remark, and Paige pushed to her swollen feet. This was a good time to excuse herself to prepare for fifth period. "So long, y'all."

She waved at Olga, who tossed over her shoulder, "Don't let Jeff scare you with his ghost stories."

Out in the hall, Olga chased her down. "I was hoping to chat privately with you." She pointed a slender finger toward the door they'd exited. "But I didn't want to do it in there. Got a minute?"

Antsy to call Ky, Paige nodded anyway. Olga's issues were more important than new homes.

"Sure. Walk with me. What's up?"

Olga lowered her voice as a few students lingered. "I have something to show you." Hand trembling, she held out her phone to show a text message written in an unfamiliar language, her back to the hallway, shielding the phone, her voice a whisper. "One of my Ukrainian students has been sending me inappropriate text messages for several days."

Paige matched her tone. "Have you reported it?"

Her already large violet eyes widened. "I don't know who's sending them. I have five Ukrainian boys in my ESL class. It could be one of them. And I could get into serious trouble if I were to engage with them in a personal way."

"True." Even after years of teaching, Paige remained astounded by the antics middle school boys were capable of. Some of those eighth-grade boys in Olga's classes already towered over small adults.

"But it's not from any of the numbers I have on file."

"So it might not be a student?"

"It might not be. There's a fairly large Ukrainian community here. Could be someone from church. But…" She shrugged. "Since my husband and kids and I all attend together, I can't imagine any man from church with the audacity to do this."

The alien words glowed on the screen. Nice not to be able to read them. "Does your husband know about this?"

Ky would have a fit if anyone sent Paige such messages. Tall, muscular Aleks, Olga's husband, would likely also hunt down his wife's harasser and make him sorry.

"Not yet." Her bony shoulders slumped. "I'm hoping the person will stop on his own if I don't engage."

"You should be honest with your husband."

"I don't want him taking matters into his own hands, though."

"But still. Honesty is the best policy." A cluster of kids rounded the corner toward them, some focused on their phones, others chattering like a mob of sparrows. Olga beckoned Paige into a supply closet and switched on the light. The old fluorescent buzzed.

Paige gripped her friend's shoulder. "First of all, I'll be sure to pray for you, for wisdom and clarity. Second, in a marriage, it's important to let your spouse be part of the solution. You should tell him what's going on."

Olga winced.

"Unless you're afraid he'll get violent or blame you or…?"

"No." Olga sniffed and fumbled for a wipe. She grabbed a paper towel roll, tore off a piece, and dabbed her eyes and nose. "Neither of those. He's the gentlest, kindest man. It would hurt him so much."

Aleks must have to deal often with male attention directed at his dazzling wife. "Has this happened before?"

"Nothing quite so…quite so…" She squinted and waved by her head, the paper towel section fluttering in her fist.

"Brazen?"

"Yes. Brazen."

"Let Aleks be part of the solution. I learned that myself when Ky's cousin started getting too flirtatious." She recapped the recent events. "When I was in their bathroom crying, I felt the Lord's comfort and sensed Him telling me to express my feelings with Ky."

Olga's head dipped. Brunette hair rustled over her shoulders with her headshake, wafting the soft scent of coconut. She unclenched her grip on the paper towel and smoothed its edges. "So what did you say to him?"

Warmed at the memory, Paige rested her palms on her baby bulge. "By the time we drove home, I had calmed down enough to tell him how neglected and invisible I'd felt. I asked him what he'd do in my place." She backed up a step, the metal shelving pushing into her spine. The cleaning-fluid scent hung heavy in the tight space, only overpowered by the buzz of those lights. "He apologized, said he hadn't realized how starstruck he'd been acting, promised he wouldn't respond to her flirtations anymore. Since then, the texts he sends her are businesslike, and he added me to the thread."

Olga wadded up the paper towel and lobbed it into a cleaning bucket. "How are things now between you?"

*Without going into detail...* "Wonderful again." She shifted, crossing her arms. "I learned from that. Like how important honesty is and how to express my feelings in a way he can hear."

The ten-minute warning bell rang out.

She clasped Olga's hand. "Thanks for confiding in me, and keep me posted, okay? I need to call Ky real quick before class starts."

Kids clogged the corridor. Absorbed into their mass, she called Ky and told him of the other teachers' teasing about the haunted house. Clip-clopping toward room 136, she zigzagged around clumps of students in no hurry to get to class.

Kyler chuckled. "Now, that's funny. Don't worry. If a ghost family lives there, I bet they're friendly. And if they're not, we'll win them over with a sizzling steak dinner."

"But what if they're vegan?"

"In that case, a crisp green salad."

His lighthearted mood lifted hers, and they talked about their dreams for their future. She hovered near the classroom door. Beyond the hallway window, dead leaves hid the lawn's bald spots like toupees.

"See you tonight, babe," he said. "Want me to bring dinner home?"

"That would be fabulous, my love. Golden Dragon?"

"You got it. Wuv you."

She grinned. "Wuv you too. I willy, willy do."

# 17

# Her

**November 2019**

Paige: We're moving to Pleasant Valley!! Signing papers next week!!

But when Paige texted, her screen remained blank. For the first time since she'd met Katrice, her friend didn't reply to her texts. So she tried again the next morning.

Paige: Hey, Katrice, thinking about you. Any more on your story?

Then again, on her lunch break.

Paige: Looking forward to reading more time-travel adventures!! When can we get together?

When Katrice still hadn't replied, Paige's stewing turned to concern. Concern morphed to hand-wringing and frantic pacing. At least in her imagination. In real life, she couldn't give expression to her angst in front of twenty-five seventh graders. Granted, two-thirds of them wouldn't notice if she hopped on the desk and wailed an aria while pulling her hair out. The other third of the desks were empty.

Including Elijah's and Tavius's. Although they'd shown up yesterday, it was only for show.

"I hope you all enjoyed the books you read. Who wants to be the first to share your book report with the class?"

Either Natalie or Kimmy would volunteer. Sure enough, Kimmy raised her hand, and Paige beckoned her forward. "Kimmy, which book did you choose, and what did you like about it?"

The tall brunette held out her chosen read. "I read *The Remarkable Journey of Coyote Sunrise.*"

Paige half listened to Kimmy's speech, having already read the content. Kimmy was one of only half of her students to have submitted their book reports. And now her worries for her two truants edged out her concern about Katrice's disappearing act. If Paige could, she'd march right down to Elijah's apartment and haul him to school by the scruff of his skinny neck.

*Lord, isn't there a way to reach these kids?*

*They need someone to come alongside them,* came God's answer as clear as if He'd spoken aloud.

*I couldn't agree more, Lord. But who? And how? I'm just one little person.*

Her words to Olga came back—*Let your husband be part of the solution.*

Really? What did Ky know about educational challenges? His specialty was technology, not academia.

As Kimmy finished, Natalie stepped forward. Paige's superstar students. They'd go far in life. If they stayed on track.

"Go ahead, Natalie."

"Thank you, Ms. Fergie." Natalie shared her book, *Focused*, with the class.

How could absentee students be reached through technology? How could school be brought to those who didn't want it or who feared they couldn't succeed? What factors played into truancy, and how could they be overcome? Who would come alongside them?

Her words to Charlene whispered in her head. *We simply don't have the resources.*

She'd talk to Ky tonight. Maybe brainstorming would release some ideas.

By the time she arrived home, however, her AWOL friend kept tempting her down a dark road.

Brainstorming with Ky would have to wait.

Was Katrice upset by their pending move? But that didn't make sense. Why would she be upset?

Paige had to check if Katrice was okay. What if something bad had happened to her? With daylight savings at an end, the sun set at four thirty now. It wasn't safe for a single woman to be walking these streets alone.

After dinner, on the pretext of grocery shopping, she told Kyler she was heading over to Safeway and would be back in an hour. She held her breath, waiting for him to insist on coming with her. But absorbed in a computer game, he merely waved at her. Why hesitate to tell him her true mission? He'd disapprove of her exploring the dark wet streets, of course, and minimize her concerns over her friend.

Her Versa, still warm from her commute home, didn't protest her haste and started right up. At Richmond Street, she bypassed the Safeway lot and turned into the alley Katrice entered that night. Her wipers shuddered under the force of the rain.

Unsure what she sought, Paige crept along the backsides of weedy yards, her headlights piercing through raindrops and illuminating sagging garages, ancient chain-link fences, Private Property signs, and No Trespassing warnings. No other cars blocked her in on the one-car lane. Snarling barks from two dogs, large and merciless from the sound of them, shot panic through her. The darkness deepened and seemed to come alive with a malevolent essence, wrapping itself around her heart. "God, help me," she whimpered. "And please be with Katrice, wherever she is." The dark aura faded, and peace flooded her. "Please help me find her, Lord, and see to it that she's okay. And please don't let those dogs get out."

She visualized her friend as she prayed. Gray eyes somber with secret griefs. Reluctant grins. Thin legs clad in sweatpants. That bag.

Straight ahead, something on the road glowed in her headlights. Something small. Yellow. She braked. Twisted her grip on the steering wheel, then twitched her left hand to hover over the door handle. Was she doing this? Getting out? Had she accurately identified it?

She parked and opened the door six inches. The barking

dogs sounded about fifty feet away, so she got out, landing in a puddle. Her hair and face soon joined her soaked feet, thanks to the deluge pounding her like pellets. Pulling her hood over her head, she rounded the car, stooped, picked up the object, rubbed off the mud, and held it to the light.

A little circle of yellow fabric. A scrunchie.

Katrice's only concession to color besides her bag.

Her eyes widened. But this held no answers to Katrice's well-being.

Paige stood on the threshold of a single detached garage, its door yawning open. Light from the yard on the left showed her nothing remained inside, save some yard implements. She craned her neck to see which property the garage belonged to. No lights shone from the small house beyond.

The snarling dogs grew louder, closer, somewhere just beyond her headlights. She stuffed the scrunchie into her jacket pocket and leapt into her car. Safely enclosed, she checked Google maps, which pinpointed this alley between Windsor and Venice Avenues. And the address of the house with the empty garage was 8701 North Windsor Avenue. Proceeding on, her car ricocheted when it hit a deep pothole, and she bit her lip to staunch the swear words. Two more houses, and there were the dogs—shadowy mounds leaping on a sturdy chain-link fence, their heads bobbing with each bark. She saluted and grinned from her fortress. "Buh-bye, doggies. Keep up the good work."

At the end of the alley, she turned right, then right again

on Windsor, looking for 8701. But the darkness hid the house numbers. "Pretty sure it was four houses from the end," she muttered, double-checking the map. Shivering in her damp jacket, she braked at the shoulder where the app directed and gasped at the rickety house beyond the broken fence. Graffiti-marred plywood covered the front windows, and swaths of chain link lay strewn around the weed-infested yard.

A zombie house.

Her headlights lit up an ancient metal mailbox—8701. Katrice couldn't live here, in this dreadful abandoned house. Her friend had never even hinted...

Movement in the shadows caught her attention. A couple stood beside a car in front of the small house next door, looking in her direction. She got out and beckoned them.

"Hi there!"

"Hey," said the young man who held an umbrella over his companion.

"I'm wondering about that house." Pointing, Paige raised her voice as rain pelted the mailbox. "I thought a friend of mine lived there, but it looks like it hasn't been occupied for a long time."

In the rim of light, the woman gestured. "Yeah, it's had some squatters coming and going." Her hair formed a high pile on her head. "I haven't seen them for a few days."

"Squatters?" A shivering started up her spine. "Can you describe them?"

"Sure. A couple of homeless folks," the man said. "Guy and lady about our age."

Paige palmed rain from her forehead. "Did she, by chance, carry a big floral bag?"

"Yeah, she did." The woman adjusted the clip holding her dark hair in place. "She was here alone for a while. Then the guy showed up one day and started arguing with her. Was she your friend?"

A grimace twisted Paige's lips. Katrice was homeless. Ky's hunch proved correct. "She might've been." But who was the man? "Did you ever talk to her?"

"No, she wasn't into drama or drugs or drinking or anything that I could tell. Just came and went from the covered porch in back, minded her own business." The woman grimaced. "Until the guy showed up. I could hear them shouting at each other."

Rain seeped down her collar. The shivering spread to her limbs, but the chills weren't from the rain, were they? "What were they arguing about?"

"I couldn't make out what they were saying. But they both sounded ticked off."

She stepped closer to their umbrella. Would they take the hint? "Then what? Did he stick around?"

"He stormed off, and she went inside the house. After about twenty minutes, she came out again with her bag and disappeared behind the garage. I didn't see where she went, and I haven't seen her since."

Well, she wasn't in the empty garage now. "Thanks

for the info." Paige spun to her car. "I'll go check the homeless shelter."

The couple's heads swiveled as she drove past them. She cringed under their gazes until she reached the corner. At the next red light, she took a right toward Willamette Boulevard and the women's shelter where her church supplied sandwiches every Saturday.

Still stunned, she prayed for the three-mile drive. She prayed she'd know what to say to Katrice if she found her. She prayed Katrice hadn't been victimized. Was the man friend the same one Katrice had noticed at Pepper's? How odd if so, assuming Katrice had talked to him for the first time only a week ago. Yet it sounded like the squatting had been going on for a while. She should've asked the neighbor to describe him. Katrice might have more than one man in her life.

Paige pulled into the parking lot of a shelter disguised as an apartment building. The guard better recognize her and let her in. The rain had ebbed to a light sprinkle, and the porch light cast a welcoming glow. She rang a bell embedded in the wall. Inside, three chimes echoed. A security guard she hadn't seen before peered out the window beside the door. He must be new.

"Can I help you?" His narrowed eyes appeared through a small barred opening in the steel door.

Time to act confident. "I'm Paige from Christ the King Church. I'm here to check on Katrice."

"Who?"

"Katrice Carpenter." And speak like you know what you're talking about. "She should've checked in here in the past couple of days. She's about my age and height and carries around a large floral bag."

"That doesn't sound like anyone I know."

Her heart sunk. If she wasn't here, where was she? Or was the guy protecting the residents? After all, he didn't know Paige. Should she come back tomorrow when a different guard manned the place, maybe one who recognized her?

Too discouraged to pray, she slunk back to her car. Katrice seemed to have vanished.

She might never see her sweet, fragile friend again.

# 18

# Me

**July 2120**

"Why do you want to go back to 2070 so b-bad?" Glim's smile disappeared somewhere back in the midst of a rare fierce argument. A silly argument about which year I should visit first—2020 or 2070. He votes for 2020. "Don't you want to see what the world was like a hundred years ago?"

But my sense of urgency to redeem the events of fifty years ago is making me dogmatic and shrill, two traits I hate in other people. I cross my arms and give him my fiercest stare. "Gotta be 2070."

"Even after we w-went to so much trouble to get that 1990s currency? I doubt it'll still be good in 2070."

"Okay, cram it. I'll show you why." We're in the Commons sipping French vanilla coffee and munching fries. I hand him my eyecam. "I saved my grandpop's journal, the one he wrote before his suicide. Read it. Then you'll understand."

I guide him to the document. With his focused intensity

in place, he's hearing the narration my grandpop spoke into an old-fashioned computer all those years ago when he exposed Bombardo. I tune my ear chip and listen along, even though I know it by heart.

> May 2080. The true story of a popular senator who got away with murder. By A. Nonimus.

"He didn't want his real name to get out," I reply to Glim's questioning look. "It would've brought shame to his family, especially his son, my father, who was a ten-year-old boy at the time."

Glim nods and resumes the narrative.

> To whom it may concern: In March of 2070, I was employed at Falling Star Inn on East Burnside in Portland, Oregon. My boss was my uncle, Mason Bombardo, the hotel owner. I was twenty-three when I began full-time employment as the assistant director. I'd been married to my wife for two years, and we had a one-year-old son. At the time of the events, I'd been employed for under a year.
> In those days, I ran questionable errands for my uncle such as delivering

unregistered drugs, though he did operate a legitimate side business of documenting and registering with the state the recreational drugs he provided for our guests. At times, he didn't bother with the red tape or was in too much of a hurry, and that could lead to trouble.

The events in question took place on March 18, 2070. In the weeks beforehand, my uncle mentioned he was considering running for the US Senate against a long-term incumbent, Oliver Brown, who was far ahead in the polls. The two of them were longtime friends and had talked about teaming up as political partners instead of rivals. What that would look like, we will never know because Brown was found dead in his car that night with his wallet missing in what appeared to be a random burglary. Brown had been strangled, garroted, and from the angle of the marks on Brown's neck, the cops believe he was tased first. The case remained unsolved, and my uncle went on to win the Senate seat.

But back to the night of March 18, after a Blind Betties concert at a nearby club, a young woman collapsed in our lobby. She'd occasionally bought the popular street drug, pink biggies, from us. In fact, before she left for the concert, I'd slipped them to her without registering them. Still, I called Emergency, but she was DOA. And her overdose was not pinned on my uncle or on our establishment. Or so I thought.

The guilt from that night has lingered with me all these years. I told my uncle, no more drugs. Knowing I caused the death of someone's daughter, someone's sister, was unbearable, and I will forever regret it.

The following night, Oliver Brown was found murdered. The next morning, my uncle called me into his office. "Alby," he began, "I'm afraid you're in a bit of trouble." I gaped, but couldn't fathom what I had done. "You know Mongo, right?"

Of course I knew Mongo, but because of my concern for my family's safety and privacy, I won't use his real name or provide any identifying characteristics as he may have family in the area. He was a street guy. Always strung out, he hung out on the block and often slept in our back doorway. He'd do anything for a fix. Uncle Mason sometimes paid him for random jobs, stuff nobody else wanted to do. Like emptying garbage and sweeping up the needles out back where junkies hung out.

"What about him?" I asked.

Uncle Mason replied, "He saw you give that Jensen girl the drugs, and he is ready to give a statement to the cops."

No way! I made sure nobody was around.

But my uncle continued, "He says he saw you through the window. Now, the Jensen family has been pressuring the cops, who in turn have been putting pressure on Mongo to tell what he knows about Lakota Jensen's OD. Since this is your problem, you should be the solution. You're looking at years in the slammer if he identifies you as the supplier. You've got a wife and small son. You need to get rid of him."

I couldn't think of a single solution that wouldn't involve bodily harm to Mongo. Still, I suggested, "Like, for instance, a lifetime supply of drugs?"

Uncle Mason snorted. "How do you know he won't snitch later? No, you need to shut him up. And there's a big bonus in it for you."

When I saw my uncle's expression, I finally got it. He was talking about getting rid of Mongo as in murder.

"How does fifty grand sound?" my uncle asked.

Well, it sounded amazing. I could make a down payment on a condo. Pay my debts.

"He's just a worthless druggie," my uncle went on. "Who's going to miss him? His only friends are worthless junkies like him."

He had a point. He went on to explain how it could be done, yet the thought of it made me shake in my boots. But fifty grand…

That night I couldn't sleep. I kept peeking at my wonderful wife's sleeping face and imagining how she'd feel with her husband in jail. She'd divorce me, and I'd never see her or my son again. I couldn't lose them. I simply couldn't.

Uncle Mason made it sound so easy: Find Mongo, tell him I had something to show him. Take him down to the riverfront and push him over the edge. Make sure it's dark and nobody's around. Easy.

The more I thought about it, the simpler the solution seemed. Nobody would come looking for Mongo, other than the cops. Street people disappear/die all the time. It wouldn't attract suspicion. And if anyone found his body in the river, there'd be no sign of foul play.

But I had to do it quickly, before the cops came back with their questions. So at 5:00 a.m., I got up—not that I could sleep anyway—drove down there, and found Mongo sleeping in our doorway. The sun wouldn't rise for another hour. I rousted him awake.

It took awhile, but he got up, muttering and cursing in his slurred voice, saying something that sounded like, "It couldn't wait till morning?"

"You don't want someone else to find it, do you?" I handed him a pink biggie. "And here's a special treat for getting up early." He swallowed it whole, no water. I wanted him in as much of a stupor as possible.

It was now or never. I could back out right now, head to my auto, but the prison cell on one hand and fifty grand on the other prodded me forward. No contest. "It's down by the river," I told Mongo. "You'll love it."

He muttered to himself as he shuffled at a snail's pace, and I wanted to shout with impatience. Avoiding Burnside, I led him on a ten-block walk along the side streets. We must have made an odd duo as we passed Mongo's street cohorts sleeping. An occasional auto drove by with its lights on, but nobody paid any attention. This would be as easy as Uncle Mason promised.

We reached the waterfront and the path alongside the river. Here, we found more people sleeping, but we ignored them. Mongo kept muttering. He probably didn't even remember why he was here. I beckoned him to the path's edge where boulders dipped down the embankment to Willamette River. "Over here," I waved to him. "Follow me."

But a security camera hung on a nearby pole. I broke out in a cold sweat. I could incriminate myself if I weren't careful. Further along the path, I sighted an answer. A public toilet—most likely too filthy for the average person, but used by street folks. I slipped my arm over Mongo's shoulder as if we were merely two guys—one tall, one short—needing a place to sleep. "Over there, behind the bathrooms," I whispered, and he switched direction.

It was all over within a minute. Mongo's body bounced once on the boulders, and then I heard a splash and a shout far below. I wasn't out of danger yet. What if he managed to rescue himself? But there was nothing except a sheer rock wall where he'd fallen. I stood around for a minute, maybe two, almost expecting him to hoist himself up out of the river and clamber up the boulders toward me.

Nothing. After two minutes, it was clear he was gone.

Later that morning, I messaged my uncle, 'No more Mongo.' The bonus arrived in my account that afternoon.

Glim stops the narrative. "Okay, so your grandpop was a murderer. You want to go back to 2070 to stop him from killing this Mongo guy?"

"Shh! Keep your voice down." Okay, good. The other customers are all in the Cloud and can't hear us. The robots' attention is focused on their tasks, stiff and precise. "That's not it. Keep listening. It gets worse."

Glim shrugs and does what I ask.

Over the next months, I couldn't forget what I'd done. I had trouble sleeping, didn't feel like eating. My wife could tell something was wrong, but I couldn't tell her.

In November, Uncle Mason won the election for Senate, prepared to move to Washington, DC, and put me in charge of his business, accompanied by a big raise. I bought a condo in the West Hills with an amazing city view, and I should have been happy. But my conscience kept getting in the way.

Life went on. My wife and I had two more kids, but grew apart and divorced after ten years of marriage. It was my fault. Keeping secrets kills a marriage. But I had no choice.

I kept imagining what might happen if I were to confess to what I'd done. Would the consequences for murder be the same whether I'd murdered a "worthless street person" or a VIP? Yes, they would. Murder is murder, no matter who the victim is.

Two years ago, while searching for an internet conversation I'd had with a client the week before, I stumbled upon an old conversation between Mongo and my uncle. The name caught my eye, and I opened it. Uncle Mason had deleted a lot of stuff he felt I wouldn't need in my new position, but he'd missed this conversation. It happened months before the internet was absorbed into the Cloud, when data could still be retrieved without fingerprint scans.

The conversation stunned me. My uncle was hiring Mongo to kill Oliver Brown and make it appear as a random burglary. How did that not occur to me, knowing my uncle as well as I did? He never did his own dirty work, but always hired others, and nothing, including morality, stopped him from pursuing what he wanted.

I called him in Washington, DC, and told him what I'd come across. "Mongo didn't see me give drugs to that girl, did he?" I challenged him. "You wanted him gone so he wouldn't snitch on you.

The cops were asking questions, weren't they? And you used me as your fall guy."

He chuckled. "Well, I guess we both have blood on our hands, don't we? We both have secrets we don't want to get out, don't we?"

It wasn't so much the words but the threatening tone that did me in. Yes, I could turn him in. But he could do the same to me. And he had evidence. He'd kept the message of me telling him, "No more Mongo." I had no leverage.

If you are reading this, it's because I am dead. When I am finished narrating this, I am going to send it to the *Portland Tribune* and K2 News along with the taped conversations. And then I am going to take a stroll to the St. John's Bridge to throw myself over the side and end this miserable existence. I no longer have anything to live for. I've lost everything—my family, my integrity, my self-respect. My morality.

There's nothing left. If there's a God, I pray He has mercy on my soul. Fare thee well, world.

I brush a tear away as Glim finishes. "Now do you get it?"

He reaches over to lay his hand on mine. "I get it. Did anything ever come of-of this?"

I twist my hand, finger latching onto his. "Nothing. Mason Bombardo got away with murder. Because the document was never received."

# 19

# Her

**November 2019**

"An app," Paige announced, sitting up in bed. "That's what I need."

"A nap?" Ky rubbed his eyes and moaned, then jerked his thumb toward the bedside clock. "At eight thirty on a Saturday morning? You just woke up."

"Not a nap. An app! For my classroom absentee problem. Remember I said I wanted to brainstorm?"

"Not right now, I hope."

Bunching up the pillowing blue duvet around her, she crossed her ankles and tilted her head at her husband. "Katrice gave me the idea. An app is one way to bring school to the students." She rubbed his head in an effort to transmit her high mood through her fingertips. "If anyone could design it, it would be you, my brilliant hubby."

His red hair, as brilliant as his mind, flamed against the stark-white pillowcase. Another moan. "I hope you don't expect me to do it this minute."

"Of course not." She tugged her sleep shirt further down her swollen belly. "These kids need one-on-one mentoring, right? Someone to walk them through their lessons and whatnot. Someone to hold them accountable." She squeezed her knees as though the gesture could release additional brainpower. "How about we make it work like a dating site? It would match up the student with a mentor based on interests, cultural factors, compatibility."

He shifted and met her gaze. "Interesting concept. But yeah, it's doable."

"It needs to serve a specific purpose, target students with unexcused absences, and match them with a mentor they're comfortable with. Most mentoring programs are generalized. For ours, the mentor would accommodate the student. For example, if the kid sleeps till noon, the lessons would take place in the afternoon."

"So we encourage laziness. And leave them unprepared for the real world."

"Somebody's got to work with them if they haven't learned these life lessons already. Once they get their degree, by hook or by crook, they might become the graveyard shift workers of tomorrow. In fact"—she snapped her fingers—"in college, some education majors completed their internships by private tutoring. We could work with local colleges to find mentors. Maybe the colleges would grant them intern credit for volunteering on this project. Extra motivation, you know." Her hand brushed his. "We just need a name."

"You could call it School2You." He propped himself on an elbow, his beard pushing around his fingers.

She lifted her palm for a high five. "You're a genius, my swee. But there would be so many details to work through."

"Plus, a thorough debugging process."

"We'd need to figure out implementation."

"Start small. Do a beta test with your classroom."

"I'd have to get the principal's okay."

"Whatever you have to do."

"The school will have to a hundred percent support me, or this will never work."

"Think you'll get any buy-in from the school? Or pushback from the parents?"

"We'll see."

At Pepper's Hot Brews, Paige craned around the group of football jocks by the door. There. Everly sat in a corner booth and beckoned Paige and Ky. Whoa. Her multicolored infinity scarf set off her gleaming golden hair and toothpaste-ad smile, and that royal-blue pullover with matching joggers was identical in every way to the one she wore to their first meeting. Had she *dyed* the garments a more vibrant color?

Nah. She bought both, because she could.

Paige nudged Ky. "Remember what you promised. You're not going to respond to her flirts."

"I won't. I won't. Remember what I told *you*, love.

Ev is like the little sister I never had. And *you're* the one I love. Not her."

Some little sister. He was even on a nickname basis.

At the brown vinyl booth, Everly stood to embrace Ky, but he feinted like a star running back and placed his arm over Paige's shoulders. "Hey, Ev. Thanks so much for driving all this way to meet us. Can't wait to see what you got."

Good to see she could trust Ky's steadfast character. Paige slid onto the bench facing the table where she and Katrice had sat last week, almost expecting to see her friend there. As her disappearance weighed on Paige's heart, she had to force herself to focus on the paper Everly handed them.

"Here's what I found out about Great-Aunt Ingrid, the one I'm presuming is your grandma." Everly fingered the column of handwritten names. Whenever her finger neared Ky's, he moved it out of her way. She continued as though she hadn't noticed. "Her first marriage was short-lived and produced a son, your father, if I'm correct. She remarried a man with the last name of Fowler from Southern Cal, and they had two daughters, both of whom still live down there."

"My aunts." Ky traced his fingers under their email addresses. "Half aunts, right? Gretchen Fowler Hanson and Bernetta Fowler Katz."

"And you have four cousins in that line too." Everly ground her perfect teeth on her lower lip. "I'm thinking at least one, if not both, of those aunts will know how to contact their half brother, Gary."

Ky's eyes brightened along with his smile.

Paige rubbed his shoulder. "This is so great, Everly," she said. "So awesome." With Ky keeping his distance, she could afford a little grace.

Everly beamed. "So my question is this—Do you want to contact them yourself? Or would you prefer I run interference? Before you answer, I need to tell you I've never met these people. But they're my father's cousins and should know who I am."

It made more sense for Everly to make contact since she had a last name familiar to the aunts. But Kyler was gung-ho to be the initiator. He scooped an arm around Paige, jostling her in his animation. "You know what, babe? This deserves a celebration. Let's go order the finest coffee this place has." He stood, nodding at Everly's cup. "What're you having? I'll buy."

"Caf-n-a-Haf, room for cream."

Kyler took Paige's hand. "Man, this is exciting. I might be this close"—he held his fingers an inch apart—"to finding my dad!"

The shop door swung open, and in walked a familiar face. The Ashton Kutcher look-alike Katrice had her eye on last week. He caught her staring and held her gaze before she turned away. She sensed him standing behind her. Heard him breathing. Did she dare turn around and ask him about Katrice? But could she risk embarrassing her friend?

Uncertain, she shuffled her feet as Ky gave their orders and led her back to their table. She glanced back at the young man, now giving his order. Maybe Katrice might join him.

She pretended to listen to the conversation between Kyler and Everly as he asked about Aunt Ingrid and her family. The dark-haired guy waited at the table she and Katrice had shared last week, frowning at his phone. Was he reading a text from Katrice? If only she had the courage to approach him, but how could she with her husband right next to her?

"Kyler?" Clarke called. Ky stood up, brushing his palms over his jeans, then strolled to the counter.

"JZ?"

The dark-haired guy followed Kyler, got his drink, then headed for the exit.

Oh no. She couldn't let him leave. "Honey?" She grabbed her purse as Ky returned with three cups. "I left my phone in the car. I'll be right back."

He searched her face as if he couldn't believe she'd leave him alone with Everly. "Okay. Don't let your coffee get cold."

She stood on her toes, her back to Everly, and muttered into his ear. "Don't let her get away with anything. I'll be right back." She hurried outside into a shock of chilled rain. Ugh, she should've brought her jacket. She pivoted toward the back lot where they'd parked—out of sight of Kyler's table. She couldn't risk exposing herself as a hypocrite.

Although this was not the same as flirting with an overfriendly cousin, Ky could interpret it that way. She hurried after the guy, who strolled along, coffee in one hand, phone in the other. He wore no jacket, and rain bounced off his Adidas shoes. She quickened her steps and caught up.

"Excuse me."

He kept walking, staring at his phone.

"Excuse me? JZ?"

He whirled, his gaze dark with suspicion. "Oh"—tiny pause—"it's you." A faint, unidentifiable accent flattened his vowels.

"No, we've never met." How foolhardy she'd been. She hadn't considered he could be responsible for Katrice's disappearance. "I heard the barista call your name. Please, I need to ask you something."

He stopped, said nothing, rain dripping from his hair.

She shivered as raindrops pelted her arms. "Do you, by chance, know my friend Katrice?"

"I already told you—"

"Look, I think you have me mixed up with someone else. My name is Paige. Last week, I saw you with my friend Katrice"—eyeing each other? flirting?—"talking. I'm wondering if you've seen her recently."

He sipped his coffee. His dark eyes narrowed. "She went home."

A tight knot loosened so swiftly, it pushed a gasp out of her. "Home? You mean, Eastern Oregon?"

He nodded, slowly at first, then rapidly, as if he wasn't certain. Was he lying?

"She went to visit her family."

"She told you that? And you've only known her a week?"

His mouth twisted. "A week? N-no, I've known her for months. We've been together for a while."

Something knocked at her subconscious. "I didn't know she was dating anyone."

His scowl loosened, morphed into a grin, and Scary Guy transformed into a harmless twentysomething guy with a charming stutter. "Nice to meet you again, Paige."

Again? Her smile faltered at the odd response. She put out her hand. What else could she do? "Glad to meet you."

A charming stutter. Just like Katrice's hero, Glim. Katrice had used her real-life boyfriend as a model for her fictional hero. Paige studied his face, olive-complexioned like Katrice, feeling like she was looking at Glim himself. "She must not have cell phone coverage where she is, yes?"

He nodded. "Yeah, she's out of range over there."

"Where is her hometown? Baker City? LaGrande? Ontario?"

A veil dropped over his eyes, and his smile vanished. "None of the above. I'll tell her I met you." He swiveled and headed toward the street. "Have a good day."

He was lying. He knew where she was, and it wasn't in Eastern Oregon.

"Tell her I miss her." She went back inside, relishing the warmth, her new wide boots leaving wet prints on the turquoise tile as she stepped around a yellow wet-floor sign.

Kyler and Everly chatted away at their booth, but Kyler's eyes lit when she slid in next to him. He put his arm over her shoulder. "You're wet, babe."

"Yeah, I got caught in a shower."

He turned back to Everly and finished what he'd been saying.

Paige savored the heat of the coffee flowing through her cold limbs. As the conversation proceeded, she tried to insert nods or comments in the right places. But...

Why had Katrice pretended not to know JZ? Why not admit she had a boyfriend? And a cute one, at that. Had he been the man she'd been arguing with at the house on Windsor Avenue? Was he heading back there now?

If she was in communication with JZ, why wouldn't she communicate with Paige? And why did JZ lie?

Paige hugged her hands around the warm mug. Had she done something to offend her friend? It could be anything. Katrice was as easy to figure out as a middle schooler on Red Bull.

At home a half hour later, Paige followed Kyler to his laptop. As he composed an email to his two newly discovered aunts, she sat beside him and helped him with the wording.

> To: Ms. Gretchen Hanson; Ms. Bernetta Katz
> CC: Ms. Everly DeLaurier
> From: Kyler Ferguson
> Subject: Ingrid DeLaurier
> Dear Ms. Hanson and Ms. Katz,
> My name is Kyler Ferguson. I live in Portland, Oregon, and am twenty-eight years old. In the process of investigating

my ancestry, I learned my biological grandmother was almost certainly Ingrid DeLaurier, your mother. I received your contact info from Everly DeLaurier, the daughter of your cousin Andrew, in hopes you might lead me to the whereabouts of my biological father, Gary. (I copied her on this email so you may address any questions to her as well as to me.)

Please forgive me if this is an intrusion. I recently found out the man I thought was my biological father was in fact not. Do you have any information on your half brother, Gary? If you are concerned about his privacy, would you be so kind as to reach out and ask if he'd like to contact me? Please assure him I am not seeking anything beyond a meeting. If he is open, I would be happy to make his acquaintance.

Looking forward to hearing from you.
I remain yours truly,
Kyler Thomas Ferguson

Per Everly's suggestion, he attached a selfie of the three of them at Pepper's that morning and a screenshot of his biological relationship to Everly and her father. They reread it, Paige gave her approval, and he clicked Send.

# 20

# Me

**July 2120**

Dusky afternoon light deepens to twilight outside the Commons windows. I sit, catatonic after hearing again Grandpop's story. Glim returns my eyecam, his fingers brushing mine. "So. Tree. Swee." His eyes bore into me. "Why didn't the message get sent?"

"Oh, it got sent. Just not received, for some reason. My dad discovered it years later and chalked it up to the fact that the contact information was incorrect in the message. You know, back then, when the internet was transitioning over to the Cloud, it happened a fair amount. I think my grandpop died before discovering his message didn't go through."

"Did your pop ever send this to the media?"

"No, he made the mistake of contacting Bombardo to tell him what he found. Bombardo denied it all and smeared my grandpop's character. In his first year of office, he'd pushed through a law reducing the statute of limitations on murder to twenty years. Solely to benefit himself, no doubt. It was too late to prosecute him. And he told my dad he'd sue him for millions if he publicized the memoir."

A robot, with the name hologram Danoid, approaches and asks us if we need anything else. Glim shakes his head, and Danoid swivels and struts off, its head down as though dejected it couldn't help us.

"So now you want to travel back to 2070 in order to prevent a murder."

I clutch his hand with all the vigor I'm feeling. "I want to at least try. Although I'm not sure how I would go about it."

Another headshake, misgivings squinching his eyes. "Are you comfortable with the idea of messing with h-history, Tree? Think about it. Your father benefited f-financially from Bombardo's administration, like my father did."

"But it was guilt money. Your dad earned his legitimately as part of his legal advisory team. My father's life was ruined from the shame of his father's suicide."

"What if your efforts result in something worse than life as it is now?"

"Like what? Are you suggesting a less radical president would've made our lives worse? I don't think so."

"I'm saying, I invented time travel to enable us to observe the past. Not to change it."

It's not like I need his permission. I clench my jaw. "Why not try?"

"Because when you tamper with the cosmic timeline"—

he draws out the words—"it could have far-reaching consequences."

Sounds ominous. But his eye is twitching. Maybe he's BS-ing me. "What kinds of far-reaching consequences?"

He speaks slowly, as though to a child, but it's only to avoid stuttering—right? "You don't know how it will impact the rest of history. What if you only make things worse, not better?"

"Well, it's not like we have any protocol for what you're doing. This is uncharted territory. You have no idea what the ramifications are." I uncross my arms and rest my fists on the tabletop. "Plus, don't you think a world in which justice prevailed would be a better world for everyone?"

He snaps his fingers and points. "Hey, instead of traveling back to 2070, wh-why not go back all the way to his birth and keep him from being born. Isn't that what you always say? He should never have been born?"

I squint at him, unsure if he's sarcastic or serious. Wondering if he'd read my mind. Bombardo was born in 2020.

"Wasn't abortion legal back then? You'd somehow have to persuade the mother that aborting her fetus, the future Mason Bombardo, would be in her best interests."

I roll my eyes and catch movement out the window. A wind gust makes the supertrees' branches look like they're bowing at us. Gallant gentleman trees. "You make it sound so easy, Mr. Sarcastic. And, by the way, you don't realize who Bombardo's mother actually was."

"Who was she?"

"Bombardo's my grandpop's uncle, right? That makes him my great-great-uncle, which would make his mother my great-great-grandma. And if she had an abortion, I wouldn't be here."

"Why not?"

"Because she was carrying twins. Bombardo had a twin sister, my great-grandma Lena. So obviously an abortion is out of the question."

He squints at me, his jaw tight.

I make one last gasp attempt. "You may be right, Swee. Maybe I can't undo what's already been done. But I won't know unless I try."

We haggle back and forth until I get him to agree that a world in which murderers get off scot-free is not a world he wants to live in. His agreement, when it comes, is reluctant and hard-won. "I can see you're not going to let this go."

I nod. "I'm not."

"Fine." He palms the compometal table and stands. "Go visit 2070, but I'm coming with you."

On my tiptoes, I kiss his cheek. "I wouldn't have it any other way—2070, here we come."

I research the Oliver Brown murder in the meantime. My grandpop's memoir left out a lot, and if I am to prevent a crime, I have to know how it was done. I daydream some what-ifs. If Oliver Brown didn't die, he'd have been our US Senator. All those radical social experiments Bombardo did wouldn't have happened. My grandpop would've probably lived to a ripe old age and given my father a happy life.

So many what-ifs are riding on this. We have to succeed.

I search the Cloud for old articles and find one from the former *Portland Tribune*. March 2070: Oliver Brown Found Murdered.

> Senatorial candidate Oliver Brown was found dead in his auto last night, the victim of an apparent robbery/murder. A witness, who was employed at a nearby nightclub, heard the crash at the corner of Grand Avenue and Northeast Davis Street and called Emergency. When the police arrived, they found the victim's wallet gone, but recognized him and made a positive identification. Marks on his neck were consistent with tasing and strangulation. The vehicle's sunroof was open, and the police surmise the perp might have gotten in that way.
>
> "We don't know for sure how the perp got in, unfortunately. It appears to be a random robbery," said Detective John Bishop of the Portland Police Bureau. "He may have been targeted because of his luxury vehicle. It probably happened too fast for the victim to do anything. An experienced perp would only need

seconds to tase someone and wrap a strangulating device around their neck. That part of town, Central Eastside, is reputed for its high crime, and we are interested to know what Oliver Brown was doing down there. We ask anyone who might know what Brown's business on East Burnside was to come forward."

After the crash, the witness saw a child with a baseball cap running down Davis Street but couldn't see the child's face or make out any details. "I couldn't figure out why a kid would be running down Davis Street at eleven at night, but he seemed to be running away from the area where the wrecked car was."

Police would like to find the child to see if he witnessed anything.

From another article the next day: Brown Visited Friend and Business Owner on Burnside.

Today police received a call from Portland business owner, Mason Bombardo, who claimed he was the last person to see Oliver Brown the night he was murdered. "We're old friends," volunteered the owner of the Falling Star Inn, a small hotel on Sixth Avenue and East Burnside, just blocks from where Brown's body was found. "He came to see me about supporting his campaign. We sat in my office, had a couple of beers, some laughs, and then I walked him out to his auto a little past eleven. He seemed sober when he drove off. I am heartbroken someone did this to him, and I regret letting him visit me here. We should have met in a safer spot."

Police are asking anyone who witnessed anything that might shed light on this crime to please come forward.

I shake my head at Bombardo's sheer audacity. Then, still searching, I pause at a headline from a week later: Brown's Family Offers Reward for Murder Info. When it became obvious the police had no leads, Oliver Brown's wife upped the stakes by offering a reward to anyone with information leading to a murder conviction. I even find a small blurb about Lakota Jensen's overdose. Police Investigate Local Business Owner after Overdose Death:

The parents of Lakota Jensen, the 20-year-old who overdosed at The

Falling Star Inn last week, are asking police to find the person(s) responsible for supplying their daughter with drugs. Police have questioned the owner of the hotel, Mason Bombardo, who turned his drug records over to the police. No record of Lakota Jensen's name appeared in his documentation. They also questioned street residents on and around Burnside, many of whom are known by police to distribute unregistered drugs, but nobody claimed to see anyone matching her image. Police are asking anyone with information to notify the Bureau.

Now Glim and I must bot the details. Glim's eyes shine, and excitement rushes through my veins too. We are about to change the course of history.

Unless, of course, there's another force at work, and Bombardo is preordained to wreak havoc on the world. I think of all the ways, all the times, mankind has wreaked havoc on this world. My shoulders sag with the weight of it all. One little vigilante isn't capable of fixing all those wrongs.

No. I snap myself out of it. Like the saying goes—one day at a time. But in my case, I say, "One mission at a time."

# 21

# Her

**November 2019**

Paige shifted in the padded church seat, trying to ease the ache in her lower back. Beside her, Kyler kept glancing at his phone, probably checking for an email reply from his newfound aunts. The pastor spoke on John 14, about not being troubled or afraid.

*I'm trying, God, but this pain isn't getting any better.* Millions of women before her, including her mother and grandmother, endured nine months of painful pregnancy and far more painful labor, and most of them survived. How they did, she couldn't imagine. Every time she moved, a jab of pain poked her. She leaned closer to Kyler as if he could absorb some of her discomfort.

He held up his phone and tapped it. There it was—an email from Aunt Bernetta. They read it together, not without some guilty feelings. *Forgive me, God, for my impatience.*

To: Kyler Ferguson
From: Bernetta Katz
CC: Gretchen Hanson
Subject: Re: Ingrid DeLaurier
Hello, Kyler.

Well, what a surprise to hear from you, a nephew I didn't know existed. Yes, I'm still in touch with my brother, Gary. He is in real estate and lives in Colorado Springs with his wife and teenage daughter. I called him this morning to see if he wants to meet you. After he got over his surprise at your existence, I told him the background of your DNA test so he knows you're legit. He promised to let me know whether he wants to move forward with this. If you are comfortable, please send me your cell phone # so we can stay in touch.

Yours truly,
Aunt Bernie

Disappointment mingled with anticipation on Kyler's face, laced with the same guilt plaguing Paige. He met her gaze, then put his phone away. The pastor wrapped up his sermon, and after the final song, they hurried to their car, Kyler supporting her with his steady arm. They rushed past friends in their haste.

Once in the car, when her backache had subsided, Paige let out a breath.

"Now what?" Ky revved the engine too hard but made no move to leave the parking lot.

"I guess we wait."

"He'll 'let her know'"— Kyler made quote marks in the air—"if he wants to meet me. What if he decides he doesn't want to? And won't that be awkward for the aunts to stay in touch with me?"

"Babe, we have to leave this with the Lord." She cringed at the platitude, but what else could she say? "He's in shock and needs time to process this."

Someone tapped on her window. Susie Edwards, one of the friends she'd ignored on the way out, stood there, her gloved finger rapping out a rhythm.

With a groan, Paige lowered the window. "Hey, Susie."

"Morning, girlfriend." Cloudy light reflected off Susie's glasses. "How are those little ones? And how are *you*?" Her cherry-red lips parted. "You rushed out of church limping. Are you all right?"

"Nothing serious, just typical pregnancy aches and pains." Paige patted her belly. "I passed my five-month mark this week."

"When are you moving?"

"Hopefully by the end of the month. We already put our house on the market." She swallowed hard at daunting visions of packing up an entire house.

Kyler revved the engine as if hinting for them to wrap it up. Paige laid a hand on Susie's fleece jacket. "Gotta run, Susie. I'll call you!"

Susie backed away, finger-waving, and Kyler saluted the driver blocking them in. "Move it, Jason," he muttered, still revving.

*Poor Kyler.* He'd had such high hopes his bio dad would be gung-ho to meet him. *Lord, please let his dreams come true. Let Gary be the dad Ky needs.*

But Ky glowered, and he'd stay that way for the afternoon if she didn't intervene. "Babe, it's ten forty-five. Let's go get something delish for brunch. Or how about a country drive? Even better, let's drive out to our new house and soak it in." If good food and a country drive didn't cheer him up, then she was out of options.

"Okay." He took off to the east, blasting Christian bands on CarPlay.

A half hour later, they arrived in their new neighborhood where homes stood on vast acreage and kept themselves at arm's length from the road. Several showed their early Christmas spirit with inflatables in their yards. Cute, grinning Santas and snowmen contrasted with the occasional giant Grinch, all gleaming in the winter sunshine. Lofty Douglas firs towered over everything like spindly sentinels.

"It's so beautiful out here." She unrolled the window, breathing deep, savoring the pastoral landscape as she tipped her face to the nippy breeze. "We ought to drive around and find out where the nearest stores and restaurants are."

Ky slowed as they approached their new home. If only they could step inside, even for a moment. But they wouldn't have their new keys until the final signing. So she had to settle for longing gazes and wishful thinking.

To their left, a new chain-link fence blocked the vacant field. "Look, Ky." She pointed ahead. "Let's check that sign to see if it will tell us what they're building here." She craned her neck. "'Future home of Pleasant Valley Bible Chapel, your new neighborhood worship center. Designed by'—"

"It's a huge lot." Ky let out a whistle. "Big enough to build a megachurch."

Something nagged her. "The church name sounds familiar. Has there been something in the news about it?"

"Not that I can recall."

"Why would it sound familiar, then?"

"Heck if I know. Do you know someone who attends?"

"How would I? It doesn't exist yet."

Ky pulled to the shoulder. "The church must already exist somewhere else and will relocate here when it's finished."

She already had her phone out, searching it. "Okay, the current church is a couple miles away. They're merging with two other area churches and forming one big church."

"Pleasant Valley Megachurch. Beware, oh ye small, weak churches. We shall devour you!"

Paige snickered as a memory emerged. "I remember now. There was a mention in Katrice's story of a megachurch in Pleasant Valley. I think the name was the same too." She whirled to Ky, who still gazed out the window. "Ky?" Her voice cracked. "Katrice must have attended that church and knew they were building here. Because she used the exact same name in her story."

He gave her that expectant look. Yep, he knew what she was about to ask. He knew every pathway her mind traveled as well as the vessels that crisscrossed the back of his broad hands.

She laid a beseeching hand on his arm. "Can we drive over to that church and find out if anyone has heard from her? Pretty please, babe?"

Ky sighed, put the car in drive, and merged back onto the narrow country road.

# 22

# Me

**March 2070**

"The autos here remind me of autopods with wheels," I whisper to Glim as we arrive fifty years in the past. Apparently, it would be another twenty-odd years before remote-control technology allowed autos to fly. Across Seventh Avenue, two streetlamps illuminate the Falling Star Inn's elaborate brick façade.

I shiver, struck by the bleakness in this land bereft of supertrees, a scene resembling a stage set of an ancient city. Concrete. Pavement. Unnatural, man-made defilements. No nods to nature except for anemic trees in carpets of dead leaves. An emotion I can't identify further chills me. I move closer to Glim and grind my teeth. Time to snap out of it. Glim timed our arrival to 10:30 p.m. on the night of Brown's murder, so now, we watch. And wait.

A cold wind slashes my bare face. I should've borrowed a cap and extra jacket. It rarely gets this cold in 2120. My toes must be turning blue.

Fingering my earpiece, I force my taut shoulders to loosen. At least I had access to my dad's storage compartment where Glim and I found the one-to-one communication devices people used in 2070. Since they're synced up, we test them to ensure we can hear each other.

One of the autos parked next to the building must be Brown's. The street is dark and quiet. Behind us on Burnside, autos whiz by and occasionally round the corner, headlights glaring at us, leaving chemical odors in their wake. If Bombardo was telling the truth, he and Brown should be exiting any moment. Light gleams from a room on the second floor, but blinds block our view inside. I can imagine the two men sitting in there guzzling beers and sharing quips. No movement nears any of the autos. Has Mongo already slipped inside Brown's vehicle?

As I stand in Glim's embrace inside a dark doorway, he does his best to wrap his jacket around me, but it doesn't quite fit all the way. Shivering, I snuggle closer, the chill penetrating every exposed part of me—hands, face, head.

Twenty frigid minutes later, here they come. Hey, Bombardo might be a murderer, but at least he's an honest one. He towers several inches over Brown as they pass under the streetlamp. Brown leans against a Honda, and Bombardo slaps him on the back. Then Brown gets in, and I wrestle out of Glim's embrace to run across the street and warn Brown. "Hey!" I yell and wave when Brown sees me. I lean toward his closed window, signaling him to open it. He does. "I saw a man get into your car," I whisper, Bombardo approaching behind me, and alarm flares Brown's eyes and nostrils. "You might want to check behind your seat."

Sure enough, the sunroof's open. I point. "He got in through there."

Glim's voice in my ear is urging me to return, his warnings intensifying. "You're putting yourself in danger, Tree."

I dare not turn and draw attention to him.

Behind me, a cleared throat. "Is there a problem?" comes a warning tone.

I whirl, face-to-face with Bombardo. Eyes shadowed in the darkness, mouth a hard, straight line. Brown's door unclicks, and all the things I could say to my nemesis pummel me.

*You're going to be president someday. Then you're going to gut the United States, merge it with Canada and Mexico to form a new nation.*

*You're going to redefine crime in order to make yourself and your policies look good, yet you're going to get away with murder.*

But I clamp down my teeth on all of it. He'd probably have me arrested, although I see no police anywhere. If this were 2120, there'd be all-seeing security guard robots patrolling both sidewalks, checking that nobody is stepping out of line. So efficient—unless the gangs riot.

*You're going to strip us of all our freedoms.*

Brown opens the rear door.

I stand frozen, unable to speak.

Bombardo scoots around me. "Ollie, is there a problem?"

"She saw someone get into my car." He shines a light

on the rear floor, and I crane my neck, but see nothing. "I left my sunroof open."

Bombardo's brow rises. "See anyone?" He braces one hand on the roof, another on his "friend's" shoulder.

Brown waves the flashlight back and forth.

Great. Nobody is hiding in the back of his car. I stand on tiptoe to check the roof. Nothing. Both of them cast accusatory looks at me, but I am already slipping away, deeper into the night, to a place where I can hear without being seen. A cargo vehicle parked behind Brown proves the perfect hiding place. I circle behind and huddle next to it on the sidewalk, out of eyeshot, shivering from more than mere cold.

"Is she gone?" Bombardo's voice carries clearly.

"She headed toward Burnside."

"What a weirdo."

As I clench my fist, I squelch the urge to hurl curses. Then a little boy appears on the sidewalk and raps on the window of Brown's Honda. Wait, no. He's not a little boy. He's a dwarf.

A grown man in a child-sized body.

"Oh, Ollie," Bombardo says. "This is Monroe, the friend I mentioned who needs a ride. His apartment is a few blocks away."

When Brown doesn't reply, he adds, "I've known this guy a long time, and he's good people. Fully trustworthy."

"Okay. Sure." Brown's door slams, and the little man climbs in the passenger seat. Bombardo goes back inside.

It's all in slow motion now. I'd almost been convinced we got here on the wrong day. But as Brown drives away, the truth crashes me to my knees.

Monroe is Mongo.

"Wait!" I yell, but Brown's receding taillights mock me. I run back to Glim. "We've got to get up to Davis Street! Right now! Brown let the murderer into his auto!"

"You mean th-the little guy?"

"Yes! That little guy is Mongo! Monroe. The 'child' the witness saw running down the street after the wreck."

"Tree, stop!" But I ignore Glim and jump in Fern, hoping to beat Brown to the murder site. Brown's Honda turns left on Davis when I am still a block behind him. A dying streetlight pulsates, trying to hold on to the bitter end, and my heartbeat keeps pace with it like clockwork.

I careen around the corner.

Up ahead, a crashed auto.

A "child" running along the opposite sidewalk back toward Sixth.

I'm too late.

# 23

# Her

**November 2019**

Pleasant Valley Bible Chapel, a stately white-brick edifice, stood empty when Paige and Kyler swung into the parking lot. "It's only eleven forty-five." She touched Ky's arm. "But there's nobody here."

"There's a sign on the door. Let's go see what it says."

Ky followed her to the glass double doors.

> Welcome to PVBC! We have outgrown our home church and currently meet at Pleasant Valley Elementary on Sundays at 8:30, 10:00, and 11:30. Hope to see you there. Pastor Lou Zeller and team.

"I take it you want to go check it out?" His elbow nudged hers.

"We might as well since we're going to be living nearby. Okay, love?"

They drove the mile to the school where vehicles overflowed the parking lot. "Oh!" She pointed through the windshield. "Look at that awesome view of Mount Hood." The snowcapped peak glowed in the winter sunshine, a perfect triangle framed by cerulean sky.

Ky found a spot near the back of the lot. "I bet we'll be in time for the sermon."

They walked the length of the lot hand in hand and into a hall designed for children. Tiny lockers, short-slung bookshelves, and murals with positive messages brightened the walls. They passed a coffee counter where a lady stood doing something on a laptop. Just ahead, a smiling usher standing beside gymnasium doors welcomed them. A man's amplified voice from inside the gym carried to her ears, followed by a burst of laughter from the crowd.

Paige hesitated before the friendly usher. "Can you direct me to the ladies' room, please?" That coffee lady.... Was it her fixation on Katrice that made her think...?

She followed the usher's direction, then veered to the counter where the fair-haired woman frowned.

As she got closer, she stifled a gasp. The woman wasn't Katrice, but she could be her older sister. Fairer of skin and hair, she outweighed Katrice by a good forty pounds and wore a bright fuchsia cardigan Katrice wouldn't be caught dead in. Yet the facial resemblance...

"Hi."

The woman, apparently not expecting anyone, startled and pasted on a smile. The name badge on a lanyard swayed as she pressed a hand to her chest. "Hi! Welcome! What can I do for you?"

"You look so much like a friend of mine, and I'm pretty sure she used to attend here."

"Oh, great. Then I might know her. I'm Karin, by the way." She pronounced her name the European way, accenting the second syllable. "And you are?"

Paige introduced herself and Ky, who now stood beside her. "We bought a house a couple miles from here. My friend's name is Katrice Carpenter, and…"

"Oh, really? What a co-inkadink! That's my last name too."

"Your name is Karin Carpenter? Like the singer?"

Her smile widened into a chuckle. "It's not spelled or pronounced the same, but yes, I get a lot of comments on that."

But the conversation was veering out of control, as it often did when Paige struck up an acquaintance with personable extroverts. Time to reel it in. "I've been worried about my friend because she's fallen out of contact with everyone. I'm hoping someone here knows where she is and that she is safe."

"Unfortunately, her name doesn't ring a bell. I would remember a name like Katrice."

"But you must be related to her. You could be her twin, and you have the same last name."

"Well, Carpenter is my married name. So if there's a relationship, it'd be on my husband's side, not mine."

Now that made no sense at all. How could someone who looked so much like her friend not be related? And what were the odds her last name matched?

Another burst of laughter from the crowd. Cool, a pastor with a sense of humor. No wonder the church was bursting at the seams.

Karin drummed manicured fingernails on the counter. "After the service, I'll introduce you to my husband. Maybe he'll know if she's a relative."

After that, they snuck into the gymnasium for the rest of the sermon on Proverbs 3:5–6. Paige couldn't resist a quiet amen more than once. Twenty minutes later, she and Ky maneuvered through the milling crowd to the coffee counter, and she helped herself to a cup of decaf. Gripping the Styrofoam cup with both hands, she willed the warmth to seep into her cold palms. Kyler poured himself a cup of regular and placed it against the back of her fingers. "Double-duty hand-warmers," he said as they shared a grin.

"There you are!" Karin approached with a little boy on one hand and a dark-haired man with aggressive features on the other. Even with the bushy eyebrows and piercing stare, he managed to attain handsome status. Not a trace of Katrice in him anywhere. "This is my husband, Theo Carpenter, and my son, Matty. Theo, this is Paige and Ky. She thinks she might know someone related to you."

"Katrice Carpenter?" Paige tilted her head. "Ring a bell? I think she used to attend here."

Theo's brow furrowed. "The name isn't familiar. But I

have some cousins on my dad's side I've never met."

"The thing is, she looks like she could be your wife's sister."

"Really? I'm confident I never saw anyone here who looks like my wife. I would've noticed."

"Unless she went to a different service."

A quick incline of his head. "True. We always attend the third service. Yes, it's possible people can attend here and never cross paths. One reason why we're building a new facility."

The little boy, who resembled his mother, hung from Karin's hand at a diagonal, as if seeing how far he could fall before landing. Only her firm grip kept him from hitting the floor.

"Matty, stop," she scolded.

"The house we bought is right across the road from your new lot."

Their eyes lit.

"The big white farmhouse, you mean?"

At her nod, Karin gushed, "Oh, what a beautiful place." She eyed Paige's belly, smiling. "I hope you guys enjoy living there. When are you due?"

Paige told her, and they made small talk until Karin said, "Once you guys move, I hope you come visit us again. We love Pastor Lou." She jerked her free hand toward the balding pastor who stood near the door shaking hands and slapping backs. "Since he's been senior pastor, we've grown exponentially."

"I can tell he's a funny guy. How long has he been here?"

"Five years. His whole family's great. His daughter, Annabelle, is attending Multnomah University, and his wife is a lovely person. They have a teenage son who's just precious."

"Well, we'll be right across the street." She squeezed Ky's hand. "I don't see why we can't visit again."

"Awesome! We'd love to have you over to our house for dinner. We're in Damascus."

Theo pulled a card from his shirt pocket. "If you could use any help moving, shoot me a text. I'd be happy to lend a hand."

What benevolence to two people they'd just met! Paige swallowed the clog in her throat and took the card. "Wow, thanks. That's so generous of you."

Ky rested his hand on the small of her back. "We were talking about going out for brunch. Know any good restaurants around here?"

Theo rattled off a couple of places, Paige's mind only half focused. The other half swirled at the improbability of Karin resembling Katrice so much, yet not being related. And her husband sharing the same last name but bearing no resemblance.

She'd never understand how genetics worked. For something God designed, He sure could do baffling things with it.

# 24

# Me

**March 2070**

I nearly weep as Glim strong-arms me into a doorway on Davis Street. He stayed right behind me as I raced here and events unfolded. A man emerges from the lit-up nightclub on the opposite corner. His lips are moving, and he's holding up his wrist.

"Tree, we've seen enough. Time to head home now," Glim whispers again, his minty breath stirring the hair over my ear.

"Sssh. The police will be here soon. See, there's the witness, calling them right now. I need to tell them what I saw."

"We need to get out of here. This is a crime scene."

I disregard him. "If I'd realized who the dwarf was sooner, I could've prevented it. That stupid police report said the perp dropped through the sunroof." I shake my head. "It threw me off."

"Even if you had figured it out, what could you have

done? Warned Brown right in front of Bombardo?"

People from the nightclub are starting to gather around the crash site, gawking and talking. "My presence would've been a deterrent."

"Maybe temporarily, but he would've found another opportunity."

Great. He's making sense. Maybe it is a matter of timing. A police vehicle arrives and lights up the crash site. Once again, I shrug out of Glim's grasp and slink toward the curb. A policewoman gestures for people to stand back and then inspects the driver's seat. As I get closer, a policeman blocks off the area with yellow tape.

I halt as an auto turns the corner, and it would've run me over if I'd stepped off the curb. The car creeps along, stopping in the street, and the driver's head cranes toward the accident under the shadow of a streetlamp. And then, from behind, an unseen force shoves me hard, and I am falling, falling, onto the pavement. The hard landing jars all my bones and knocks the breath out of me. Next to my head screeches a tire, and I scream to be heard over the crowd noise.

Pain mauls me as a pair of hands lifts me and drags me to the sidewalk. "Swee," says the most beautiful voice ever. "G-get in Fern right now and go home. Bombardo p-pushed you. You need to disappear before he comes back and tries again."

Blood oozes from my hands. I touch a nasty bump on my forehead.

"Plus, you need medical treatment." He lifts me to my feet. When I stagger, my breath coming in rapid gasps, heart pounding, his grip tightens around me. He tucks me into my autopod with a decisive thrust. Over my protests, he resets her panel for home. "I told you this was dangerous, Tree, but you didn't listen."

In the few seconds it takes for Fern to take me home, a depressing realization stuns me despite the pain.

What if it's not possible to alter the past?

Back in my home year, during my overnight hospital stay, I mull over the sequence of events. My headache has ebbed, and the doctor is finished taking images of my head. But my ribs still throb like a woodpecker is perched on my chest.

According to Glim, Bombardo appeared around the corner of Grand Avenue on foot, saw me, and acted so fast Glim couldn't react in time. After he pushed me, he ran back the way he came, and the police never saw a thing. Considering the dark of the night and the drama of the crash site, that makes sense. Yet something's off in the narrative—a piece is missing. I think so hard my brain hurts. But it's useless. The memory won't come. What did I see that isn't penetrating the fuzz where my brain should be?

Glim marvels that Bombardo recognized me from the side, in the dark. It must have been my clothing and my hair, he says. He suggests Bombardo walked to the site after

Monroe returned, mission accomplished, wanting to see it for himself. Theory is the perpetrator is often present during the aftermath of his crime and blends in with the crowd like a regular spectator. Maybe Bombardo did.

"But why would he do that to me? Did he think I was a threat?"

A robot wheels in my meal tray and leaves it beside my bed.

"Yeah, of c-course." Glim rolls his compometal hospital chair to make room for my breakfast. "He realized you were the lady from earlier and panicked, thinking you may have witnessed M-monroe getting in the car. He wouldn't know for–for sure, but he didn't want to take any chances once he saw you there."

"You could have reported him to the police."

"Uh-uh." His gaze follows the robot's departure. Then he scoots the chair to my side. "I wasn't going to take the r-risk. I didn't know how badly injured you were, and my only thought was to get you home and to a-a hospital."

"Well, thanks. That was thoughtful."

He helps me sit up, then moves the tray to my lap. After I poke at the oatmeal, choke some down, and give Glim the rest, he downs it in three big bites.

I pick up a purple grape, then put it back. "And now, Bombardo is still a fixture of our past, having wreaked havoc and mayhem over all of us."

"Not over me or my family, Tree."

"I know, I know. But you have to admit the United

States our grandparents grew up in was a better place than Normerica."

Glim shrugs, staring off into space. What *is* he thinking? "*You* have to admit there are plenty of ways life is better now. Crime is reduced, so is unregistered drug use. Hardly anyone is hungry or sick. Most of us will live well past the age of a hundred."

What's the point in arguing? I lay back, close my eyes, and plop my head to the side. I feel him watching me, but I stay in my self-imposed cocoon. Our points of disagreement have ramped up lately. Weren't we on the same page about Bombardo and time travel? Now, he's backtracking.

"So we're going to let Bombardo get away with murder?"

"No." His voice sounds nearer, and his breath warms my cheek. "You should write a book about what you've learned, Tree. Exposing him posthumously is better than not at all. The whole world will soon know who he was."

What a great idea. "You're brilliant. I'll start the minute I get out of here." I infuse sincerity into my tone so he won't think I'm being sarcastic. "Which means I need to travel back to 2020."

"Why?" His shoes scuffle. He must've jolted.

"Research." I peep one eye open.

Yep. He's frowning. He rubs his temples. "What kind of research?"

I open both eyes. "I have an ancestor who played a significant role in all this, and I'd like to visit her before she passes."

"Are you going to tell her who you are?"

"Probably not. I just want to get to know her, pick her brain. In the interest of research. Subtly, that is. Do you want to go with?"

He's silent. Then he gazes out the window again. What is out there so compelling? Whatever it is, it's out of my sightline. "Why don't you go ahead, Swee?" His voice softens as he meets my eyes once more. "You know how this works now. You've got enough cash to get you by for a while. I'd be in the way."

Taken aback, I nod, feigning nonchalance. Inside, I'm anything but.

# 25

# Her

**November 2019**

On their drive home, Paige, her tummy full and happy from the delicious brunch, could feel her thighs and rear expanding with all the extra calories, and not only from baby weight. She'd be a whale by the time she gave birth. Her appetite had never been so out of control. She glanced at her puffy face in the visor mirror. Great. Chipmunk cheeks, a sure sign she was retaining water.

"When is your next doctor appointment?" Ky asked as if he'd read her mind.

"Tomorrow."

He swerved around a pothole on Foster and spun gravel on the shoulder. "Hello, Pothole. Fancy meeting you here."

Giggling, she released the visor she'd been gripping as he settled back into his lane. "We should stop and say hi to Mom on the way home."

"Yes, let's do. She'll be so excited we're going to be closer to her."

Paige texted Doreen and received an affirmation that she was home. Ten minutes ticked by on their way to Southeast Shane Lane and Doreen's dog-friendly home. After the dogs got their exuberant greetings out of the way and Doreen served coffee, the subject turned to the new house.

As Kyler predicted, Doreen threw her hands up in ecstasy when he shared the news of the home inspection and closing. Eyeing Paige, she sobered, tilting her head, then stretched across the cocktail table to touch Paige's shoulder. "Honey, are you sure you can handle moving?"

Paige shrugged. She had no idea. "I hope so."

"Plus, you still have to sell your house." Doreen resettled in her seat. The recliner creaked as she swiveled side to side. "Have you hired a Realtor yet?"

Nodding, Paige kneaded Caitlyn's fur with her stockinged foot. The dog lay curled, content, at her feet, Siobhan next to Ky. "The real estate office over on Lombard sells a lot of homes in the area. We're—"

"That's it!" Doreen snapped her fingers, and Caitlyn raised her head, cocking her ears.

"What's it?"

"Gary's last name. Remember I told you his last name reminded me of a major Portland thoroughfare? It was Lombard, the one that goes through your neighborhood." She palmed her forehead. "I can't believe it took me this long to remember, especially since I've driven that road umpteen times on my way to your place. But I guess, since we recently talked about it, it's fresh in my head, and—"

"My father's last name is Lombard?"

"No, not Lombard. But something like it. Lombardi? No, Lombardo, I'm almost sure. Like the bandleader from the forties. Guy Lombardo."

"Yeah, I know who he is. By the way, I contacted my biological aunts yesterday." He launched into the events leading to the email exchange, all the while studying his mom's face.

Paige sipped her coffee. Gary Lombardo? It sounded like Katrice's fictional bad guy, Bombardo. She'd love to giggle over that with her friend—if only she knew how to find her.

Pulling out her phone, she searched the name. Two Gary Lombardos popped up on Facebook, neither of them in Colorado or the Portland area. Next, she tried Gary Lombardi, still with no success.

"Babe, I'm not finding him on the internet."

Doreen rocked faster. "I could be wrong about the name. It's been almost thirty years."

"I'll email my aunts for his name." Such yearning deepened Ky's tone, despite his efforts at casual. "It would be cool if he wants to meet me."

Doreen got up, came over, and hugged her son's neck. "Just remember, hon, if he doesn't, it's his loss."

"Yeah, yeah."

"Seriously. If he doesn't want you in his life, he's a double fool. First, because he couldn't see what a great catch I was"—she winked at Paige over Ky's shoulder, and Paige grinned back—"and second, because he's missing out on the best son a father could ask for."

At Emmanuel Birthing Center the next morning, Paige still basked in warm memories—meeting the Carpenters, spending the day with Doreen, culminating in a fried chicken dinner—so she almost didn't notice Dr. Anthony frowning at the blood pressure cuff. When the doctor cleared her throat, Paige tried not to attach a worrisome meaning to it, but Dr. Anthony, a smiley ob-gyn in her forties, rarely frowned.

"What is it?" Paige shifted her hips to a more comfortable position on the hard clinic chair.

"Why don't we take it one more time." The cuff inflated again, and Paige practiced the deep breathing she'd learned for when labor came.

"Hmm, one eighty over one oh six." Dr. Anthony tucked her bobbed salt-and-pepper hair back from her face, her frown deepening.

Whoa. "That's unreal. Why is it so high?"

The doctor set the BP device aside. "It could mean you have preeclampsia. But I'll have a better idea once I get your urine test results."

"I've heard of that." Paige's pulse spiked. It sounded scary. "But is…is it dangerous?"

"It is treatable. You—"

"What about my babies?"

"We'll keep a close eye on them. Now, let's check for swelling in your legs and ankles." The doctor pulled Paige's feet onto her lap and felt the skin around her ankles and calves. "Yes, there's a bit of swelling starting." She lowered Paige's legs, then reached into a drawer, and found a pamphlet. "Here's some information on preeclampsia. And here's what you're going to do, young lady, to make sure it doesn't develop into full-blown eclampsia. You're going to rest as much as possible between now and your due date. You're going to cut your salt intake and drink sixty-four ounces of water a day. How much water do you drink?"

"Not enough." Paige couldn't bring herself to look at her doctor. She hadn't been diligent in watching what she ate, and this was the price she'd pay. She had to give up delicious restaurant meals and those snacks that kept her hands and mouth busy all day.

"Make yourself drink eight glasses a day. I'm going to prescribe you magnesium sulfate, which you'll take every day between now and delivery. And no more work. I'll write you a note to excuse you."

"I can't work?"

"You can't do anything that will tax your system."

"I can't quit my job. I—"

"Your school will hire a substitute."

*But the kids. Moriah. Elijah. Kimmy. Natalie...*

"But we're moving next month."

"Then your husband will get to do all the packing. I

bet he'll enjoy that, won't he?"

How could this be happening? No way would Kyler be okay packing up the entire house. "He has a job too."

Dr. Anthony's eyes softened, and she patted Paige's shoulder. "I'm sorry this is happening. I know it's a disruption. But you and your babies have to be your priority right now. And your husband's. Not your job or your new home." She pointed to the leaflet Paige held. "Go home and read that, discuss it with your husband. And I'll need to see you once a week until your symptoms subside."

After Dr. Anthony handed her a cup for her urine sample, Paige shuffled to the bathroom. Her school was required by law to give her medical leave without jeopardizing her position, and she'd get up to fourteen weeks of paid leave. She did the math. She'd lose a month of pay. The loss of income would be hard. How could she explain this to Ky? Would he resent being her caretaker and sole breadwinner? This wasn't the ideal time to find out what he was made of.

What terrible timing. She'd have to shelve the app design. But, when she returned to the classroom, would it be too late for kids like Elijah and Tavius? What if they gave up on school before she returned sometime next year?

She set the urine sample in the slot and then washed her hands again, dreading the conversations with her husband and her principal.

Before she headed home, she sat in her car and skimmed the pamphlet about what she faced: "A serious complication of pregnancy characterized by high blood pressure and fluid retention." The rest of the words blurred, except for one phrase—"potentially fatal."

Yet it didn't answer the most important question: Would she and her babies survive this?

After a Google search, the pressure in her head eased. The odds were in her favor. A small percentage of mothers with eclampsia died, but the vast majority survived.

Breathing a desperate prayer, she started the car and headed to school.

# 26

# Me

**July 2120**

It takes a week for the pain from my injuries to abate. I'm able to return to work after three days since I can't exert myself sitting at my workstation and billing MedicAll. My boss, Beta, is sympathetic and tells me to take as much time off each day to rest as I need to. How forch that she's so understanding. Glim, Eartha, and Bestie spoil me with TLC, but I still have an abundance of time to think, to search my memory for that elusive missing piece. It teases me, buried beyond my consciousness like an unearthed treasure. The Cloud can't help me. I can't capture camera footage from the corner of Sixth and Davis in the year 2070.

But I can pretend I'm a camera looking down on the scene. While Glim is in his dorm working and Eartha is out, I take advantage of the rare solitude. Lying in bed, Bestie warming my feet, I allow my imagination to drift, float, seek, coming to rest above the intersection where I stood that night. In my mind's eye, I see the cops scurry through their investigation. I watch myself shimmy out of Glim's restraining embrace, emerge from the doorway, and move toward the curb.

And what is Glim doing?

He's trailing me, out of sight.

I look to my left, toward the oncoming car. And there it is. I remember what I saw at that moment. Or rather, what I didn't see. Glim claimed Bombardo came around the same corner on foot. But when I glanced over, the sidewalk was empty and still. Shouldn't I have seen someone? A movement, at the very least? If Bombardo didn't come up behind me, who did?

The truth knifes through me, slashing my insides, and I see. I know who pushed me.

Glim.

I gasp, my heart doing a desperate dance. Glim, the man I love, who I thought loved me. Why would he do that?

The way his gaze darkened when he warned me not to "mess with" history—wait. He did it to stop me.

He was desperate enough that he was willing to risk great injury to me. He had to have had a huge stake in stopping me.

Of course he did. His family benefited from Bombardo's administration. He couldn't risk Bombardo getting arrested, his future political career nonexistent.

Then why pretend to go along with it?

Was he merely excited about the idea of time travel, but when I got too close to messing with his past, he balked?

No, wait. He only agreed because he was determined to obtain twentieth-century currency, and I held the answer. And he was determined because…

He wanted to return to 1995, implying he wanted to stay awhile. To spy on his ancestors. "Among other things," he'd said.

What other things?

What about the time I caught him time traveling?

I suck in a sharp breath.

I think I know what he was doing in 1995.

I can't let on that I've figured him out. But it'll be difficult to play dumb. I need to talk to someone, yet at the same time, who could I tell? I can't tell Eartha. She'd just tell me "I told you so."

Yes, she did tell me so, and Brook did too. But I didn't listen.

After what seems like hours of mulling, I hit on a plan. But it won't work until I'm pain-free, so I'll have to stay put another day or two. I can manage a couple days of pretending. I hope.

In fact, here comes Glim's signal now. Turning to my side, I give him what I hope is a sweet welcoming smile. He sits on my mattress beside me, caressing my hand, asking me how I'm feeling, and as I answer, I scream inside—*How could you do this to me!*

I search his eyes for any signs of humanity. Were they always so dark and inscrutable, and did I only see what I wanted to see in them—warmth, affection, benevolence?

Curse my unwillingness to see his true colors! The waving red flags popped up here and there and should have been clues, had I bothered to examine them. For instance, his basic selfish streak. I dismissed it as part of the normal human condition.

Closing my eyes to signal my weariness, I stiffen as, to my horror, he lies beside me and takes my hand. Is he going to finish what he started and murder me? He rubs my shoulder blade. "Relax," he whispers. "You're so tense." He pulls me into the spoon position and holds me, massaging my head.

I grind my teeth against the urge to wrest myself from his possessive grasp. But I don't dare.

Time to pretend with all my might as his caresses slow, then stop.

I fight sleep until I hear his rhythmic breathing, each sigh punctuated with a soft whistling snore. Incredibly, I fall asleep, the comfort of his arms overpowering my repugnance. When I awake, he's gone, the privacy wall is up, and I'm alive. I pinch myself to be sure. Faint doggy snores drift from the foot of the bed, human snores from across the room. Breezy and Skye sleep as soundly and untroubled as my dog.

I flex my limbs, feel my ribs, and rejoice—the pain is nearly gone. I won't have to wait two days to implement my plan.

I'm leaving today—before Glim realizes I'm gone. He'll never find me.

After tossing and turning for half an hour, I give up sleeping and go into the Cloud to research life from a hundred years ago. Apparently, everybody owned two things: a smartphone, and some sort of computer like a tablet or laptop. For writing a book, I'll need one. I have roughly two thousand dollars of their cash. That better be enough to buy those two basic items. I have no idea how much they cost. And who will teach me how to use them?

In old images of computers from back then, the screen looks like the hologram of a Cloud portal, except it's a physical device. Maybe it won't be too hard to learn.

Next, I search for details of my ancestor's life, the woman who holds the key to my past. Her full name, where she lived, whom she married, when she died. Her obituary is fascinating reading, and I peruse it for any clues. It might take a while to find her once I get there. I don't have an exact address, but "social media" was the big thing in 2020. I might track her down that way. Funny how the Cloud precursor, the internet, was so segmented back then, compared to our Cloud today where everything is in one gigantic cyberspace.

Step 1: Message Beta to let her know I need extended leave to deal with a family emergency. By the time she sees it and asks questions, I'll be gone.

Step 2: Persuade Eartha to look after Bestie without telling her why.

My opportunity presents itself at 6:30 a.m. when I go out to the living room to watch the sunrise. She awakens and stumbles into the kitchen for coffee. She never brought up the missing meds again. She must believe it was Breeze, and I'm still in her good graces.

"Tree! You're up early."

"I woke up at three and couldn't get back to sleep."

My voice and face give me away, for she scoots over and touches my arm. "What's wrong?"

I sigh. "I need a huge favor."

"Uh, how huge?"

"Can you watch Bestie for a few weeks?" More like a few months, but I can't tell her. "I have to go somewhere."

Her brow furrows. "Where?"

"I can't tell you. I don't want Glim to know. Because when he finds out I'm gone, he'll ask you where I went. You can tell him I refused to say."

"Why don't you want Glim to know where you are?"

I stretch my hands high over my head. "It's a long story. Please don't tell him that." I slap my hands down to my side. "Just say I'll contact him at some point."

"Hmm, okay. Are you going to visit your parents in Bend?"

"Can't tell you that."

"But can't you take Bestie with you?"

I pause. "Well, I may come back for her if the place I'm going can accommodate her. That's the most I can promise."

"So I'll need to tend her at the most three weeks? But

possibly less?"

I shrug, as clueless as she is. "If all goes well."

"Message me when you get there."

That's an agreement, right? I express my gratitude with a hug. Now for the practicalities. I stuff as much into a suitcase as I can. Bestie, sensing something going down, sits staring, then stands, paces, and sits again. After grabbing blankets off the bed before my roommates awaken, I make a bed in the back of Fern and fill a cooler with sandwiches. I have plenty of cash to buy food and other supplies when I get there, and if I don't have to pay for lodging, the money should hold me for a while.

I hug Bestie, and tears fill my eyes as I whisper. "Not sure when I'll see you again, sweetie pie."

Bestie licks my face.

Hmm, 7:04 a.m. Time to go.

I climb in Fern and set the time accelerator to June 2019. I need extra time to master the era's technology before I contact my relative. Plus, Glim will assume I'm going to 2020. So I'm dialing it back to a year where he won't find me. I leave the return time open so, in real time, my sojourn to the past runs parallel to the present. If I spend three months in 2019, I'll be gone from 2120 for three months. I will set the return time later.

I'm on my way. Buh-bye, Glim.

So long, 2120.

# 27

# Her

**December 2019**

As soon as Paige saw Dr. Anthony's face drooping behind her perky bob, Paige knew. She clutched Ky's hand even harder, her pulse revving.

"Good morning, Paige," the doctor began. Was it her imagination, or did a note of resignation ring in those words? "We got your urine test results back, and the news isn't good."

Paige twisted her hand, clasped in Ky's, the veins sticking out of hers, the tiny blond hairs bristling on his fingers.

"We found protein in your urine, which means you do have preeclampsia. The good news is your blood test showed normal platelet counts and liver enzymes. But we will want to keep an eye on those." Dr. Anthony propped the laptop against her chest, crinkling up her baby blue scrubs. "The ultrasound images showed two normal babies, a bit on the small side but with no visible anomalies."

Paige's shoulders relaxed as relief erupted in a sigh.

"Have you been taking the magnesium and drinking all the water?"

She nodded, and Ky cut in, "I've made sure of it."

"You haven't been overdoing it with the activities?"

"No, I spend most of my day in my recliner. Hubby here does all the cooking and TLC."

The doctor loosed her grip on the computer, skimming it. "Your BP is still one forty-five over ninety-three. Not as bad, but still too high. I'm concerned about that."

"But why me? Do I have any risk factors?"

"Yes, cases of primigravida and multiparity are at greater risk. In other words, first pregnancies and multiples. So you have a double whammy."

"What else can be done?"

"Well, historically, we solve the problem by inducing early labor. But only after the baby's developed enough. We can't do that in your case at only twenty-five weeks." She scrolled down. "I see you're having headaches accompanied by nausea, which are typical symptoms. I can prescribe you a gentle pain reliever that won't hurt your babies."

"Thanks."

She rolled her chair closer and touched Paige's hand. "You're in a stage of life when you have to take very, very good care of yourself. Two little lives are depending on it."

"And two big lives," cut in Kyler.

"Yes." The doctor chuckled. "Two very important, big lives." She wrapped up the visit, adding additional instructions, then sent them on their way with a "Take care, you two."

"We will."

Paige wept all the way home, bowed under waves of panic. "Why me?"

"Calm down, babe."

"I hate when you say that!"

"Remember your verse? First Peter five seven?"

"Yeah." She sniffed. "But even if I cast my cares on God, maybe this is His will, and I'll have to endure it. Women die from this, you know."

He made that scoffing sound she hated almost as much as his attempt to calm her. "Death is quite a stretch, babe. Most women who have preeclampsia recover. You're not going to die."

Despite her common sense telling her Ky couldn't know the future, his matter-of-fact confidence reassured her. She wiped her face with her palm. The MercyMe song "Even If" played on the radio. God must have heard her cries and sent the song especially for her. She clung to the lyrics that claimed God could save her through the fire. And even if He didn't, He was still her hope.

Easy for her to say she believed it. But with her life and her babies at stake, could she put it into practice?

"Want me to stay home with you today?" Ky shot her a look, then back to the road. "I've got some vacay days to use."

*Thank you, God.* "Yes, please."

"We can take a drive through the Gorge or to Mount

Hood. Anywhere you want to go, my lady."

"Take me to the beach. The most windswept, stormy one you can find." The better to mirror her emotions.

"Devil's Punchbowl?"

"Perfect choice, babe."

"It's 'cuz I wuv you."

"Aw, I willy wuv you too."

Her wonderful husband summoned help with their move from their church family, and four of their friends, plus Doreen, now filled the house, sorting, packing, tossing, laughing, while Paige lay in the recliner giving final approval on the donations and throwaways. The local Christian station provided background accompaniment.

She shifted uncomfortably. They must think she was a lazy slug.

Ky had assured her they all understood her situation, but guilt still cropped up. Like the time she'd given Tavius an F on a test—although he deserved it, she felt she'd contributed to his delinquency.

She'd lain around all through Christmas festivities also, enjoying the rest yet feeling like a leech while Ky and his mom decorated the tree and the house, shopped, baked, and waited on her. Now everything Christmas was packed up as if it never happened. But the beautiful memories stayed fresh in her mind. She looked forward to wearing the cute maternity smocks Doreen had gotten her—paisleys and florals, pastels and polka dots. And Ky looked forward to her wearing the skimpy black maternity lingerie he'd gotten her and laughed at her blushing face when she opened his gift in front of Doreen. The memory brought a smile.

After Ky furnished the crew with pizza and fruit beverages, the guests all trickled out, leaving them alone finally. Ky pulled up a chair next to her and patted her baby bump. "Look how much we got done today."

They'd stripped the living room walls and left the tables bereft of décor. Storage crates piled high in waiting mode in the corners, nearly to the ceiling. A house in flux. When they moved in, the bare house waited for them to imprint their personalities on it. And now, its personality was packed away and hidden until it could blossom in a new environment. Tomorrow, the moving vans would arrive and haul everything to the new house.

Ky got up to fill her water bottle. "Your medicine." He handed it to her and sat. "Drink up."

"Yes, Dr. Ferguson." Paige drank deep, forcing it down, missing the sweet, bubbly tang of her favorite Diet Sprite. Dr. Anthony had urged her to avoid sodas, at least until the birth. Ky had been tyrannical in enforcing the doctor's instructions—monitoring her salt intake, refusing to buy any soda, filling her water bottle, despite her protesting she had to use the bathroom twice as often now. "Which means getting up from my mandatory rest," she'd reminded him.

"I can't let anything happen to you or the babies," he'd said, his somber mood contagious.

So she'd zipped her lip. After all, this was only temporary.

Now he clamped a hand on her shoulder. "I got an email from Gary. Finally." With him so consumed by the move, he'd seemed to forget his previous obsession: his biological father. Now, his eyes lit.

"Oh, babe, that's so great." In the weeks since he'd contacted his aunts, he hadn't said a word about it. "What did he say?"

"He asked me questions about myself and mentioned things about himself. One interesting thing he told me was that, before he was in real estate, he'd been an electronic engineer." He shook his head. "How do you get real estate agent and electronic engineer into the same person?"

She caught up both his hands, sharing his enthusiasm. "He must be a multifaceted person. Like you."

"That must be where I get my love of all things IT."

"Is he a *Star Wars* aficionado too?"

"I wouldn't be surprised."

"I bet he has a great sense of humor."

"Do you want to read it?"

"Of course!"

He handed her his phone, and she skimmed the email for something to catch her interest.

I see you take after my father's side of the family.

Your half sister is Zadie. She's sixteen and enjoys cheerleading for her school's basketball team. She looks a little like you.

I was raised in California but attended Portland State University before moving to Colorado and have been here ever since. I haven't visited Portland in many years, but now, I'm thinking maybe a trip back would be in order. I'd like to meet my son. Although my daughter is an amazing young woman, I always wished for a son. I'll make arrangements and reach out to you. I have attached a photo of me and my family.

I hope you and your wife had a warm and enjoyable Christmas.

Yours truly, Gary

"He wants to meet you! That's wonderful." Paige clattered the phone onto the empty side table. "You should tell him he's got two grandbabies on the way."

"Good idea." His grin stretched wide as he keyed in

a reply, narrating as he went. "Gary, thank you for your kind reply. My wife, Paige, and I look forward to meeting you. You will be a grandpa soon as we are expecting twins in March." He turned to Paige. "I want to ask him what his family would think, but I don't know…"

"Awkward, isn't it? He didn't say if he told them about you."

"Yeah, but these days, there isn't the same stigma over out-of-wedlock babies there was decades ago. He ought to be able to tell them."

"On the other hand, consider this. If I found out you had a kid somewhere, it would be huge bombshell for me. I might be a little upset. I'm curious if he told them and how the wife took it. If you ask him, maybe he'll tell you. But be subtle about it."

"Good idea. How about: 'Do you think your wife and daughter would like to come with you? It would be good to meet them.'"

Paige nodded her approval. "Perfect."

"Let's check out the photo." Kyler tapped the screen a couple times, revealing a family of three—Dad, Mom, teenage daughter. Gary stood tall, a handsome man in his fifties.

She stole the phone back and zoomed in. "I see you in him. You're built like him. Zadie does look kind of like you, but she takes after the mom."

"I'm still wrapping my brain around the fact that this man is my biological dad and this girl is the sister I never had. Blows me away."

"Oh, and is his last name Lombardo, like your mom thought?"

"Actually, no, it's not. Close though." He brought the screen nearer his face. "His last name is Bombardo. Gary Bombardo."

# 28

# Me

**June 2019**

"You have reached your destination and may now disembark."

"Not quite yet, Fern. First, I need to get my bearings."

I've arrived, shivering, in the year 2019 on a cool, cloudy June morning. In my beige short-sleeved jumpsuit, I hope to blend in. Summer in the twenty-first century is the warmest time of the year. Yet it feels chilly with the temperature in the upper fifties or so. In 2120, a typical winter temp. Shifting from side to side, I gauge the pain level in my ribs: almost nil. But the pain in my ribs has transported to my heart, the fresh ache over Glim's backstabbing nearly paralyzing me. But I must keep moving. No time for luxuries like tears.

My head is still spinning from the trip, during which my dorm fell away and disintegrated as time whirred by so fast it could be a scene break in a film. Then Fern and I materialized in someone's back yard. I crane around, secure in the knowledge nobody can see me as long as I stay inside

Fern. Glim's explanation reassures me: people in this time dimension can't see autopods. But as I step out, I turn to see an old house with boarded-up windows. Next to me, an ancient, empty garage, perfect for storing Fern. Rooftops march on for blocks and blocks. Squat shabby houses line up side by side like gigantic toys.

When my dorm was built, all these houses must have been razed. My complex spans several blocks, and sky bridges connect it to the dorms on all four sides. I let out a low whistle at the sheer number of houses destroyed to accommodate all those dorms.

Shaking myself out of my ponderings, I consult my mental list. First thing to do: find a place to buy a smartphone and an electronic tablet. Second: find someone to teach me how to use them. Third: find Great-Grandma Lena's mother.

After I move Fern the few feet into the garage, I set off down a narrow lane toward a street where autos speed by. Some building must have stores, and one will sell smartphones. Too bad I can't go to the Cloud and order drone delivery. They do things the hard way in 2019. In the distance, the graceful St. Johns Bridge soars above the rooftops, its gothic green spires piercing the gray skies. The familiar sight cheers me—some things remain the same, even after a hundred years. Sure, the 2120 version is shabbier, but its famous elegance remains unchanged. The raw beauty of the unspoiled West Hills across the river looks so familiar and welcoming in this alien environment.

I want to climb up there and hug them.

A heap of discarded items lies next to a fence. I draw closer to a bag of some sort, made with fabric imprinted with gigantic flowers in blue, crimson, yellow, pink—clean and new. Why would someone throw away an almost-new bag? I grab it and check inside. Empty, except for a little round stretch of yellow fabric, a small gift of sunshine on this cloudy day. I yank it over my wrist, relishing the satisfying snap. Back at the autopod, I throw in my hairbrush, toiletries, odds and ends, the heart necklace from Glim. No, the necklace is going back. I'll never wear it again. Digging the money out of my pocket, I start to put it in the bag, then stuff it back into my pocket where it's safer.

On the street where autos rumble by, a brick building rises up ahead, and red letters form the word *Safeway*. It resembles the images of twenty-first-century stores on the Cloud. Maybe it sells phones and tablets. I'll need to cross the street, but those ancient metallic beasts known as cars are coming at me from both ways. None of them have radar causing them to stop at obstacles.

A block away, someone stands at the corner, peering as though she wants to cross the street. So I follow her to a crosswalk and a flashing light and safely across the street, the stopped cars grumbling at us as though angry we interrupted their journeys.

Inside, Safeway smells like a chilly greenhouse. Stacks and stacks of fruits and vegetables explain the smell. The rest of the store could pass for a goods warehouse. We have it so much easier in 2120 with robots and drones doing our shopping and delivering.

Shivering again, I add a jacket to my mental need-to-buy list.

A lady with red glasses and a pale face stands behind the customer service counter. "May I help you?"

"Hi," I say. "Do you have smartphones here?"

She tilts her head and gives me a funny look, her smile frozen. "Um…"

"I need to buy one."

"Oh." With her baffled stare, I must've said something wrong. She's eyeing me like I'm an alien.

I suppose I am.

"We don't sell electronics here," she says in the tone of someone talking to a child, "just groceries and pharmaceuticals. But AT&T across the parking lot could help you." She points behind her, and I thank her and leave, feeling stupid.

I find the smartphone store and stop inside the door. Devices cover the walls. I make a beeline to a display, and my brain spins, overwhelmed by the myriad of shapes, colors, sizes. At least the screens all resemble the Cloud portal. How can I know which one to buy?

"May I help you?"

I spin toward a dark-skinned woman about my age, eyebrows raised. Is my jumpsuit causing that haughty expression? I smooth my hands over it, but nothing appears out of place. Her jacket and skirt are impeccable. Even her Maria name tag is polished. I straighten to my full five-foot-six height and meet her arrogant expression with my own. "I need to buy a smartphone and a tablet, please."

She softens. "You betcha. Do you know what you want?"

I wave toward the display and all the choices. "What's the most popular?"

She moves to a different display and picks up a sleek, shiny model. "This one. It's the latest iPhone. Very popular."

"I'll take it. How much?" I pull out my wad of cash, and Maria's eyes bug.

"You want to pay cash for it?" Her voice squeaks at the end.

"Sure." My heartbeat quickens. Did I stick my foot in it again? "Is that a problem?"

"Well, no." Her gaze, darkening, flicks to the cash. "It's just... most people put them on their account."

"Oh."

"It's seven ninety-nine with trade-in. Do you have a trade-in?"

Not sure what she means, I say no.

"Then it's nine ninety-nine." Her tone turns challenging, almost daring me to dispute her.

I calculate my cash, the result worrying. "Do you have anything cheaper?"

"How fancy are you going for? What's your budget?"

"I don't need fancy. I'd like to stay under five hundred if possible."

Without a word, she replaces the fancy phone and pulls another from the shelf.

"This one's ninety-nine. It's just your basic phone, no apps or internet access. It does have a camera and texting capabilities."

"But I'll need the internet for social media."

"Look, if you want those you have to pay more, I'm sorry to say."

I sigh. "Okay, what about a tablet? I'm writing a book so I'll need, um…" What was that term?

"You'll need a Word app. I can sell you a tablet with everything a smartphone has and Word. It's on sale for five ninety-nine, with an additional hundred for the accessories."

Weary of haggling, I agree. But after I fork over the cash, she asks me, tight-lipped, for my name, address, and ID. I give her my name and use my home year's address, though it probably isn't valid here. Then I gotta come up with a reason I have no ID—well, no ID she'd recognize. "I got my wallet stolen."

She tosses me that skeptical look again but doesn't argue.

I tuck the box with my tablet into my new bag and hurry to the exit. Once on the sidewalk, I take it out and open it up.

Then my shoulders fall. I have no clue what to do now, cram it. But the last thing I want to do is go back inside and face the suspicious Maria again. So I explore the neighborhood. In a hundred years, the buildings on this block, plus the Safeway, will be replaced by a ten-story dormitory/apartment complex. Strange how most families in the twenty-first century lived in houses. I squelch a twinge of envy with fresh anger at Bombardo for making us live like zoo animals.

A whiff of something delicious besieges me from a nearby door. Pepper's Hot Brews according to the big white letters on the picture window. My tummy growls. I haven't eaten for hours. I follow my nose to a counter displaying pastries and a coffee menu full of names like "Moka's Hot Sister" and "Whole Latte Luv." I order an Al Cappuccino, which only comes in small, and a sprinkle donut from a hairnetted, multipierced person. The name tag says, "Hello, my name is Chaz. My pronouns are they/their." Chaz asks for my name, and then I find a seat by the window, one of the empty seats. A diversity of people as amazing as the pastry display has me ogling them—some dark-skinned, some with clumpy hair or no hair, even a few with ripped-up jeans. One young woman is clad in black from head to toe, including the tattoos snaking around her bare arms. Everybody looks and dresses differently from everyone else. I blend right in.

I'm no sooner settled than Chaz calls me. On the way to the counter, I pass a friendly face belonging to a woman in boots and a flowered dress mostly hidden by a shapeless brown sweater worn one time too many. She's about my age with a round face, curved-up mouth, and clear green eyes behind big blue-rimmed glasses. The perfect anti-Maria. She has a tablet like mine open in front of her.

Ah! Why not?

After retrieving my goodies, I sidle up to her. "Hi."

She smiles up at me, confirming my first impression. "Hey."

"Mind if I sit?" Her smile falters, but she bravely pastes it back on and shrugs. One of those chirpy people who refuse to let a bad day or interruption get them down. Exactly the person I need to help me complete item number 2 on my list. I set down my drink and donut and take out my new tablet. "I noticed you have one of these, but I'm having trouble with mine. Can I ask you some questions?"

"Okay." She's too nice to say no.

I swivel my tablet toward her. "I've never had one before. Can you tell me how to start it up?"

"Oh!" She touches the side of the device and slides it back to me. The screen flashes multiple colors. Now what? When I touch it, the colors disappear, and there's the portal!

"Hey, thanks. Sorry if I seem ignorant, but I'm new at this. Wasn't raised with computers and smartphones and internet."

"Really?" Her eyes light. "Neither was I. We lived in a tiny town in Eastern Oregon with spotty Wi-Fi, and all I had in the way of technology was a clunky old computer from the nineties. I only was able to use the internet at school and the library. I can tell by your accent you're not from around here."

My accent? She's the one with the accent. Every word came out precise, each letter defined. Has English really deteriorated so much in a hundred years?

I bite into my donut. "Can you show me how to use Word? Buy you coffee."

"Oh, don't worry about that." She lifts her black paper cup. "I'm good." She reaches for the tablet and frowns at it. "You still need to download it."

"Is that a problem?"

"Not at all. It'll just take a minute." As I sip my rich cappuccino, music plays overhead, a pretty tune by some female singer. Last night, I looked up popular singers from this era, names such as Adele and Rihanna and Bruno Mars. Maybe this is one of them.

"Here you go." My new friend startles me. "All set."

I stare at the screen, still not knowing what to do. "You're a star. How can I make this up to you?"

"No worries. Just pay it forward."

Pay it forward. Interesting concept. "Just show me how to use Word. Please? And then I'll leave you alone."

She's stuck giving me a tutorial, probably silently judging me. Her cordial expression reveals nothing. But when she sees how I struggle on the keyboard, she suggests using the talk-to-text feature. What a perfect solution! I want to hug her.

We're wrapping up my intro to twenty-first-century technology when I remember the third item on my mental list. "If I'm trying to locate a relative, what's the best way?"

"Oh, Facebook, I'd say." She opens up a browser. "Do you have an account already?"

"No."

"By the way, we never introduced ourselves, did we?" She pushes her big glasses up on her nose and sticks out a hand. "I'm Tiffy. And you are…?"

I shake the hand she offers me. "You can call me Tree."

"Tree? Is that short for something?"

I nod but don't enlighten her. She's too agreeable to object, so she helps me set up a Gmail account, then walks me through the Facebook setup. I'm now a proud member of the social media community. And now it's time for item number 3: search for my great-grandma Lena's mother.

Tiffy shows me the search box, and I hunt for each letter, painstakingly keying in the name I know so well.

Paige Ferguson.

# 29

# Her

**January 2020**

Paige gasped, her heart shuddering. What in the world was going on? How could Katrice have come up with an unusual name like Bombardo for her story, which just so happened to match Ky's father's name? She couldn't have known. Her friend must possess a clairvoyant streak. She had to find Katrice and get her to explain. Or...

Was she overreacting and a logical reason lay behind the coincidence?

If, however, Katrice had the gift of clairvoyance, it could only originate from one source. And it wasn't the Lord. Had Katrice dabbled in New Age thought? If only she could ask. But her friend had disappeared.

Someone had to know where she was. "Honey?"

"Yeah?"

"Can we make one last trip to Pepper's tomorrow morning so we can tell them goodbye?" On the off chance JZ was hanging around.

"Great plan."

If she could talk Ky into driving over to the zombie house, she'd talk to the neighbors. Maybe Katrice had returned. Because if she couldn't find Katrice, this was going to bug her for all eternity. And her health didn't need this kind of stress.

"What's up, babe?" Ky loomed over her. "You look like you've seen a ghost. You all right?"

"Fine." She loosened her tense facial muscles and forced a grin. No reason to tell Ky about Katrice and have him freaking out any more than he already was.

"Let's check your blood pressure."

For the fifth time today? Seriously? "Okay."

Ky retrieved the BP pump from the bedroom and slapped it around her arm. A Trail Blazer game blared over the TV as the device tightened. "One fifty-two over one oh one. A little better but still too high."

She cringed at the worry in his eyes. Leaning back, she practiced her deep breathing and relaxation techniques until she felt her tension ease. "Let's take another reading now."

Her blood pressure read a few points lower. *This is only temporary. This is only temporary.*

But the things she'd learned about preeclampsia… Women did still die in childbirth. How could she be sure she wouldn't be one of them?

While she was at it, how could she be sure the tiny boy and girl inside her would turn out normal? Too many risks vied for moms-to-be to fret about. She leaned back again, her hands resting on her baby bulge, enjoying the little dances of baby feet and hands, the ripples of their womb waltzes. Or were they wrestling in there? Jockeying for space? Was one of them more territorial than the other? *Little boy, are you being nice to your sister?*

A vision of their future played through her mind—a best-case scenario, a warm summer day, the smell of fresh-mowed grass. A sixteen-year-old girl, dark-haired like Paige, on the lawn of their Pleasant Valley home, throwing a Frisbee at her twin brother, red-haired and brawny like his dad, catching it in one swift motion. Carefree affection radiating between them. She and Kyler watching from their big wooden veranda. Mason and Emmeline.

Her worries banished, she smiled, closed her eyes, and slept.

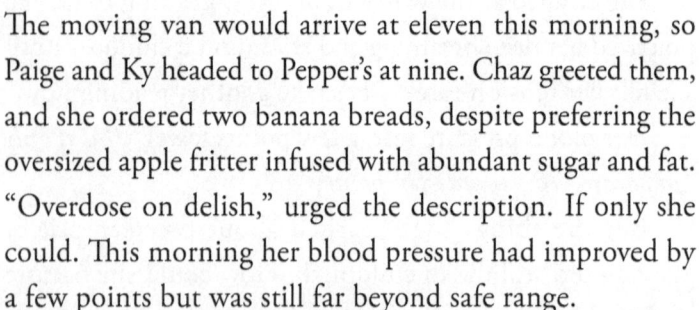

The moving van would arrive at eleven this morning, so Paige and Ky headed to Pepper's at nine. Chaz greeted them, and she ordered two banana breads, despite preferring the oversized apple fritter infused with abundant sugar and fat. "Overdose on delish," urged the description. If only she could. This morning her blood pressure had improved by a few points but was still far beyond safe range.

Ky ordered the apple fritter she was lusting for along with his usual Talldark, a name more like a British TV show than a coffee. "Babe!" she scolded. "You're going to eat that fritter in front of me?"

"Um, yeah. I'm in the mood to overdose on delish." He led them to a table in the back, and she scanned the room for JZ. But then, even if he were here, how would she talk to him without Kyler seeing? Maybe Chaz could help.

She spread a napkin on the square wooden table and set her bread on it. "Babe, I'll be right back." She retraced her steps to the counter and waited for Chaz to finish with their current customer. Another barista, a new one apparently, stepped forward and eyed her. "Can I help you?"

"Need to talk to Chaz for a minute."

"They're helping someone."

What was with that just-this-side-of-snarky tone? "I know. I can wait."

Seconds later, Chaz turned to her. "I understand you want to talk to me."

"Yeah. Do you remember my friend Katrice?" She held her hand level with the top of her head. "Yea tall, always carries a flowered bag?"

"Oh right. I do remember her. But I thought her name was Tree."

Paige jolted. Tree. Short for Katrice?

The jumbled pieces that comprised her friend sorted together and clicked into place. Katrice had used her nickname for her main character. And she'd used her boyfriend as inspiration for her protagonist's love interest.

Her story read like a memoir. Yet how could it be? The fictional Tree lived in the far-distant future, in a world frighteningly different from her own. Time travel wasn't scientifically possible, not in a million years, much less a hundred. A desperation to find her friend surged through her. But right now, Chaz still stared at her.

"What about her?" Chaz waved their hand under her nose. "Paige? What about Tree?"

"Oh. Yeah. She seems to have disappeared. Has she been in here recently?"

"Bummer." Chaz held up their palms. "I haven't seen her for, like, months."

"What about her boyfriend? JZ?"

The dark brows leaped. "He's her boyfriend?"

"That's what he said."

"He was in yesterday. He…"

She didn't wait for him to finish but hurried back to Ky. Trying to still her rapid heart rate, she breathed deep and plopped to her seat, then broke off a piece of banana bread. It stuck to the roof of her suddenly dry mouth, leaving her chewing in vain. Now what? *God, show me what to do. I'm so confused. What is happening? Is Katrice safe? Is she even who she says she is? I have to know why…*

"What were you talking to Chaz about?" Ky's voice cut into her prayer.

"Nothing important." The lie escaped before she could stop it. She scrutinized the bread, her finger tracing the walnut ridges along the edge.

"Then what's wrong? You've hardly said two words."

She needed to take a leap of faith and trust Ky to be on

her side. She met his worried stare. "Remember the alley where we watched my friend Katrice disappear?"

Ky nodded, his brow furrowed.

"Can we drive over there after this? I want to tell her goodbye, but I haven't been able to reach her lately."

"You know where she lives?"

"I have a good idea. Please?"

He shrugged, his way of agreeing without agreeing. "I guess."

She forced herself to keep the conversation going as she waited for him to finish. Finally, they headed out and down the street to the alley.

Paige kept her focus on the spot where she'd found Katrice's scrunchie. Nothing. And there was the empty garage to her right. No sign of her friend.

"So where are we going?" Ky slowed at a pothole, his questioning stare boring into her.

She pointed to the zombie house. "She was squatting there. Let's drive around to Windsor and see if there's any sign of her."

Ky made the circuit, his truck tires sinking deep in the ruts, jostling them to and fro. Two right turns brought them to the paved Windsor Avenue where he pulled to the shoulder at the spot Paige indicated and then braked. In the soft morning light, the zombie house took on an even eerier vibe, its desolation a dramatic contrast with the sunlit day.

"Are you serious?" Ky shaded his eyes, craning toward the graffitied plywood covering the windows, the brambles and tall weeds overrunning the once-green lawn like a victorious army. "No way anyone lives here."

"But the neighbors said they saw her."

He shifted his full gaze to her. "You talked to the neighbors?"

No. Don't sink into defensive mode. "Yeah, those people over there." She gripped the door handle. "In fact, I'm going to talk to them now to see if they've seen her hanging around."

"Paige, wait."

She stopped, but her gaze snagged on a sight up ahead. JZ! A block away, sauntering straight at them. She grabbed Ky's hand. "Babe, I've got to talk to this guy. He knows Katrice, okay?"

Without waiting for his reply, she exited the truck and waited until JZ drew near. Thrusting her hands into deep jacket pockets, she felt Ky's gaze on her but resisted the urge to look. Icy January wind stung her face and whipped needles of hair into her eyes. Her quarry stared at the ground, his hands in his pockets, until she stepped forward.

"Hey, JZ?"

He startled, peering at her blankly, and kept walking.

"Wait! JZ?"

His face twisted. "Are you talking to me?"

She flipped hair from her eyes with gloved fingers. "Of course I am. Who else would I be talking to?"

"Do I kn-know you?" Same flat syllables, same veiled gaze.

"Don't you remember? I'm Paige, Katrice's friend. We

chatted at Pepper's."

"Pepper's?"

Was the guy an imbecile? Or was she mistaken and this man was just an astonishing JZ look-alike? "Do you have a twin, by chance?"

He shook his head, still with that baffling expression.

"You don't remember talking to me at Pepper's a few weeks ago?"

His eyes sharpened. "Did you say you know T-tree?"

He must be playing dumb. Maybe hoping she'd give away Katrice's whereabouts. "Of course I know Tree, but she's still missing. I was hoping you'd found out where she is." She gestured toward the truck where Ky watched them. "My husband and I are moving today, you see, and I wanted to tell her goodbye."

"Oh." He continued to study her as unease snaked up her spine. What was going through his head? "Where to?"

"Out in the country, east of here. A place called Pleasant Valley."

Something flickered in his eyes. At last, he was showing some sort of emotion. "Well, I'm looking for her t-too," he said. "So if you see her, tell her to c-come home."

"I haven't seen her for weeks. I need to talk to her."

"So do I." He shot her a sharp look. "How long have you known her?"

"Just a few months. We met at church." Could he harbor the same suspicions of her as she did for him?

He stared off into the distance. "A few months. Like

when? September?"

"Sometime in the fall, yes. I can't remember exactly. Why?"

"Not important." He waved away her question, then faced the way he'd come. "I g-guess it won't do any good to look for her today, then." He waved and retraced his route back toward Richmond Street, leaving her to ponder the strange conversation.

Paige fought dejection as Ky drove them home. He kept glancing at her, no doubt hoping she'd answer his unspoken question. But she was the one with the questions, and the only person who possessed the answers had disappeared. Obstacle after obstacle impeded her quest for her missing friend, unlike her husband's, whose quest for his father met with resounding success. Well, the latter was more important—wasn't it? Of course it was.

They'd been home for only five minutes when the moving truck pulled up. Time to leave her life here, her memories, and launch into an unknown future. She sighed. She might never see Katrice again, might never find the answers she sought.

# 30

# Me

**June 2019**

I spend the next days exploring the neighborhood, practicing using my tablet, and listening to people's conversations. It's important I sound like everyone else so I don't keep getting funny looks. Or worse, being asked if I'm not from around here. The English language has devolved so much in a hundred years. We speak less precisely and use fewer words. When I first use the talk-to-text on my tablet, it corrects my 2120-style speech such as leaving out filler words and slurring my consonants, and it even inserts proper punctuation. Just like the Cloud does.

On my second day when the clouds clear away, I glimpse Mount Hood and nearly trip over a rock. I'd seen images of what it looked like before the glaciers dried up, leaving it an eleven-thousand-foot pile of dirt. So the monstrous vanilla ice-cream cone rising into the eastern sky leaves me breathless.

What a shame to realize what will become of the

mountain in a hundred years. From stunning beauty queen to barren old matriarch.

I occasionally recognize a building or landmark, but most of the time, I'm in an alien land, unaccustomed to the autos and their constant roar. At night, ringing in my ears makes sleep a struggle. During the day, the St. John's Bridge cheers me and grounds me. Pepper's is my favorite place to people-watch and practice technology, and after a few days, I'm feeling comfortable. Too bad the talk-to-text can't be spoken silently like in my home year. You see people everywhere speaking into their holograms, but you can't hear what they're saying.

Glim never leaves my thoughts though, dampening my sense of adventure. I even imagine I see him in the distance. But then I blink, and the person proves a stranger. Sorrow mingles with relief. I miss him, yet I can't forget the terrible deed he committed. The pain in my ribs has ebbed, but will the fissure in my heart heal?

No matter. I must focus on why I'm here.

Paige Ferguson.

If the obituary is accurate, I don't have much time— time for what, I'm not even sure, other than to getting to know the woman who would birth Mason Bombardo. What's she like, and are any of his traits evident in her?

The old ambition to redeem the past rears up as I recall the details of her life. Could I succeed in altering history? It must be possible. Otherwise, Glim wouldn't have tried to stop me. How, in Paige's case, would I go about it? Would

Mason Bombardo be a different man if he'd been raised by his biological mother? Possible scenarios play through my mind as I locate her.

Mostly public posts fill her social media page, so anyone can track her whereabouts. She loves selfies. A lot of images include her husband, a big red-haired guy, and they look happy. How those expressions would transform if they knew what their future held.

If Paige had enemies, they'd have no trouble homing in on her. She publicizes the school where she teaches, the friends she hangs out with. I ask the barista where St. Johns Middle School is, and she directs me to a brick building blocks away, another edifice lost to time. My peers and I didn't attend schools. We congregated in a common room on our dormitory floor for lessons in the Cloud. Multiply this by dozens of floors and hundreds of housing units and thousands of cities. You get the idea. Our sports facilities span the top floors of each housing unit—gymnasiums, tennis courts, weight rooms, what have you. Each neighborhood has its football field everyone shares.

Anyway, at the middle school, I sit on a bench near the main entrance as if I'm waiting for someone. It's midafternoon. I shift, tempted to go inside to ask when school is out, but I fight the urge. It'll generate more suspicion. I'm getting sick of suspicious looks, whether due to my clothes or speech or cash use.

I jitter my leg, antsy to get up, pace—*do* something. What am I doing anyway? Is it the right thing?

Glim's left me limited options.

I work on my tablet, brush up on twenty-first-century English, worry.

The door slams open, and kids pour outside in a rushing stream—tall kids, dark kids, pretty kids. Yet they all manage to look alike. The girls wear jeans full of holes, their eyes scanning phones or friends' faces, all smirks and giggles. The boys wear scruffy hoodies, faces arranged in cooler-than-thou masks, backpacks showcasing their favorite bands and brands. *If you love conformity so much, wait until you're all 110. You ain't seen conformity yet.*

Big yellow autobuses line up in front, interspersed with autos, the ugly chemical scent reminiscent of a distant fire. How can this be fine to breathe?

I stand. Dare I go inside and look for Paige? After all the photos, I'll recognize her.

But I can't risk it. I drop back onto the bench, a wooden splinter poking through my jumpsuit, and wait. I wiggle so the splinter stops its torment, but the splinter in my thoughts keeps poking me.

The students have dissipated when the door opens again and three adults exit. Despite the green streaks in her hair, Paige's pixie face stands out as she lags behind, easing the door closed, then hurries down the steps on the heels of the other two. "See you tomorrow."

At her voice, the splinter jabs into my heart. My very own great-great-grandma stands twenty feet away. She doesn't notice me, so I trail her until she gets into a small white car and drives away.

I failed to plan for the inevitable moment of truth.

What do I do once I find her?

For the next week, I fall into a comfortable routine, always with my mission foremost in my mind. Each morning, I wake up on Fern's black floor, then head inside the vacant house to get ready for the day. Shuddering, I sidestep the appalling trash. What happened to the previous residents that they would leave all this?

Nothing in here works except the toilet, so I make myself a sandwich with vegetables and fixings I bought at Safeway and keep in the cooler. Next, I catch a taxi to the Y where I take a hot shower and change into an outfit from a secondhand store. I wear quiet clothes so as not to draw attention to myself. Lastly, I go back "home," work on my story, practice my twenty-first-century English, and sightsee.

On the boulevard, missing Eartha and my other friends, I turn my head from a group of girls our ages. Then I scoot around a group wearing leather and chains. No reason to get jittery. I'm safe here, even without security guards to watch people's every move. People come and go freely and don't need fingerprint ID to enter buildings. Life is simple and primitive.

A mop-haired guy passes. Cute and sparkly-eyed like Glim. What's Glim doing now? Pestering Eartha on my whereabouts probably. A weird sense of his lurking presence pervades my awareness, but he couldn't have figured out when and where I am. If he's contacted my parents, they'll be worried. I should've told them I'd be gone for an indefinite period. But they'll have contacted Eartha, and she'd have told them.

It's eighty degrees outside, but ten degrees cooler inside Pepper's. I pull my sweater tighter around myself. How can these people in shorts and tank tops handle the cool temp? They must be used to it. Pepper's comforting din fades into the background as I sip my cappuccino. Except for the lack of robots, it's not that different from sitting in the Commons. I hold my cup in midair. I met Glim on a Thursday much warmer than this one. I glimpsed him from afar at the Commons, sipping coffee and, from his grin, enjoying his interaction with the robot server. He was, by far, the most eye-catching man. The other female patrons posturing around him must've agreed.

I set my cup down and tap out a name on my laptop. The Facebook screen fills with Zellers. Which of these are Glim's ancestors? Which of them is responsible for passing down their corrupt genetics?

A single-minded focus on getting him to notice me took on a life of its own. I ordered a drone from Finity, a tiny thing resembling a baby sparrow, unobtrusive. I set to work botting it, and the next day in the Commons, he was seated twenty-five feet away with two other guys. The programmed drone beamed in on them and picked up every word. I followed the conversation on the Cloud.

His name was Glimmer.

And he worked for Finity Drones.

I gasped and spun toward him. But with his profile toward me, he noticed nothing. I had to know what he did at Finity. Was he able to discern what I'd done?

For two days, the drone followed him and told me where he lived and where he parked his autopod. Yeah, I know, what a stalker. But hey, it worked for Eartha, and it worked for me. Glim never knew—he either didn't notice the drone or didn't bother to trace it. On the third morning, when the drone told me he was headed for his autopod, I made my way over there, succeeded in reaching it before him, and leaned against it, arms crossed, in waiting stance.

There he came, strolling across the pavement. His face shifted when he saw me. "Hey, what are you doing leaning on my pod?"

I made a mock-startled face. "Oh, I'm sorry! This is yours? I'm waiting for my friend, and I thought this was hers." I shook my head, then pretended to check the Cloud hologram. "But now she's telling me she's been delayed. So…" I shrugged and gave him my friendliest smile. "Where are you off to?"

His suspicious expression faded, replaced by a disarming grin. "Running a work errand. Meeting a delivery at the Port."

As he spoke, I pretended to reply to my friend but instead disarmed the drone. Couldn't have that little thing, which he'd recognize, disrupt the moment or, worse, blow my cover. "Funny, that's where my friend was going to take me." I tilted my head at him, arranging my face with its most sincere expression. "I'm thinking of moving over that way. We planned to check out some dorms."

"Well, hey, hop in," he invited, and I did. And that marked the beginning of what I thought was a beautiful relationship. Until the red flags started waving. Flags like messages unreturned until the next day. Or fits of temper. Flags he tried to explain away with various excuses.

I pick a random Zeller account, someone local. A young guy named Jared Zeller in Pleasant Valley, Oregon, bears some resemblance to Glim. But nothing on his account tells me if he's the one responsible for a descendant like Glim.

I sigh and log off Facebook. If only I'd heeded those bright red warnings.

Now, I'm stalking Paige and the Zellers with the same single-minded focus. Maybe I should've learned my lesson already.

Each afternoon, I return to Paige's school. Each time, I wait in a different spot for her to emerge. Sometimes I sit on the grass with my tablet, disguised in sunglasses and cap. One day when the students flow from the building, excited screams rush from a pack of girls, then frantic yells screech from a black-clad boy, his cool facade breached by another furious boy chasing him. They jump the steps, attack each other on the grass, and get pulled apart by headshaking, finger-wagging adults. How can any parent send their sons to such a lion's den? Sure, bullying exists in the twenty-second century, but doing school in our dorms dilutes the opportunities.

Paige leaves in her little white car, and I stroll back home. It'd be nice to have the simple luxury of a drone to follow her. But drone technology is still in its infancy. So I fantasize imaginary conversations with her, which, of course, will never happen. *Hi, Paige. I'm your great-great-granddaughter. I know when you are going to die and who your husband will remarry. Your children will be influenced by the DeLaurier/Bombardo family. Due to their encouragement, your son will grow up to be United States president.*

*And I am here, if the fates are willing, to alter your destiny.*

## 31

# Her

**January 2020**

At Pleasant Valley Bible Chapel, the rousing worship, the pastor's warm, casual delivery, and the welcoming atmosphere convinced Paige they'd found their church home. She cuddled under Ky's arm during the sermon on spiritual armor, and afterward, Karin guided them to Pastor Lou Zeller and his family.

The pastor's college-aged daughter, Annabelle, shook their hands, her mouth stretched into a stiff smile, then her younger brother, Jared, stepped forward and shared a fist bump with Ky.

Naomi Zeller, Pastor Lou's wife, hugged Paige, her highlighted hair brushing Paige's cheek. "We're so glad you're here." A flowery scent wafted from her, and the smile lines around her mouth and eyes deepened. "A few of us are going to lunch at Heidi's. You two are more than welcome to join us."

Soon, Paige scooted into a booth there and pressed

tighter against the back to accommodate her ever-expanding belly, even sucking in her tummy out of habit though it did no good.

Across from them, Theo and Karin focused on Matty, whose scowling face threatened a fussing session. Karin shot them an apologetic look. "We might not be able to stay after all," she said to no one in particular.

To Ky's right, Pastor Zeller gave his feedback on the best dishes. As Paige perused the menu, her mouth watered at the selection of pancakes, waffles, and omelets. Even though they'd waited half an hour for a table, each bite made it worth it.

Annabelle, a pretty girl of twenty with a somewhat formal way of speaking, sat beside Paige. With her smooth hair and elegant style, she seemed somewhat like Kyler's cousin Everly. She touched Paige's arm. "I understand you're having twins."

"Yes! Who told you?"

Annabelle indicated Karin who was still attempting to placate her son. Theo had turned away from the drama as he enjoyed bacon and eggs while chatting with Jared. "How are you feeling?"

"Better, actually. But my doctor fears I might have preeclampsia and has ordered bed rest for me."

Annabelle's jaw dropped. "Well then, shouldn't you be at home resting?"

Oops. TMI. Paige shook her head. "I feel fine. The occasional socializing is okay, as long as I don't overdo it."

She rolled her eyes. "It can get boring lying in bed all day."

"No doubt." Annabelle's grin flashed even white teeth likely fixed and straightened from childhood braces.

"Enough about me. Tell me about you. What are you studying in college?"

"I'm in the prelaw program at Multnomah. Then I plan to apply for Lewis and Clark's Law School."

"Impressive. I wish you the best. What kind of career are you aspiring to?"

"I'm not sure yet." She placed her hand over her heart, crinkling up her yellow blouse. "The Lord has given me a burden for the disenfranchised of our world, the people who need an advocate but can't afford one."

"Probably not much money in that, right?"

Soft hair swished over her shoulders. "It's not about the money. It's about helping people who can't help themselves."

"That's great, admirable. There's a need."

Annabelle chewed a chunk of Belgium waffle before sipping crystal-clear ice water. "Especially among undocumented immigrants and their children. The current system is inadequate for those who need it most."

Not knowing how the law worked in the state, Paige nodded along, caught up in her new friend's passion. "We need more people like you. Most of us are too busy trying to meet our own needs to consider others'."

Annabelle put her fork down. "Yet the apostle Paul told us to consider others as more important than ourselves."

"He sure did. But so few of us think that way."

Karin stood, holding a furious Matty, who kicked and tried to wriggle out of her grasp. "Theo, we need to get this little guy home."

Theo got to his feet, a stressed frown clenching his face. "Matthew Theodore Carpenter, what in the world is the matter?"

"He's tired," Karin said.

"Not tied!" screamed Matty, hurling another kick at his mother's thighs.

At the next table, a teenage couple stared agog, but Paige barely noticed. Her ears had perked up at the son's full name.

*Matthew Carpenter.* She'd heard that name before. She racked her brain to remember Katrice's words. Her friend had mentioned tracking down her ancestors, one of them by the name of Matthew Carpenter. Something prickled the back of her neck, but Matthew was a common name, right?

It had to be coincidence.

Since she'd met Katrice, how many instances had she chalked up to coincidence? Three, four, five? A lot for one friendship.

The prickle, more intense now, crept up her spine. Seeking relief, she clutched both knees with tight grips, her breath coming fast. If Katrice wasn't clairvoyant, then something even more sinister was going on. If she did dabble in darkness, then it was good Paige found out now—

"Are you okay?"

Annabelle's voice halted her churning thoughts. Paige

turned her full focus on her new friend. Her plastic smile had morphed into open-mouthed, genuine worry, her attentive eyes had grown wide. Paige shook away the gloom and forced her own smile.

"Just tired, I think. Like poor little Matty."

Karin and Theo were exiting the restaurant, their son's wails fading out the door.

Kyler, oblivious, still chatted with Pastor Lou.

Annabelle leaned over her and poked his shoulder. "Hey, hubby. How come you're ignoring your pregnant wife?"

Ky jerked around, eyeing Paige's hot face.

If only she could slither under the table and hide! How dare this well-meaning busybody put her and Ky on the spot? Annabelle barely knew them. "I'm fine," Paige nearly hissed at Ky. "I don't need a babysitter."

"Still, we should get home." He pushed back his chair. "You look like you're not feeling that great."

And her blood pressure must've shot up by ten points from pure humiliation. Ky put some cash on the table, but Pastor Lou thrust it back at him, insisting on paying. They gave hugs and handshakes to their new friends and headed to their grand new home. "Nice people," Ky said.

Paige kept her eyes closed and, too confused to pray coherently, begged God to tell her what was going on with Katrice.

# 32

# Me

**June 2019**

When summer break for schoolkids arrives, I no longer have the opportunity to keep an eye on Paige. Even worse, Safeway, taxi rides to the Y, meals at neighborhood cafés are depleting my cash supply. Since I have no way to cook for myself, restaurants are my only source of hot meals. I need to raise some serious cash.

On Lombard Boulevard, people hold up signs asking for money. Many drivers stop and comply. One of my new YWCA acquaintances, Simone, encourages me to try it. She's out there every day, and sometimes ends her "workday" with a hundred bucks. One morning, she stands on one corner, and I stand on the other holding a sign: Wallet Stolen. Please Help. Some people yell at me, and the first time, I nearly throw my sign down and walk home. But Simone calls to me across the street to ignore them, that most people are decent.

After a week of panhandling, I have another five

hundred in cash. After two weeks, I have enough for a smartphone, so I return to the AT&T store. Maria isn't in sight, and a nice young guy helps me pick out the perfect phone. Throughout that long warm summer, I monitor Paige through social media. But I rarely find anything to help me pin down her whereabouts. I'd need to connect with her on social media, but of course, I can't. She doesn't know me yet.

Panhandling keeps me flush with cash, yet my living situation is still subpar. I sleep in Fern, invisible to the outside world, and when it rains, I stay in Fern and work on my story. Simone is my guide to the world of the homeless, directing me to shelters where I can sleep on cold nights, food pantries that serve hot meals, pointing out the campsites to avoid. "They're all druggies in there," she says, indicating a thatch of trees across a side street where colorful tents peek through. She and her small family sleep in a double tent further down the alley. I have to be careful when I go back to my "garage," so she doesn't see where I go. She'd freak if she saw me disappearing. Occasionally, a homeless person wanders into the yard, but the barking dogs two doors down discourage them from staying.

Life is free, uncomplicated, lazy, and if not for Simone's friendship, it'd be staggeringly boring as well. After all, how much more excitement could life hand me, holding up a sign all day, eating meals wherever I can, writing my story? It's only temporary. Yet how temporary? I can't imagine going back to 2120 and facing Glim now. Things will never be the same between us.

But if I can find a way to prevent a tragedy for Paige and Kyler... Then, perhaps, I can go home with my mission accomplished, and Glim won't be able to do anything to stop me. His past will already be altered, and so will mine. For the better.

Weeks go by, then months, before I get a breakthrough. I've grown comfortable with life in the twenty-first century and written several chapters on my Bombardo exposé when I see a public post on Paige's social media. Paige Ferguson is attending Christ the King Community Church, St. Johns.

I call a taxi and whoosh off to church for the first time since Bombardo's funeral, which happened to be my first time ever. I arrive late but slip into the back.

Paige and her partner—I mean, husband—are in the section to my right and a couple rows ahead. What a cute couple they make. Some invisible conduit between them proves they're madly in love.

I pretend to listen to the man on the platform speaking, but all the Bible talk is unfamiliar. He mentions Jesus and God as if they're real, as if they're standing up there on stage.

People yell the name of Jesus when they're mad, but no one in the twenty-second century owns a Bible. Not that it's illegal, but most Normericans aren't interested in such an archaic, irrelevant document. These people, though, are as rapt as children at a magic show. And just as gullible.

When the service is over, I hover near Paige, and she brushes by without seeing me. She hurries into the ladies' room.

Right behind her, I dodge clusters of chatting parishioners and kids being kids. I lean against the counter, studying my phone as if oblivious to my surroundings—like everyone else in this era—until Paige comes out. Because I'm in her way, she's forced to say "Excuse me" in a somewhat childlike voice.

"Sorry." I scoot to the side, continuing my phone perusal, then put my phone away, and turn to her. "Have you been attending here long?"

She meets my eye in the mirror and displays a white-toothed smile. "Just about two years." She shuts off the tap and shakes water off her hands, spraying shiny droplets on the counter. "How about you? Are you new here?"

I nod. "It's my first time." So surreal to talk to my great-great-grandmother. Already her graciousness reels me in. Is it a familial bond, or is she like this with everyone?

"Welcome!" Paige reaches for a paper towel. "I'm Paige."

"Katrice."

"Are you new in town too?"

As the door whooshes open and a little blonde girl enters, pulling on her mother's hand, I nod again. "Yeah, I've been here since June. How about you?"

"I've been in Portland almost six years."

I make a show of crimping my hair in the mirror. "Do you have family here?"

"My parents are in Montana, but my husband grew up here." She leans against the counter facing me, making no move to leave.

"Any kids?"

I hold my breath as she hesitates. "Not yet. How about you?"

I get it. I'm still a stranger. Why would she mention her pregnancy to me?

"Not married, no kids." There's gotta be a way to introduce the subject of her occupation. "But I've heard this is a good neighborhood for kids and the schools here are highly rated."

"Really? Who told you that?"

"A neighbor."

I justify the fabrication by reminding myself why I'm here. Other women and girls are coming in and leaving, stall doors are swinging back and forth like robonic gates and we step to the side away from the sinks while the other ladies wash their hands. It's such an ordinary scene—the ladies' room, so everyday—and they have no hint as to the momentous event taking place.

Paige chuckles. "You could say I'm biased, but I think the school where I teach is awesome. I teach middle school English."

I widen my eyes, crack a huge smile. "You do? That's so great. I've been looking for someone to help me with a fiction-writing project."

She steps back, her smile less bright. "Well, I'm not sure I'm that person. I'm pretty busy."

I lay a hand on her arm in a show of solidarity. "I get

that. But I promise I won't take a lot of your time. I just need a little guidance." My smile stretches wider. "It takes place in the future."

Her eyes brighten. "Sounds intriguing. What do you need from me?"

"Just some feedback on what I have so far. It's only a few chapters."

She's reluctant, but curious, judging by the gleam in her eye, the way she takes her time wiping her hands. Then we exchange phone numbers, and I leave, striding along on the brink of history.

# 33

# Me

**October 2019**

Paige and I stroll through Pier Park, the vast fall leaves whispering above us. She stoops, one hand holding closed her sweater, and selects a veined maple leaf, the colors as vibrant as the Thomas Kinkade painting in her living room. She brings the leaf to her nose, the morning dew dribbling on her chin. "Ky and I met with Everly DeLaurier yesterday. She's my hubby's distant cousin apparently."

As she speaks, so open and eager, my vision glosses. I've grown so fond of her so quickly—and not only because her DNA contributed to mine, but because she's a lovely person.

"We met up at Pearly Gates Coffee Place. You ever been there?"

I shake my head.

"You and I will have to go sometime." She twirls the leaf. "It's a darling place. A friend, Norma Daily, owns it. But it might have been too much for Everly. She was sweet about it, but the religious atmosphere put her off. I should've thought of that when Ky suggested it."

Yep. That's Paige. Sure, she's religious, but she's also upbeat, as friendly as Bestie. Hard to hear the DeLauriers are already homing in. Is there a way I can stop that? Warn her? She and Kyler are so sweetly in love that I want to weep.

But I get it about Everly and whatever the Pearly Gates place was. Since I'm not religious, it chafed me to attend Paige's church. I managed a couple more times. Then I was done. All the talk of God and the Bible was a foreign language. My lack of religious fervor, having met at church and all, bewildered her. But I made some excuse, and that was that.

She drops the leaf and wipes her hand, then gestures to the bench ahead. "But you said you had another chapter for me?"

"I do, indeed." I wipe an edge of the bench for us, then sit, hand over my tablet, and clutch my bag while she reads. Having her read my story makes an excellent pretext for our friendship, as I'm confident she will eventually put the pieces together.

While she reads, I search her features for any trace of me but find little. I take more after the Carpenter side of the family. In my father's old photos, I found the closest resemblance in my great-grandfather Matthew Carpenter. Yet still I observe Paige's smile, her gestures, her body language, her speech. It might be hopeful thinking or it might be genuine when I notice split-second likenesses in the simple choice of a word or a cute chuckle or the way she rolls her eyes at her husband.

With this bond, my previous faint sorrow intensifies into grief at the fate in store for her. And she has no idea, which is the most tragic piece of all. Yet although I know something will go wrong, I have no idea what it is. The information in the Cloud was not specific except for the date of her death. I can't warn her, obviously. And in the early days of her pregnancy, no problems present themselves.

If I only knew the details, maybe I could figure out a remedy. We citizens of the twenty-second century have acquired a lot of knowledge over the last hundred years. Surely, there's information on the Cloud about her condition, whatever it is.

She's finished with the chapter, her comments spot-on. She's such a whiz with the 2019 version of the English language. But more than that, it's so forch to be with her as her belly swells with unborn twins—my great-grandmother and her brother are curled up inside her, maybe even hugging. I tuck my tablet away. "Have you seen the doctor again?"

She giggles. "You should have been there when I told Ky the ultrasound showed twins!"

I zip my bag, and Paige pushes to her feet. We head back the way we came as Paige talks about her doctor appointments. Best I remember her doctor's name and office location, on the off chance I might use the information someday. How many times have I compared her experience to Eartha's, looking for any similarities, anything I can use?

Eartha had a number of issues when she carried Heather, all of which were treatable with recently developed medications.

As the weeks go by, it becomes harder to keep my knowledge to myself. And then one day, something happens that changes the entire trajectory of my mission.

Paige and I are in Peppers talking about ancestry when a familiar face peers in the front window. *Oh no.* My heart gives a giant lurch. It can't be Glim. But it is. How did he find me? I come up with a story for Paige, and she chooses that moment to leave. Then I beeline to the restroom. My heart in my throat, I peek out and watch Glim wander around the tables, obviously hoping to see me. When he leaves, my shoulders sag, but I wait another half hour before I head back "home," my heart shuddering with nerves, my brain humming with speculations.

Before I can talk myself out of it, I've directed Fern to take me to the day Glim visits the inn—February 4, 1995, for 4:00 p.m., plenty of time to work out any glitches—and set my return for two seconds from now. Or should I leave it open-ended? Will I want to return here, or flee to a different year? This trip will either confirm, or negate, my suspicions. After Glim's sudden appearance, it's vital I learn how he's been using his time machine. I leave the return setting as is since I can change my mind later.

I throw on a hoodie over sweatpants and shirt. But Fern's warning light beeps—"Obstruction ahead."

Cram it. This garage was likely occupied by a vehicle in 1995. I hit abort, drive Fern a couple blocks down the alley to a vacant lot, and hope it was also vacant twenty-four years ago.

After a successful landing in the 1995 version of my neighborhood, I swoop back down the alley to check out "my" house. Fresh paint and shutters, a well-tended lawn, cheer me. Whatever misfortune happened later to turn it into such an eyesore, I will never know.

I return Fern to the vacant lot, which now contains a small house, and leave her behind a tree. I need to call a taxi, but my 2019-model phone might not work here. Or I could drive Fern to the inn.

I slap my forehead and rub my temples. Why didn't I take time to think this through? Throwing up my hands, I stifle a groan and guide Fern to Falling Star Inn to scope out the area for the perfect landing spot.

Minutes later, I find it.

On the roof.

Several buildings in these blocks have flat roofs bordered by parapets, and some even have doors exiting to the roof. Including the inn. If the door is unlocked, I will leap for joy.

I park near the doorway jutting from the rooftop, pleased at the clear blue winter sky above. No rain in sight, but I wrap my jacket more tightly around me in the chill breeze and pull the door handle.

It opens into a dark abyss. I linger, my eyes adjusting enough to see a ladder descending who knows how far down. But since this is a two-story building, it can't be too far. I prop the roof door ajar with a wooden wedge so

I can escape if need be.

At the bottom of the ladder, I stop at a wide steel door—the kind you'd never want to be trapped behind because nobody would hear you screaming. Again, I pull the handle. This time, I step into the end of a red-carpeted hallway lined with doorways.

A bolt of adrenaline leaves me weak-kneed. I'm inside the hotel, where, this night, a murder will occur.

On the street where Glim will land his time machine.

I creep along the hall, clutching my bag, the plush carpet swallowing my footsteps. Recessed wooden doors line the rich golden hallway, three on each side. Whimsical murals of falling stars raining down the walls—stark white against a deep purple background, some with grinning faces, watched over by a big winking sun—give the place an oddly playful vibe. I pass another mural, this one of a hand-painted constellation suggesting high school geometry class. I follow a set of stairs descending to the lobby. At the counter, a blonde woman sits with her back to me, a computer lit up in front of her.

Somehow, I need to sneak by her. I peer around the corner. She still hasn't heard my approach. To the right, an ornate lobby spreads out, its décor reminiscent of ancient movies Glim and I watched from the 1940s during our research on twentieth-century life. Semisheer red curtains frame wide windows looking out onto Seventh Avenue. I plop into an inviting velvet armchair as though I'm a guest and cross my fingers the employee doesn't study me too closely.

Two other chairs are already occupied by a hand-holding couple—the only other signs of life.

I jolt at a blaring noise.

"Falling Star Inn, this is Alissa. How may I help you today?"

My heart rate relaxes. It was only the phone, 1990s style. Glim's presumed arrival is still hours away, so I need to occupy myself until then. At the other end of the lobby, a little café with paneled, windowless walls, its tables swallowed up by shadows, offers the perfect observation spot.

Alissa's phone conversation whirls my attention her way. She's speaking in a fierce whisper. "Babe, I'm sorry.... I told you it's over." Long pause while the person on the other end launches an emotional protest. I visualize the mean lookout guy Glim mentioned. She keeps reiterating not to bother her anymore. I cheer her on: *You go, girl.*

When she slams down the phone, I make my way over. "Way to stand your ground, girl."

She rolls her large blue eyes and grins, tossing her glowing blonde mane over her shoulder. "Men!"

"Trust me, you'll find someone great someday. You deserve it." I give myself a mental pat on the back for my oh-so-1990s speech.

Her gaze darts to an unseen spot beside her computer, and her eyelids quiver so quick, I nearly miss it. "Yeah." Only a photo of someone she loves could give a girl such an expression. I adjust my angle, but still can't see what she's seeing. She reaches over, her face contorted, and a thud tells me she's knocked over whatever it is.

"By the way"—I lean closer, having established girl-bonding—"who's on duty tonight at ten?"

Alissa gives me a tilted-head, skeptical look. "That would be me. Why?"

I stifle a gasp, keeping my expression still. Will Alissa be killed tonight? From the conversation, someone has reason to hold a fierce grudge.

I hope it's not the mean lookout guy. Yet Glim didn't see anyone else, so the sentry fits the part.

But I have a plan to save her if it's possible.

"A good friend has a reservation here for tonight, but she's disabled. She's supposed to arrive at ten p.m. Do you think you could meet her in the back parking lot to help her inside?"

Alissa responds by punching some computer keys. "Is your friend Ms. Knight?"

No. "Yes."

"Funny, she didn't request assistance. She can just call us herself and ask."

"Well, she forgot. And I was in the neighborhood, so…"

And if Alissa is not at her desk when the shooter arrives, maybe she will survive this evening. My hope is, she will wait as long as she needs to for Ms. Knight to arrive and miss the big event.

But if the shooter doesn't find his quarry, will he try

again another time? Or will he find a new quarry? I don't remember the victim's name—it could be Alissa.

"But her arrival window is supposed to be between nine thirty and ten thirty. If she has a car phone, she can call me when she arrives."

Dang. "I doubt she does. She'll be driving a rental. But she told me she expected to arrive at ten. If she hasn't arrived by then, can you…?"

"Yeah, I'll check every few minutes." Her gaze travels to her computer screen, sending a clear message our conversation is over.

It was the best I could do to protect her. With my gut twisting, I wander toward the café, drawn by the aroma of cooking, enticing my newly acquired taste for meat. I need a fine, hearty meal after weeks of skimping on food. I down their largest bowl of clam chowder, which tastes far better than the Y serves, and some Italian bread with vinaigrette, savoring every bite, ignoring the handful of other diners.

This world without electronic devices or the Cloud is a strange one indeed. People talk to each other, not to their hands, not to the air. A door leading to an outdoor patio beckons me. After paying the bill, I head there. Hanging baskets displaying bright blooms waft their scent across the big-beamed structure. Here in the quiet rear, the whiz of cars on East Burnside drones on.

Somewhere above me, Fern waits. A wood-planked staircase leads from the patio to the hotel's second story, and I start up. The door at the top opens to a lobby-type room, sofas and chairs, shelves filled with paperback books like the Librarium. A lone occupant, ignoring me, relaxes with a book, and I stroll down the hall I started from, seeking assurance I can get back to Fern when the time comes. I don't plan to be anywhere inside the building at ten tonight. The big steel door at the end of the hall, to my relief, opens, and I make note of the open door at the ladder top. Someone better not close it before I'm ready to leave.

I will worry about that when the time comes.

Soon, Glim will arrive, and I'll see whether his version of this evening's events is true. I can't shake the suspicion he met a girl while he was here, that he didn't leave as quickly as he said.

Back in the lounge room, I cross to the windows overlooking Burnside. On the nightclub across the street, a neon sign blares the words—Third Degree. Drinks and Dancing Every Night.

I won't be going there. But I'll be watching through the parapet on the roof. If he goes into the club, I will see him. He came to 2019 to look for me. Now, I'm flipping the gate on him.

Returning to the bookshelf, I scan the titles. My finger stops at Stephen King. I pull out his book and settle in for a nice long read. My reading has improved over the past five months, not having the Cloud to assist me. Within the first quarter of the book, I've surmised it's a story about vampires. Riveted, I don't notice darkness falling until someone turns on the ceiling light. The whole time, people have been coming and going, conducting soft conversations, but nothing of importance.

It's six thirty. I'll get dinner in the café, then resume my vigil.

Three hours later, it's probably thirty-five degrees up on the roof, and my face is frozen stiff. It might crack if I smile. The rest of me is bundled in a thick parka I found in 2019 and matching gloves and cap. I'm struck by the clarity of the starry, starry night sky. Pricks of light poke through the blackest of canopies, glittering like snowflakes. Through a carved hole in a parapet column, I have a flawless view of Burnside. So far, no sign of our scary sentry/probable murderer. I do hope Alissa is making her way to the back parking lot. I cross the roof to the other side but see no activity below me.

After twenty minutes of pacing from one side to the other, I finally see Alissa in a fuzzy coat and stocking cap emerge from the back door to the parking lot. She merely stands and looks around, hands on hips, in waiting mode. Swiveling, she retraces her steps to the lobby. I'm tempted to call to her, to warn her. Instead, I race to the other side and peer down. Glim should be here any minute. But where's the brawny lookout guy? Glim said he was in front of the door.

There's Glim, crossing Burnside, heading to the front entrance. Still no intimidator standing guard—simply Glim, visibly shivering, looking through the front window into a no doubt well-lit interior. He'd have a clear view of the front desk. Is Alissa there? I run to the parking lot side. No Alissa. So she's at the front desk.

Back at the street side, I overlook the top of Glim's head as he peers through the windows. Why would he lie about the lookout guy? Does he embellish everything for thrills? Inserting a nonexistent bad guy to his narrative would amp up the thrill value.

Glim spins and recrosses the street and disappears.

I slump. That was a whole lot of nothing.

Except for adding the other guy, his version of events fit reality.

But what about the shooting? Shouldn't that be taking place? Yet the sidewalks on this side are deserted.

Did I get the day wrong? Or the year? I make my way back to Fern. When I return to 2019, I'll Google it.

A noise on Burnside recaptures my attention. Whirling, I peer through the hole.

A man, his face and hair hidden under a ski mask, stomps toward the inn with decisive strides, dressed in military-looking slacks and a thick jacket. Something bulges under his coat.

The killer!

My breath catches as he pounds on the door, opens it, and shouts. "Alis-ssa, you get over here. I-it isn't over t-till I say it is!"

I know that voice. Spots swim before my eyes, channeling the stars above, and I fall to the roof, clutching in vain at empty air.

Coming to slowly, I feel around the rough surface I'm lying on. Pat my palms over a sandpapery expanse. Utter dark surrounds me.

Awareness flows to the surface.

My heart is doing a crazy dance in my chest. Tingles skitter through my veins. Sirens pierce the night, growing louder. Nearer.

I'm lying on the roof, alone. Glim gave himself away, and I fainted.

# 34

# Me

**October 2019**

The first thing I do after I hobble to Fern, gasping like a drowning woman, and return to 2019 and our garage is look up the Falling Star shooting on the internet, something I should've done before I left.

I'm shivering so hard, despite the spike in temps from thirties to eighties. This calls for something warm to drink, but I don't dare return to Pepper's lest Glim is still hanging around. I fling my bag over my shoulder and head to Safeway's coffee counter. I take my hot cup of brew to the least noticeable corner, my back to the human traffic, and, within seconds, have my answer.

> Last night a female employee of Falling Star Inn on East Burnside was fatally shot by a man presumed to be her lover. Alissa Hamilton, 23, the hotel's receptionist, had a relationship with

a man known only as JZ, according to hotel employees. Eyewitnesses told police that at approximately 10:15 p.m., a masked man entered through the main hotel entrance, shouted at Alissa who sat at the reception desk, then pulled a gun, and shot her. Unfortunately, he turned and ran across Burnside, and it is not known where he went from there.

"I could tell it was JZ by his voice," said an employee, who wishes to remain anonymous. "He has a noticeable stutter. It was a big mistake for him to open his mouth."

A close family member of Ms. Hamilton told this reporter Alissa and JZ had been dating for around six months, and he'd moved in with her last month. "But she had decided to kick him out. I don't know if she had yet, but if she did, that could explain why he came after her."

Tears roll down my face. I grab a napkin from the dispenser and scrub them away, but they keep dropping. How many other victims are hidden in Glim's past?

I jump to my feet, desperate to get back to Fern and figure out which year to escape to before I end up as another of his victims.

Because breaking up with him now is out of the question.

I shuffle along the alley toward Fern, thinking hard, puzzling over his 1995 timing. The article said he'd known Alissa for six months, which meant he traveled all the way back to August of 1994 after his initial visit in February of 1995. How many trips did he take during those six months? Or was it one continuous visit?

Was it before or after we traveled to 2070? It had to have been sometime in the two days between obtaining the currency and takeoff. Because afterward, he was by my side every waking moment. Shaking my head, I start to shiver. He must've already done the dirty deed when he shoved me to the street.

I'm fortunate to be alive.

Did he plan to leave me after I helped him obtain that currency? Maybe he had to flee to his home year at the last minute in order to escape justice.

Despite what I've seen of Glim's dark side, it's hard to believe he'd stoop to murder just because someone broke up with him.

The shivering stops, and every bit of me stills. Frozen on the alley, I suck in a sharp breath. He saw her from the window that night and decided he wanted to get to know her. Most straight, single guys would want a woman like Alissa. So he sent Zeph further back, to a warmer season, when he most likely wooed and charmed her. That day I suspected he'd time traveled? His expression? Well, someone could interpret it as an I-just-met-a-girl face. Which is why he was so desperate for US currency. He'd decided to stay indefinitely. Until she ended things.

The way she looked at something just out of my sight—maybe it was a photo of her and Glim.

Funny how my heart grieves for Alissa but is hardened to the lies and backstabbing from my former boyfriend. He can rot in hell, for all I care. The phrase from a Stephen King book expresses my sentiments perfectly.

At a noise, I jolt.

And there he is, standing beside the garage as I arrive. He steps forward and snatches my wrist with a painful grip and a curse. "Where've you been?"

"Glim!" I try to smile, but it's gotta be as authentic as his fake concern.

"Why'd you take off without saying anything to anybody?"

My heart pounds. Is my terror showing in my face? "I told you I planned to track down an ancestor. Remember?" The dark glint in his eye… a trait I never bothered to concern myself about. Until now. The wind sighs through the ragged elm above us.

"I've been l-looking all over for you. You said you wanted to go back to-to 2020." He still has my wrist in a vise grip, and I relax it in hopes he will too. Then I can make a run for it. But he doesn't. "When I landed in January, I found F-fern empty and abandoned, but no sign of you. So I went back further, then further again when I still didn't find you. I ran into your friend Paige a couple times. Your ancestor, right?"

He doesn't wait for me to nod, just keeps speaking, each word a whip lashing me. "She asked me where you were. She-she told me you'd been out of touch for weeks."

His hand pulls my arm closer, wrapping around my back, so I have no choice but to stand inches from him unless I want to create a scene. Which I don't.

"She also s-said you guys had become friends in September o-or so. That's when I realized you'd l-lied to me. You went back to 2019, not 2020." Behind the opaque darkness in his eyes, the brittle spark shows through. His voice rises to a dangerous pitch. "Why did you lie to me, Tree?"

I try to yank my arm free, but he only squeezes harder. "It wasn't a lie, Glim Zeller." Do my gasping words give away my fright level? I cannot let him see my fear. "I was off by a few months, okay? I wanted to meet her before I lost my chance. I thought I told you that."

"You c-could have told me when you left."

I shrug, a desperate attempt at casual. Tightening my leg muscles, I will them to stop quaking. "I'm sorry, Swee. I didn't tell anyone, even Eartha. I wanted to do this on my own without anyone trying to talk me out of it."

"Why? What's the big s-secret?"

I sigh and subtly move my wrist, still in his grip, away from my back. "It's not a secret, and I don't want to argue about this."

Movement flits in the house next door. A shadow appears in the neighbors' window, then scurries away.

Lowering my voice, I say, "Look, I'm getting to know Paige, and I like her." He's released my arm, and I resist the urge to shake the circulation back into it. "I want to stay here a few more months. Then I'll come home. Okay?"

"And how do you plan to do that?"

"Come home, you mean?" I gesture at the garage. "In Fern, silly."

A half grin flits across his face. "I d-disabled her. So if you don't want to be stuck here for the rest of your life, you'll have to come home with m-me."

A gasp nearly escapes. Did he check my trip history? If he did, he'll know I know.

But he's glaring at me as though I'm a naughty runaway, not like I'm a threat to him.

He's not even trying to hide his true colors anymore. As close as I am to slipping into shock, I force normality into my tone. "You said Zeph can only transport one person at a time. Remember?"

"No, I didn't."

"You did." My voice amplifies toward shouting level again, so I gentle my tone. "When I asked if I could go with you, you said you didn't include the passenger confirmation in the time accelerator."

"It's fixed." He folds his arms and braces a shoulder against the wall. The spark in his eyes darkens. He lied. Then had the nerve to accuse me of lying.

What a despicable…

But I have to pretend to go along. I have no choice. As much as I like Paige, I don't want to be stuck here forever. And maybe, just maybe, I can confide in Eartha. My parents. And come up with an escape plan. I force a grin, surely as wooden as the garage wall he's leaning against. "All right."

He smiles and tweaks my nose. If only he could be arrested and thrown in prison for the rest of his life. "Portland of 2120, here we come."

# 35

# Her

**January 2020**

"You've got to come over and see our new place, Olga." Paige rocked in the blue recliner, her legs extended on the footrest. She tipped her head back, her hair snagging along its suede. Boxes still lay unpacked in their new home, but her heart swelled every time she took in the view from their big picture window. "Our yard is amazing. Big enough to invite all our coworkers over."

Tall evergreens framed a sky that varied in color based on the weather's mood. This time of year, the mood manifested itself in various shades of gray, from ethereal silver to rain-soaked pewter.

"I'm kidding, girlfriend. I have no plans to throw a party anytime soon. It's hard enough getting through each day."

Once winter ended, her little family would spend much more time on their big wraparound porch, basking in green serenity. Until then, she'd put up with unpacked crates, bare walls, and pearly-gray skies. On days Ky worked, Doreen popped in at least once to check on Paige, usually ending up staying two or three hours chatting, working on the house, finishing chores. When he was home, her wonderful husband took care of most of the food preparation and spent a portion of each day pawing through their unsorted belongings.

Speaking of husbands… "I'm glad you told your husband about Pavlo." The eighth-grade boy, already the size of a grown man at the age of fourteen, had given himself away one day when a female classmate overheard him bragging to a friend and she told Olga. "And I'm glad Aleks didn't freak out."

She laughed at the story Olga told of her husband calling the boy and scaring him half to death, all without uttering a single threat. "I'm sure he'll never do it again. Oh, and keep encouraging my substitute. She's got a tough job."

Paige hung up, thankful for friends who stuck by her. Without her coworkers staying in contact, she'd battle loneliness, which she'd attempt to combat by eating and drinking things she shouldn't.

As January transformed into February, her health improved. Her blood pressure stopped rising and stabilized at around one forty-five over ninety. Dr. Anthony encouraged her to keep doing whatever she was doing because it was working. During this time, Ky had several phone conversations with his father, and the two of them were hitting it off. Paige rejoiced yet sensed her husband's attention being pulled in another direction.

One soggy Saturday afternoon as she reclined in her chair knitting a baby bootie—a former hobby she'd relearned during her forced downtime—Ky let out a moan and an "oh no" as he paced up and down the narrow unlit hallway with his phone fastened to his ear. "How bad is she hurt?"

She sat up as he strolled with agitated steps, back and forth as though his legs had taken over his will. "What's wrong?" she ventured, though he wouldn't answer.

He held up a hand to her. "I'll get over there right away. Thanks."

Ending the call, he regained control of his legs and came to her. "My mom is in the hospital." Before she even opened her mouth to ask why, he shoved the phone in his pocket. "She had a bad fall while she was out walking the dogs and broke her hip."

Paige gasped. "Oh, poor Doreen. Did someone find her?"

"Someone saw her fall and called 911 right away. She's at Adventist." He grabbed his black Jedi-master hoodie from the coatrack and brought over her blue parka. "How about we run over there quick to see how she's doing?"

He helped her hoist herself up and put on her coat. "What terrible timing for her." Paige had to bend forward to tug the zipper over her bulging belly. "She was so excited about being a grandma. How is she going to enjoy grandbabies with a broken hip?"

"And how is she going to help you out?"

Seriously? She huffed. "Her medical needs are more

urgent than mine right now."

He drove her Versa the twenty-three minutes to the hospital, joining Doreen as she was being wheeled into surgery, only half awake, looped up on painkillers. Ky grasped her hand. "Mom, we're here. Paige and I."

She sent a weak smile their way, and the attendants directed them to the waiting room.

The forced wait dragged on and on until they were called back to the nurses' area where they learned Doreen would stay there for four more days before they transferred her to rehab. They'd have to either bring the dogs to their house or arrange for boarding.

At Doreen's release from rehab, Ky insisted on moving her temporarily into their home while she recovered, into the empty bedroom on the first floor, across the hall from the master suite. Although Paige enjoyed having Doreen there, she balked at their reversed roles. Most days, the dogs ran free in the back woods, where the fence contained them.

"Ky." She stopped him one evening about a week after Doreen had moved in. After recentering the framed photo on the end table of a young and energetic Doreen with three-year-old Kyler, she reached for his arm but missed. "I love your mom, but she's not following doctor's orders. She's trying to do too much. This morning I caught her in the kitchen, propped on her walker, doing the dishes. She's supposed to be resting like me. Can you talk to her and tell her to take it easy?"

The tightness in Ky's face betrayed his strain at having

two invalid women in his house, plus two active dogs. He searched her face.

"Are you sure there isn't a better solution?" She reached forward again, clutching his arm. "I'm having to take her to her doctor appointments. I wouldn't mind, but my blood pressure has been going up lately."

She released his arm and poked her cheek. "Look at this. I have chipmunk cheeks. I almost don't recognize myself anymore." She lifted one bare foot. "And my ankles are tree trunks. I'm worried, Ky. Aren't there other options for your mom?"

He shifted from foot to foot. "If I could take time off work to take care of you, babe, I would." He shoved his hands in his jeans pockets accompanied by the metallic clang of keys. "But we have a mortgage payment and other bills, and without your income, I can't afford to take any time off."

A knot twisted Paige's gut. What was she to do? She couldn't burden Ky any more than he already was.

Casting all your cares on Him...

Time to put that verse into action. Oh, but it was so much easier said than done.

# 36

# Me

**July 2120**

"In 2120 terms, I've only been gone two days," Glim tells me after we arrive home. "So it'll be like you were hardly gone."

I want to ask him why he chose to return two days after the original takeoff day, but I don't care. At least my roomies will believe I did leave and came back earlier than expected. I swallow hard. "Eartha and Bestie will be happy to see me," says my voice.

I don't look at Glim as I exit Zeph and tote myself and my flower bag across the skybridge to my dorm with him at my heels. The landscaped road stretches on below. I visualize all the houses once in this expanse. Over there, where the bench is, the cute little yellow house across the alley used to sit. Below and to my right is where Simone pitched her tent. Already I miss her—and Paige—and my life in 2019. I hope she won't be too frantic at my disappearance.

Lord willing, to borrow Paige's phrase, I'll be back.

When I open the door, Bestie jumps all over me, and

Eartha's jaw drops. "You're back early!"

Oh, how I long to confide in her. Even she would be shocked by Glim's true nature. "Yeah, change of plans."

"You got a new bag! Pretty. How much did it cost?"

"I found it, practically new." In 2019 terms, I'd been gone several months. Was I two days older or five months? Had my twenty-fifth birthday come and gone without my realizing it? My mind chews on these baffling questions as I grip my wrist. My yellow wristband is gone. Glim must've wrested it off during our tussle. I glare at his back as he and Eartha chat in the kitchen. I want to warn her, to scream at her to be careful. Instead, I go into my room so I don't have to see him and then go to the Cloud to research Paige. I pause at Kyler's obituary.

> KYLER THOMAS (FERGUSON) BOMBARDO—date of death: May 1, 2069 (age 78), Portland, Oregon. Kyler Bombardo is survived by his second wife, Annabelle Zeller Bombardo, and their two sons, Moses (Rachel) and Aaron (Misty); brother-in-law Jared Zeller; two children from his first marriage to Paige Ferguson, Mason (Rose) Bombardo and Emmeline (Matthew) Carpenter; five grandchildren, and two great-grandchildren. Born in 1991 to Doreen Ferguson, he discovered as a

> young man a blood relationship to
> the famed DeLaurier jeweler family of
> Portland, resulting in the reunion with
> his biological father, Gary Bombardo.
> Taking his father's surname after the
> death of his first wife, he became known
> as Kyler Bombardo until the time of
> his death.

Jared Zeller! Was he Glim's ancestor, and was he a bad guy too? The obituary fails to mention how soon after Paige's death Kyler remarried. Which reminds me: I need to obtain her medical records.

Breezy sits at her desk beside her bed, botting robots for her patient visits, so I tap her shoulder. She turns a startled, annoyed face to me. "Yeah?"

"Hey," I begin. "Which medical center are you with?"

"Emmanuel. Why?"

Perfect. Paige's clinic was on the Emmanuel campus. Just maybe, her records will still be in cyberspace one hundred years later. "My great-great-grandma was a patient there, and I always wondered what she died of. Would her records still be in the Cloud?"

Breezy cocks her head, probably surprised I'd spoken so many words to someone I rarely speak to.

"If I give you her name, can you find her for me?"

"How long ago did she die?"

When I give her the date, her mouth tightens, but she

proceeds to hunt down Paige Ferguson's cause of death. "I doubt a patient from that long ago will be here."

"If you find her, I'll rent you a massage robot for a week." During busy times at the hospital, she often comes home with sore feet and back.

She smiles, then shakes her head as the portal fills up with tens of thousands of names. "Ferguson, Alfred... Ferguson, Alice...Ferguson, Gloria...Ferguson, Lucille... Ferguson, Nancy...Ferguson, Peter..." She points in the air. "Her name would be right there if she were listed. But it's not there."

Dejected, I plop on my bed and randomly go to the Cloud, unsure what I'm seeking. I might as well message Beta that I'm back and can resume my work. She's overjoyed, and I throw myself back into my job in a vain effort to occupy my overactive brain. However, I'm rusty since I've been away from it for months in real time. In 2019, I got accustomed to the unwieldy technology. This is way too fast and slick, and reacclimating'll take effort.

My brain chews on Paige's nonexistent medical records. Why am I surprised? Did I really think I'd find data that old? As I access patient records, an occasional name gets alphabetized as maiden name-married name. Something clicks, and I call over to Breezy. "Try Mason. Paige Mason-Ferguson."

Longing thickens my voice. I better not be setting myself up for a crash.

"'K."

It's so quiet I can hear us breathing. I need to become reaccustomed to our much quieter twenty-second-century living.

Twenty seconds tick by. "You were right, Tree. Here she is. Paige Mason-Ferguson."

I hop to my feet to peer over her shoulder as Breeze holograms up a primitive medical chart, the clunky, wordy type with old-school fonts and heavy black lines commonly used in the last century. "Cause of death?"

Enlarging the image, she hunts around the cumbersome record. "Cause of death: Hypertension-induced stroke.'"

I gasp. "Wow. Poor lady. If she lived now, what kind of meds would you give her?"

"Sounds like she might've had eclampsia, also known as toxemia. Nowadays, we'd treat her with Predsomaril. It lowers blood pressure without harming the baby and eliminates all the excess fluid buildup. It sure has saved a lot of women's lives. Didn't Eartha take it during her pregnancy?"

"I think so, but it was to prevent eclampsia rather than cure it."

"Yeah, it's become routine to prescribe it to pregnant women as a preventive measure. All it takes is one drop a week. But for a full-blown case, the dosage is four drops per day."

If only Paige could've had such a cure before it was too late. "Isn't that the med you borrowed from Eartha?" I ask her. "Borrowed" sounds so innocuous when in reality she stole it.

"No, no. Stop asking me that. That's what she thought too, but I swear I didn't."

A sudden urge to return to 2019 grips me. I no longer have Fern, and a vision of her, lonely from disuse, in that decrepit old garage breaks my heart. What will happen to her? It's only a matter of time before all those houses are razed to build dorms. And Fern along with them.

I need to buy a new autopod, but even more urgently, I need to get out of here and return to Paige. Yet without Fern, it's a futile, impossible dream.

I might as well teleport myself to the dark side of the moon.

# ✦—•  37  •—✦

# Me

**July 2120**

I must have fallen asleep with impossible dreams on my mind, for I dream of Glim and me traveling back to the Middle Ages. Dream Glim reverts to the nonscary, jovial Glim he portrayed himself as. We joust with knights and bow our knees to kings. Fun stuff. It's just like Glim to impose himself into my dreams, the same way he imposed himself into my bed tonight. I did my best to hide my fright, remembering poor Alissa after she told him they were through. But he plops beside me as if entitled to my time and energy, and it's decision time.

He falls asleep before I do, which is typical, but also gives my mind a chance to flicker with ideas and plans. A suggestion will present itself, but then I discard it as it proves too lame, too unconvincing, too unbelievable. I fall asleep with my brain considering, then discarding, over and over.

Then I wake up and know what I have to do.

To implement my plan, I need to pretend to be his

girlfriend a little longer.

When Glim awakens, I've just opened my own eyes, my brain aflame with purpose. He props himself up on his elbow and searches my face, his dark eyes droopy with sleep. "Hey," he says in his smooshy morning voice, running his finger along my lower lip. It takes great effort not to bite down hard on it. "What do you remember about the night we went back to 2070?"

At first, the question jolts me. Then a shiver snakes through my gut. There's only one reason he's asking me—he's suspicious I've figured out who shoved me. My body language or vocal tone must have given me away. "Why?" is all I can say.

"Just because. I'm curious." His opaque eyes watch me, and I squelch that shiver. "Have you remembered anything else about that night?"

I make a show of furrowing my brow as if pondering. What would the Tree he knows say? The question grounds me, and my voice cooperates, taking on an edge of challenge like the former Tree. "Am I supposed to remember something? Is there something else you recall?"

His gaze darts upward, a sure sign that whatever is about to come out of his mouth is being made up as he goes. "I was thinking about that man, Monroe. Mongo. Whatever his name is. He must've run twenty miles an hour back to the inn after the crash."

Still in character, I punch his upper arm. "Glim, you silly. Whatever made you think of that after all this time?"

Actually, not that long ago. Only a week and a half, not five months. Glim doesn't know how long I stayed in 2019, and I don't plan to tell him.

"Just thinking about how Bombardo showed up afterward. So Monroe must've run three blocks in five minutes…"

He drones on, and I let him dig himself a hole. If he's trying to gauge my suspicion level, he's doing a good job. Yet I arrange a smile of detached interest for his benefit. "You're right. I'd rather forget that night, if you don't mind."

His gaze bright, his shoulders relax, and he kisses me. "Okay, I'll drop the subject, Swee." He gets up, then reaches to hoist me up, catching me in a hug. "Where in time should we go next?"

I smile up at him, swallowing my revulsion. "Great question, Swee!" I tell him about my dream traveling to the land of knights and medieval kings. "But I know that's not possible."

"We could visit the 1960s during the flower-child movement. San Francisco."

My snarky smile better be convincing. At last, he leaves, and I slurp coffee in the kitchen. A little spills over the rim as I grip the Antarctic rosenbleeter mug with trembling hands. My racing heart subsides, and my breathing slows. My scheme, bright and clear, invites me to its ambitious path.

Bestie begs for a walk, so I take her out, up and down the familiar, yet no-longer-familiar streets. It's blazing hot and humid. I need to get used to the heat all over again.

Bestie steers me to the corner where the Safeway used to be. I crane my neck at the tall dormitory dominating the block now, and across the street to the building replacing the store where I bought my tablet, which is still hidden in my overnight bag along with my smartphone. When I get home, I need to check them both to see if they're working. If I can finish my story, the trip back in time will have been worth it.

To implement part 1 of my plan, Glim needs to be on his work shift. I holomessage him.

Me: Have a good workday, Swee.

Glim: Shift starts in fifteen.

I stand under a hot shower for the allotted ten minutes while my dormmates are stirring and starting their days. As I towel off, Eartha is walking Heather to the community classroom for school lessons. Moss is still here, so they must've decided not to split up. Until they do. I dress and make my way across the skybridge, sans my dog, to Glim's dorm, then up to the top level and the podlot. Sure, I could ask Glim to borrow Zeph. But he'd disable the time accelerator to make sure I don't run off again. I scan my fingerprints—he hasn't thought to restrict my access yet—and climb into the autopod's front seat.

Either he trusts me implicitly or he's naive regarding human nature. Otherwise, he would've checked my trip history in Fern and disabled my access to Zeph.

Now comes the tricky part—How far back in time must I travel to grab Eartha's Predsomaril before Breezy does? Despite her denial, she must be the one who took it. It was the weekend I went to Bend to visit my parents, which is perfect because I don't want to get distracted by an accidental encounter with my other self. On Zeph's operating panel, I punch in the date of that weekend and time it for Saturday morning in hopes I get to it before Breezy does.

Off I go to last month, but you'd never know I'd gone anywhere. After Zeph stops humming, the only changes are some autopods have shifted slightly in their spots and others have disappeared. I cross to my dorm, pondering whether Eartha is home. She and Heather should be at the kids' gym on the top level where they spend almost every Saturday morning. It would be awkward trying to explain what I'm doing there. I'll sneak in, grab the bottle, and sneak out.

My other self is in Bend right now. I try to wrap my brain around that, but it gives me a headache. Makes me feel like my noggin is flipping upside down. By some magical, impossible miracle, a person can exist in two places at the same time. The phenomenon threatens to undo me.

I reach the bathroom without a hitch. Eartha's medicine cupboard is next to mine, so the security panel recognizes my fingerprints and opens with no protest. As I dig through pill bottles, something dings in my mind, but I'm too focused on my task to explore the déjà vu sensation. Examining each bottle, I find the one I seek and open it to see how much remains. It's half full of tincture, so I pocket it and recross the bridge.

Halfway across, I stop, my spine prickling with a dawning awareness. Eartha's accusation that I took her medication propels itself into my consciousness, and I clutch my chest to still my spiking pulse.

I am the one who took that bottle. Not Breeze.

My head spins. Do I truly inhabit July 2120 at this place and time? Or am I only visiting, and my real self is in Bend? When Eartha accused me, my theft was still in the future, yet in her timeline, it had already happened. So am I in the past or in the present? If she hadn't said anything, would I have still chosen this specific day to steal the medication? My heart thuds. I'm trapped in a time warp. The horror of it grips me. I run to Zeph, hop in, and make my escape back to real time, already plotting the next leg of my plan.

# 38

# Me

**July 2120**

With the precious medication in hand, I have to persuade
Breezy to let me borrow one of her nursing smocks. One
of the few things that hasn't changed in a hundred years:
medical garb. She's in the same spot, squinting at a hologram
only she can see. "Hey, Breeze," I say, and a real breeze wafts
through the window screen, warm and smelling of damp
foliage. If only it were so easy to conjure up other wishes.
Hey, Currency. Hey, Promotion.

Hey, Man of My Dreams. I sigh. I have yet to meet him.

Breeze turns my way. "What?"

"Halloween's coming up, and Glim and I want to dress
up as doctor and nurse. May I pretty please wear one of
your smocks?"

She returns her attention to the invisible screen. "Sure,
help yourself. But you have to bring it back afterward."

"Of course. Thanks, my friend, I owe you one."

She grunts a "you're welcome," and I thumb through

her collection of about ten off-white nursing scrubs, all embroidered with her name on the lapel. I'll blend right in at Paige's hospital bed.

"If you damage it, I expect you to replace it."

I don't dignify that one with a response, just grab a smock and put it on. To add credence to my request, I rummage through my closet and locate a long black wig and fake glasses from a previous Halloween and model them for her. She nods her approval, and I return to Glim's autopod with my floral bag stuffed with cash, tablet, phone, and some jackets I bought in 2019. Zeph is still warm from my previous trip ten minutes ago, and I climb in. I punch in the date and time of March 1, 2020, 10:00 a.m. The day Paige brings her twins into the world.

Within seconds, I'm transported to someone's lawn and relief overwhelms me. I breathe in the sheer pleasure of being back in the twenty-first century. Later, I'll worry about what to do when I have to return to my home year. The empty garage, my previous home, is several houses down. Is that a barking dog I hear?

But no, the dog is across the street behind a fence. Zeph is lodged beneath a tree. If anyone spots me, they'll think I was hiding. The street is six feet from where I stand, so I sprint forward without a backward glance. It's freezing cold, and a layer of white blankets the grass, but this time I'm prepared with extra warm layers. My smartphone lights up—such a lovely sight—and my tablet still works.

Disguised as a brunette, bespectacled nurse, I visit

Safeway for the final touches to my new look. I purchase eye shadow, brow pencil, blusher, and lipstick, and draw myself a new face in the ladies' room, a face nobody, including Paige, will recognize. I toss the makeup in the garbage, then catch a taxi to Emmanuel Medical Center and rush through the front entrance as if I'm late for work. I'm not sure where to go, but I don't dare show it. Wishing I'd taken time to scope it out, I stride down hall after hall until I spot a nurses' station. They better not ask questions.

I slip into a patient room near the nurses' station. If I can access a computer, I can find Paige's room number and obtain her records. The only thing I know for sure is that she is here today. Over my shoulder, a mound's bunched under a sheet, but no other sign of human activity disturbs the room. The patient's chest moves up and down, so the person is alive and sleeping. If only it were Paige, but the face is aged and whiskered.

A few nurses mill around the station, chatting, working on computers, or talking on phones. I wait five minutes, but it is never unoccupied. Okay, so this isn't going to be as easy as I'd hoped. Slipping out of the room, I keep my profile turned away from the nurses and make my way down the hall.

This is a big hospital with hundreds of rooms. How will I find Paige in time? But I can't give up. As I walk up and down the dozens of corridors, scanning the names beside the doors, personnel scurry around, some pushing wheelchairs or gurneys, some studying clipboards, none paying me any attention. I must look like I belong.

Then a young doctor peers at me as he rushes past, stops, and takes in my smock. What's he thinking? "Can I help you find something?"

"My friend is here, but I'm not sure what room."

"The front desk can help you." Then he hurries off. What did he see to make him stop and question me? My smock is a different style from the other nurses. Maybe those who notice will assume I work at another facility and I have reason to be here.

Where is Paige? I don't dare ask anyone.

"...pregnant woman admitted to Emergency..." A speed-walking nurse's telephone voice snaps me to attention, and I swivel, follow her back the way I came, and catch up at the elevator, listening in to her conversation with an unknown listener. "Her husband brought her in a few minutes ago with dangerously elevated BP. I was in the middle of my break when I got summoned.... See ya there." We descend one floor, and she turns as if finally noticing she's not alone. "Going to Emergency?"

I merely nod, not trusting my voice, and tail her through a maze of corridors. She seems oblivious to my presence, but at least, she knows where she's going.

She takes me straight to Emergency, then zips to a figure on a cot, lying beneath a sheet. Paige's husband hovers nearby, and I slide into a chair in the shadows to wait unnoticed yet observe. The nurse I followed takes Paige's vitals and hooks her up to an IV. I stifle a gasp when

I see Paige's face. I barely recognize her puffy features, her frightened eyes pleading without words. Hands groping in my pouch, I ensure the precious tincture is tucked away and await an opportunity to administer it.

The nurse speaks in a soothing tone as she works. "We've got a call into your doctor to see if we need to induce labor or perform an emergency C-section." I don't catch Paige's reply. But the murmurs subside, and the nurse leaves, giving Kyler full access to his wife. Voices from the other alcoves float behind partially closed drapes.

I check right, then left.

Nobody is paying the slightest heed to me.

Taking a deep breath, I screw up my courage. Act like you know what you're doing. But what if the husband questions me? Memories parade through my mind of Paige's "arrow prayers"—quick little requests to the God she believes in. Can't hurt to try it. Because if God does exist, He'll hear me. And if He doesn't exist, which I was taught, then no real harm done. I'll have only myself to rely on, as I've had to do my entire life.

God, if You're really up there, please help me save Paige. Getting to my feet, I inhale a deep whiff of sour hospital-room air, then march to Paige's side.

"Hello, Paige." I elevate my pitch to disguise my voice.

"Katrice?" Paige's gasp startles me. She clutches the pearl-gray sheet, her knuckles white against the drab navy hospital gown. Her eyes give off an alarm, but why is she so scared of me? And how in the world does she know it's me? I glance down through fake black glasses at the strands of fake black hair draping over the front of my smock. The Katrice she knew looks nothing like this. How could she recognize me?

I have only one option. I point to the name on the smock, hoping she doesn't notice my shaking finger. "My name is Breeze. You can call me Nurse Breezy."

The fright in her eyes dials down a notch, and she relaxes into the pillow.

Kyler steps closer. "Your name is really Breeze?"

"My parents were into nature names," I explain with a smile.

"Do you, by chance, have a sister named Windy?"

Paige giggles.

Yes, Ky's a jokester, but how can he crack wise at such a solemn moment? I force a laugh and put on a friendly-nurse smile. "Paige, I'm here to give you your medicine."

She blinks up at me, her smile flickering, her brown eyes nearly disappearing inside pillowy puffs. Green streaks in her hair form a flowerlike effect against the stiff white pillow.

Tears sting my eyes, and I blink them back.

Kyler launches a question. "What's the medicine for?"

I hold up the bottle. "This will help reduce the swelling and lower her BP. It could mean the difference between life or death." Putting as much force as possible into the words, I hold the dropper near her mouth. "Say ah!"

She stares with a question in her eyes.

Kyler leans toward me. "Did Dr. Anthony order that?"

"He did."

Kyler narrows his eyes.

I somehow erred.

"Dr. Anthony is a woman." He steps closer.

Cram it! "Oh, I'm sorry. Of course. I've never met her. I went by the instructions in your wife's records. You see, if we don't get her blood pressure down, she could die." I practically spit the words, and when he backs up a step from the force of my determination, I somehow keep from sighing out my relief. It worked.

"I might die?" Paige opens her eyes wide, and her jaw gapes like a cavern. I squirt four drops onto her tongue. My biggest fear was that she or her husband would object. But she swallows the medicine, her eyes wide and fearful, and my shoulders slump.

"That's a good girl," I say in the tone I've heard Breeze use on her Cloud patients. "I'll come back in a few minutes to check on you."

"What about inducing labor?" Ky has recovered his watchdog persona. "Or the emergency C-section? Is she on her way?"

"I haven't heard anything yet."

He stares me down with his intense green gaze, his red beard jutting out. In his kelly-green University of Oregon hoodie, he gives off a fleeting impression of an overgrown leprechaun. "What was it you gave her again?"

"Predsomaril." Despite my efforts to stand my ground, it's my turn to take an involuntary step back this time at the unexpected role switch. Paige described her husband as a "lovable teddy bear," leaving me unprepared for this husband-the-bodyguard side. "It treats the symptoms of preeclampsia."

Maybe it's my imagination, but has the swelling on her face subsided?

He smirks as though challenging me. "Why don't you go ahead and take her blood pressure again? Let's see if it's going to work."

Can he tell I'm a fake? Feeling wrong-footed, I blurt out, "Her assigned nurse will be monitoring that. I'm the medication nurse." I punctuate my words with a false-confident grin.

"O-kay."

Does he accept my answer?

Soft footsteps shuffle nearby. The other nurse is returning, so I spin and flee. The sound of a curtain swept aside tells me I had a narrow escape.

"How's Mommy?" says the nurse.

Ky's voice stops me in my tracks. "That other nurse gave her some medication I've never heard of."

"What other nurse?"

"Breeze. She told us if she didn't take it she could die."

As I sidle away, I pull my smartphone from my pocket to have a point of focus, heart shuddering at the close call. The voices fade as I put distance between me and them. If any of them is suspicious of me, they could send hospital security to hunt me down—actual people, not robots, which means there's a chance I could outrun them. No need to try outrunning a robot programmed to run twenty miles an hour.

I keep my head down, walking aimlessly until I catch the aroma of cooked food. My stomach growls. I haven't had a meal yet, so I follow the scent to the employee cafeteria on the ground floor and purchase a veggie sandwich, my stomach too unsettled for meat. But I can't sit. My thoughts spin like electrons out of control as I munch my sandwich.

Beyond the window, spindly trees stretch out their winter limbs over a frosty lawn. A handful of other patrons are scattered around the room, their voices undulating. I resist the urge to pace. I don't want anyone noticing me. My agitation must show.

Has the medication worked? Because if it didn't, Kyler will never let me near his wife now. And I don't have the motivation or energy to keep doing this, trying to change an unchangeable past. I can only pound my head against an immovable wall so many times before I give up.

A prickle vibrates my scalp. Any moment now, I could be grabbed and hauled away.

I need to return to Paige's room to know if this is the day she gets a second chance at life. I toss the remaining sandwich in the garbage and leave. When I near her room, again nobody notices me. The nurses are occupied with computer screens or clipboards, hurrying here and there with purpose. I reach ER alcove 2, then hover out of sight.

"One forty-four over ninety-five," the nurse marvels.

"Wow, she might be coming out of the woods."

"The other nurse, Breeze, said the stuff would reduce her blood pressure. She gave it to her in a dropper."

I sense, more than see, the nurse's bewildered headshake. "Do you remember the name of the medication?"

"It was a mouthful."

"Pred-something." Paige's voice croaks. "Not prednisone, but similar."

"She better not have given you prednisone."

"She said Dr. Anthony authorized it."

The nurse mutters something that sounds like "rookies," and I clench my fists. "I don't know of a nurse named Breeze. But I'm pretty new here. Let me go look her up, and then I'll page her." The nurse leaves the alcove, and I slide around the corner out of her sight line. It's time for me to leave before the nurse discovers there's no one employed named Breeze.

I make my escape into the freezing March morning, tip my face to the gloomy sky, and breathe deep, the air scented with twentieth-century fumes, my taut muscles loosening. The medication appeared to work. But what about tomorrow? Dare I go back after her babies are born to check on her?

Besides braving the ER again, I must do one more thing before I return home and face Glim. I hail a taxi and direct the driver to my old hangout. Pepper's.

# 39

# Her

**March 2020**

"Hello, Mommy Mommy." The sunny nurse nearly sang the words as she brought tiny Mason and Emmeline into Paige's room for their first feeding.

Paige, sore from the C-section incision and groggy from drugs, forced a wimpy smile. Mommy. The word would take some getting used to. And juggling two nursing infants, even more so. The nurse helped her balance her babies, one at each breast, but it was awkward. What if she dropped one?

"We're happy how well your body has bounced back from the toxemia," the nurse went on. "The swelling is nearly gone, and your blood pressure is almost normal."

Paige forced out her next words. "Nurse…Breezy…"

"That name is not in our employee database. We don't know who she was, and—"

"Well"—Kyler propped against the foot of the bed, crossing his arms—"whatever she gave Paige worked fast."

"It's odd," said the nurse. "We don't know what medication she gave you. Dr. Anthony didn't authorize it."

Locking onto the nurse's face, Paige strove to make her understand. "She was…a…angel."

The nurse chuckled. "Okay, maybe not a literal one."

"Yes. Angel. Sent by God." Paige grabbed a breath. "Lots of people…praying. God sent a…a…angel."

The nurse smiled the indulgent way adults do with children. "However it happened, your prayers were answered."

Voices nearby, one deep and unfamiliar, the other Doreen's, yanked the nurse's attention away. She closed the privacy curtain, blocking the visitors from Paige's view. "Can you come back in a while?" the nurse said. "It's babies' dinnertime."

Doreen's words carried over the barrier. "I have someone here she and my son are going to want to meet."

Paige gasped, her exposed skin turning cold. With babies filling her arms, she could only gape helplessly at her naked chest. "Ky, can you cover me up please?"

His warm gaze taking in the scene, he lay the sheet lightly over the babies' heads, brushing her chin.

More murmurs. Then Doreen peeked in.

"Oh, Paige. Ky. I brought you a visitor."

"Not now, Mom. She's nursing."

"I'm almost finished," Paige croaked. Both babies' eyes had closed, yet their little mouths still moved. She eased them away, nestling the babies close. "Ky," she whispered.

"Go on out there and talk to your mom. I'll be fine."

Nodding, he tugged the curtain open, and Doreen rushed inside. A handsome gray-haired man smiled in the background, hesitating.

Ky's jaw dropped. "Gary?"

"Surprise!" laughed Doreen.

"Mom, you sneak. Did you arrange this?"

"We both did!" She hauled Gary forward, his face both bemused and apprehensive. "You've been so occupied with your little family, Gary has been unable to reach you. So he contacted me and arranged a visit. He wanted to see his new grandbabies."

Doreen rearranged the sheet to expose the babies' faces but nothing else. Paige, too weary to ask what she was doing, lay back on the pillow with a sigh. Gary smiled down at her and the sleeping babies as Ky beamed beside him. Gary's arm rose and slipped across his long-lost son's shoulders. Paige clung to the picture in her mind as tightly as if she'd snapped a photo. Then Doreen came to the rescue, holding up her phone.

"Okay, everyone. Smile. It's selfie time!"

# 40

# Me

**March 2020**

At Peppers, still in disguise, I find a seat near the window and check out the clientele. It's so great to be back, basking in the aroma of coffee and freshly baked pastries. I hadn't realized how attached I'd gotten to this place. Chaz is behind the counter along with a dreadlocked woman I don't recognize. Tiffy, whom I haven't seen since my first day here, sips her drink at a booth across the way and studies her laptop. I open my own and finish my story, then approach the counter. Chaz looks at me without recognition. "Help you?"

With my tummy protesting the partial hospital lunch, I order another veggie sandwich. "Is there a place nearby where I can print a document?"

Chaz points. "Yeah, try FedEx over on Lombard."

I thank them, clutch my lunch bag. Then, my laptop tucked under my arm, I go in search of the shop. Thirty minutes later, I'm holding a folder with a sheaf of papers inside—my exposé of Bombardo. Next, I take the tincture from my pocket and place it in a shipping envelope along with a note to Paige.

> Hello, Paige. Here is the rest of the Predsomaril. I suggest you take four drops a day to prevent your symptoms from returning and use until empty. God bless you and your little ones.

I think back to the sentiments Eartha received from friends and family after Heather was born. This needs to sound genuine.

> May they bring you many years of joy and happy memories. ~~ Nurse Breezy.

I put her name on the front, then open Google Maps for her address. I saw it across the street from Pleasant Valley Worship Center after Bombardo's funeral.

There it is—a large white farmhouse with black shutters. After Kyler Ferguson passed away at age seventy-five, it reverted to his second wife's side of the family. They've owned it ever since.

I address the tincture shipment and pay for overnight delivery, then put the manuscript in a separate envelope, address it to Paige, and order regular ground shipment. The tincture will arrive tomorrow, and the manuscript anywhere from one to two weeks later.

With my last task complete, I make my way to the alley where I spent five memorable months. Nobody is out on the street today. Nobody but me is foolish enough to brave the cold. But I press on, needing one last glimpse of my Fern before I return Zeph to Glim.

And there she is, forlorn and neglected. Already a layer of dust has collected on her clear round surface. I reach up to touch the fingerprint sensor, missing the sensation of compometal on skin. So it shouldn't be such a surprise when the door opens and Fern speaks.

"Please state your destination."

Laughing, I hop in, and even though Glim claimed he disabled her, I relish the memories of sailing through the sky in my autopod. Absently fingering the operating panel, I jump when Fern hums to life.

"Please state your destination," she asks a second time.

Did Glim lie when he said he disabled her? No. The time accelerator is missing from the panel. Oh, if only I could return home in Fern. But then how would I get Zeph back?

Maybe I can take Fern for one last joyride.

"I don't care where you take me," I tell her, which I hope doesn't confuse her. But she lofts into the sky and hovers, waiting for further instruction.

"Fern, take me on a tour around the city."

"Instructions verified."

We sail north for a bird's-eye view of three magnificent snowcapped peaks. I want to photograph them and solidify their memory before I return to my home year. Because once I return, there's no coming back.

To the east, Mount Adams and Mount Hood dominate the horizon. To the north, Mount Saint Helens crouches like a tamed lion, giving no hint she is going to erupt again in fifty-five years. You'd never know by looking at her that she has the power to cause a massive earthquake, but she does. She'll level nearly half of Portland's older westside buildings, wiping out vast sections of infrastructure. But the majority of the people living here now won't be around then anyway.

Below me, canopies of trees drape over the city like fluffy green area rugs. Neighborhood parks are dotted here and there, interrupting the geography of houses and streets and autos. I snap photos and commit the sights to memory. Because a hundred years from now, the Portland I know is a dull shadow of this nature's showcase. To think I once thought it green!

In the meantime, Paige waits, hovering between life and death. On impulse, I call the hospital and ask if my friend Paige Ferguson has been released.

"One second," the lady says. I hear her breathing and muttering as computer keys click. Then she says, "Looks like she'll be going home tomorrow."

Thank You, God! "How is she doing?"

"Your name, please?"

"Um, Katherine."

"What is your relationship to the patient?"

"Just a friend."

"I'm not authorized to give out any information. I can put you through to her room."

"No thank you." I end the call, then return Fern to her hiding place. What will become of her? In seventy years, maybe even sooner, that garage will be demolished. I have a vision of a robodozer sweeping her up into a heap, never to be seen again.

I can't leave her behind. Is it possible to stow her someplace that won't be disturbed or demolished in a hundred years? A place where I can retrieve her after I return home? When I bought her a few months ago, one of Glim's Zeller relatives was upgrading to a ten-seater model and needed to sell Fern. I asked if he bought it new, and he said the oddest thing. "My son-in-law found it in the woods behind their home. Someone had abandoned it there. But it still runs fine. Here, give it a test run." I didn't think to ask him or Glim where the son-in-law's home was.

But I have a feeling I know.

The woods behind Paige's home. Could this be another situation where time moves in a circle? The same circumstance I experience with Eartha's medication?

Shaking my head to dislodge the knot in my brain, I return to Zeph, still on the neighbor's lawn. Seeing nobody about, I hope it means the residents and the neighbors are all at work. If someone were to spot me, they could call the police, then I'd truly be stuck here. But without incident, I move Glim's autopod to the site where Fern waited so long and climb inside her. She's still warm from the mountain viewing, and I navigate her to Pleasant Valley.

In ten minutes, we're swooping over Paige's new home and the thick woods surrounding it. Since she's still in the hospital, the house will be unoccupied, and there are no spying neighbors nearby. "I'm leaving you here, Fern." I pat my autopod's front panel. "Nobody will bother you for at least ninety-five years, and you'll be safe. Rest in peace."

"Instruction noted." Fern rests under some trees in the acreage behind Paige's new home, in a corner of the back fence that separates the property from the wilderness beyond, far back enough that it's unlikely anyone will happen upon her. I give her one final pat and make my way through the woods, alongside the house, and to the road. I start walking west next to the construction zone for the future home of Pleasant Valley Bible Chapel, then call a cab as cars speed by, leaving fumes in their wake. I sneeze while I wait at the stop sign for the cab.

In thirty minutes, I'm back at the garage and climbing into Zeph, setting the time accelerator for the same moment I left. Glim will never know. And if, when I return to my dorm Fern is missing, I'll know where to find her. And if she's there…

I'll always wonder when and how she came into being.

I'll have proven time can be circular as well as linear.

# 41

# Her

**March 2020**

The doorbell rang. Nudging open the screen door with their snouts, Doreen's dogs bounded into Paige's living room and skidded to a stop on the hardwood floor. Baby Mason's swing barely missed colliding with Siobhan's wet nose, pulling a cute chuckle from him and a soft woof from the dog.

Paige, nursing Emmeline, laughed at the comical canines' expressions of wonder as they danced around sniffing the unfamiliar, miniature human. Siobhan, still attempting to leap at Mason, strained against Kyler's strong grip. Kyler grabbed the other dog's collar while Doreen hobbled inside, gripping her walker.

"Mom, we're gonna put the dogs out back." Kyler practically dragged both setters to the back door, their claws sliding across the polished floor. During Paige and Doreen's convalescence, they'd explored every inch of the back forest but had been banished from visiting since the twins' birth two weeks ago. Kyler feared their presence around the babies since Doreen was still recovering from her fall. He'd relented and let her bring them today with the promise she'd keep them under control.

"You said you were pretty much back to normal." Kyler's tone was almost accusatory. "I wouldn't have let you bring them otherwise."

"I know. That's why I said so," she wheedled. "I had to see my precious grandbabies."

"Well, can you take the dogs to a kennel next time? Please?"

Their voices faded through the back door, and Paige gazed at her daughter's tiny face, her round mouth grasping for nourishment. A feeling unlike anything she'd ever experienced filled her to the brim. Euphoria. That's what this was. She'd fallen madly in love with her babies and stayed on an oxytocin high twenty-four seven.

She'd never dreamed of the joy motherhood would bring.

Not for the first time, she thanked Angel Nurse Breezy for the medication that had most likely saved her life and gave her a chance to be a mother with all the highs and lows she would face in her future. Breezy had even mailed her additional medication with instructions, something Paige hadn't heard of a nurse ever doing. But she wasn't going to question it. Every time she took a dose, she felt better.

Mason, his tummy full, had fallen asleep in his swing, as she knew he would. Grateful God had blessed her with two low-maintenance babies, she breathed a prayer of thanks.

When Emmeline had fallen asleep on her shoulder,

Paige joined her husband and mother-in-law on the back porch, and then Kyler brought out the baby swing holding the sleeping Mason. With both babies out, the three of them settled into the Adirondack chairs watching the dogs gallop into the woods, stop, and sniff everything, and soon disappear into the thick underbrush.

The March sun cast unseasonably warm rays over them as they visited. Doreen's euphoric smile split her face every time she gazed upon her two-week-old grandbabies.

Seconds later, loud, excited barking interrupted their small talk. "Sounds like the dogs found something interesting." Ky stood. "Let me run back there and make sure everything's okay."

"Careful, honey. Could it be a wild animal that somehow got through the fence?"

"Possible." Ky glanced at the garage door. "Maybe I should grab my rifle, just in case." After exiting the garage, gun in hand, he beelined toward the rear fence at the south end of the nearly one-acre property where the dogs' frantic barks punctuated the still air like two out-of-sync drums. Soon, the barks morphed to yelps, and Paige braced herself, waiting to hear a shot. It would wake the twins. But so far, their eyes stayed closed, their breaths even.

"There's got to be an animal back there." Doreen shuddered. "I pray Kyler and the dogs are okay."

"I hope it isn't a bear." Paige snuggled her baby girl tighter against her chest. She needed to get up and look for herself, but she couldn't leave Doreen alone with the babies in her state.

Someone thrashed through the brush, Ky and the dogs probably running from whatever they'd found. Then he emerged, ashen-faced, and alarm bolted through Paige. She rose, clutching Emmeline close. "What did you find?"

"In a minute." He held up a hand as he returned his gun to the garage and Paige dropped back into the chair. When he'd settled himself between her and Doreen, he didn't remove his gaze from the thicket of tall firs. "I think I know why this house went for a song."

"Really?" The lurch of her heart must have sent a signal to Emmeline, who shifted and frowned, the kind of scowl preluding a wail.

But the baby relaxed again with a soft snore.

"Yeah. There's some sort of alien spaceship back there."

Paige blinked at the last thing she expected to hear. "Oh, come on, Ky. That can't be true."

"Oh yeah?" He raked through his hair, dislodging pine needles, then tugged at his beard. "I followed the dogs to that far southwest corner, you know where the fallen tree is, but I didn't see anything. As I got closer, something rammed me in my chest. I felt around, and something solid materialized out of thin air. But it's apparently invisible."

"Ky, that is preposterous. How can that be true?"

"Why don't you go see for yourself? You go ahead. I'll watch the babies."

Dare she? Did she want to discover something that could give her nightmares for years? Did she want to know?

She shook her head. "Maybe another time, babe." She injected a soothing tone into her words. "I'm sure you found something. And I bet there's a reasonable explanation. Right, Doreen?"

"Right." Doreen laid a hand on her son's arm. "If it's invisible, why were the dogs barking at it?"

Ky shrugged. "They picked up the scent of aliens. No wonder the previous owners were anxious to sell. Who'd want to share their property with invisible aliens?"

"Ky, if anybody should share property with invisible aliens"—Doreen chuckled—"it would be you, my Star-Wars-loving son."

Through the pounding of her heart, Paige slid her hand into Doreen's and relaxed at the woman's firm squeeze. She wasn't spooked by the idea. She didn't consider it an act of aliens. "What do you think it is, Doreen?"

Doreen patted Paige's hand with her free one, her face untroubled. "It may be something made out of glass. Or it could be—I saw a video recently about a man in China who makes panels out of see-through material. Transparent aluminum as I recall. So there's a reasonable explanation, nothing alien at all."

"But I felt around it, Mom. The thing is round like a spaceship. But invisible."

She smiled at him as though he were still a small boy. "Someone who used to live here was getting inventive, apparently. As for why they left it here, well, maybe they plan to come back for it someday."

# 42

# Her

**March 2020**

A thick FedEx parcel lay propped against the door when Paige returned from a stressful soda run with the twins. She should've waited for Ky to get home from work. But the craving for Diet Sprite was too strong to overcome, so she put the sleeping twins in their car seats and headed to the nearest convenience store. If she'd known they'd both noisily awaken at the same time while she waited in the long checkout line, she would've stayed home.

The admiring oohs and aahs from the others in line almost made up for it.

Doreen had furnished her and Ky with one of those strollers that converted to car seats, which made Paige's job as baby transportation coordinator a whole lot easier. With the two-liter bottle of soda tucked between the twins, she reached for the FedEx parcel, then wrestled the whole load inside her front door. After setting the fussing twins into their swings, she examined the parcel—about an inch thick, it sported no return address. In the kitchen, she poured herself a glass of Diet Sprite on the rocks, savoring the bubbly sweetness cooling her parched throat.

She zipped open the parcel and pulled out a folder of bound papers, and a gasp erupted. She held a printed copy of Starry Starry Night by Katrice Carpenter. Hardly aware of her movements, she plopped into a chair and laid the bound manuscript on the kitchen table.

She thumbed the pages, hoping Katrice had left a note. Where had she been all this time? At least, she was still alive, likely holed up someplace where she'd finished her story. But why drop all contact? And why send this to her after ignoring her for months?

The manuscript was printed in small font on both sides of the paper, and she skimmed through the first quarter or so, keen to know the reason for so many coincidences—the church. Ky's father's name. The Carpenters. When she got through the section she'd already read, Glim and Tree were preparing to travel back to the twentieth century. A sense of anticipation gripped her. Finally, she'd learn what happened next.

She checked the clock. Hmm, past 4:00 p.m. Almost time for Ky to come home. And the twins were starting to fuss again. A wave of fatigue washed over her. Sighing, she left the story on the table next to the unfinished bottle of soda, wearily stood, and picked up the fussier baby, Mason. Lying on the couch, she nursed him, then Emmeline.

And before she knew it, she'd fallen asleep.

A sharp cry jerked Paige from her dreams, and she lurched upright. Both babies nestled beside her, but Emmeline's feet dangled from the edge. Any slight movement from Paige might have sent her daughter right over. Paige gasped and scooped her to safety, but the baby kept fussing. Her heart thudding over the near accident, Paige felt the baby's bottom. Soaking wet. Still groggy, she tucked Mason into the back of the couch and then carried Emmeline to the changing table and fixed her problem. She yawned, no less exhausted than before the nap. Trying to catch up on sleep during this phase of her life was a losing battle. "I'll sleep when I'm dead," her mother used to say.

Speaking of… The doctor told her she had almost died. Which made her grateful every day for the angel God had sent to save her life. God must've had a reason to keep her around longer. Obviously, her babies needed a mother. But did He have a larger purpose?

Her eyes drooping, she swallowed as her dry throat cried out for a drink of something cool. The Sprite. Where had she left it? Oh yes, the kitchen table. She'd been reading Katrice's manuscript, hoping for answers. Cuddling sweet-smelling Emmeline to her chest, she made her way to the kitchen. Any moment Ky's truck would grumble into the driveway. She kissed her baby's velvet-soft head. Ky'd be home soon, and she should start dinner. Unless he was bringing dinner home. She started to retrace her steps to the living room where she hoped her phone waited. Had he texted her while she slept? Such a deep sleep… She still wasn't fully awake.

But first, a drink. She reached for the soda, her taste buds tingling.

Her weary hand missed the neck of the bottle and knocked it sideways instead. Right on top of the manuscript. Sticky liquid spilled everywhere, and she choked back a scream. Then moaned as the papers soaked up the advancing liquid faster than she could grab a rag with her free hand.

When it was all over, she lay Emmeline down next to her brother and examined the mess. Katrice's story was soaked, its edges stuck together and impossible to separate. Tears threatened, and she let them fall. She'd never know how Katrice's story turned out. She'd never get the answers she sought.

When Kyler walked through the front door, she greeted him sobbing. At the alarm widening his eyes, she sought to reassure him that the babies were fine. "It's just me. I spilled soda and had a big mess to clean up."

He tugged her into his embrace, and she clung there, soaking up his comforting presence as thoroughly as a stack of paper soaks up liquid. But despite his noble intentions, he couldn't fix this.

He couldn't bring back the story.

It was gone forever.

# 43

# Me

**July 2120**

"What are you doing in my autopod?"

Glim is standing a few feet away, glaring at me. I gasp, then scream. My scream curdles my own blood, so it must be churning his.

"S…sorry, Swee," I gabble, launching myself from the seat before he murders me.

"Swee?" The word undulates, disbelief stretching it to three syllables. Glim steps back, an unreadable expression in his eyes, holding his palms out as though I'm the bad guy. "You'd better leave before I call security."

But I sense a different kind of energy in him. He's staring at me with an unnerving intensity, but in a bewildered way, not the scary/angry way I expected. "Call security, Glim?" I blurt. "Really? Why would you do that?"

What is wrong with him? And what's wrong with me, that I'm not running for my life back to my dorm? I should be in a panic right now. But he's putting out a calming vibe that settles my heart and soothes my fright.

His brow furrows, eyes narrow as he surveys me. "How do you know my name? And what were you doing in my pod?"

My heart gives a giant thud. He doesn't know me. It's my turn to step back, and I land on my backside in Zeph's front seat. The control panel beeps, and then I notice.

The time-travel mechanism is missing.

"I said, get out of my pod. Or I'll call security." Somehow, Glim doesn't sound as fierce as he should.

Does he have a clone? Is this his good twin?

From the corner of my eye, I see robots headed our way, and I scramble to my feet. "Cram it, Glim. I'm going."

"I asked you how you know my name."

I don't even know how to answer, so I don't. Instead, I stalk across the skybridge, people and dogs and the crowd below scurrying about their business. But something's off. The sky is a clearer shade of blue today, and no supertrees shade the street. I feel every blazing 120 degrees clear to my bones.

Strange. Other differences in the world from before I left—a few minutes ago in real time—slow my steps. A different energy zaps the air. I glance down at the twenty-first-century garb I'm wearing. Wait. Nobody's wearing jumpsuits. Some are clad in garments of thin, mesh fabric, the easier to stay cool in on hundred-plus-degree days. Others wear hardly-there pieces, exposing mostly skin.

The street is more crowded than when I left five

minutes ago.

Where did all these people come from? Or are they robots?

A subtle hunch worms its way into my head. A hunch that's stunning if it's true.

Have I stumbled upon an alternate universe?

What—or who—will await me at my dorm? Please, please, God, let Eartha and Bestie be there.

Did I just pray like I've been doing it all my life? Like I believe in a Supreme Being?

Dear God, what is happening?

Yep, a genuine prayer.

My dorm looks the same, and I let out a pent-up breath. The moment I walk through the front door, as familiar and comforting as my Fern, Bestie gives me a welcoming lick, and Eartha, stroking Heather's tiny head, pounces on me. "You still stalking that Glim guy?"

"Stalking Glim?" I hear the crazed relief in my voice, the gratitude that Bestie and Eartha, at least, haven't changed. "You have to be kidding. That guy is evil. He's…"

I clamp my jaw shut at her disconcerting gaze. She tilts her head and surveys me as if she's trying to decide if I'm for real or a humanoid, while I'm wondering the same about her.

"I can tell by your face," she says. "You always get that little squint in your eyes, the clench in your jaw. He's gonna think you're weird, you know, if you don't knock it off. You better hope he never finds out you bought a drone from his own company to follow him."

"Worked for you, didn't it?"

She casts another odd look my way. "What are you talking about?"

I wave away her confusion. "Never mind." So, in this strange new world, Glim and I are not dating. Eartha didn't chase Moss. Maybe I should play along, see where this is going. I work to relax my jaw and my stalker eyes. "Anyway, he caught me."

"And…?"

"And, nothing. I made some lame excuse and came back."

"Why did you say he's evil?"

I shrug. "'Cause he's got the biggest and nicest autopod in the whole lot."

Eartha shifts Heather to her other shoulder, adjusting the burp rag. "He's probably already coupled. Or if he's not, I have no doubt you have a lot of competition. I heard his ground-floor apartment is very nice. The perks of being related to the worst president ever."

The smell of Breezy's fresh-brewed coffee wafts our way. I inhale deeply and will Eartha to clarify. As far as I'm aware, Glim is not related to Bombardo.

She pats her baby's tiny back with quick little beats. "If he's anything like his ancestor President Zeller-Blair, then you're asking for trouble."

President Zeller-Blair? I dare not say anything. Eartha will know something strange is happening.

My earpiece pings, indicating a calendar event. Great-grandma Lena's funeral is in one hour. In all the drama of time traveling, I forgot all about it.

I edge toward the door, in a hurry to leave. To see if Fern awaits me in her podspot. Please…

"Where are you off to now?" Eartha asks.

"Heading to Grandma Lena's funeral. My parents will be there too." At least, I hope so. In this odd world I've landed in, I can't be sure of anything. "Haven't seen them for ages."

"Isn't your grandma Lena the one whose twin brother ran for senator against Zeller-Blair and lost?"

I wave my finger over the door opener as I nod, trying to squelch the raw panic building inside at this alien world I've landed in. A world where everything appears almost normal, nearly the same. Yet nothing truly is.

But Eartha doesn't notice my odd state of mind. "Something you and Glim Zeller have in common. You're both from important and distinguished families."

Not that his credentials impress me one iota. In my peripheral, Breeze turns her head our way, not bothering to hide her curiosity. The door swings open, and I head up to the rooftop lot and my autopod.

But Fern isn't in her spot. A different autopod sits there. I connect with it on the Cloud, which tells me to call him Otto.

Otto? As in Ottopod? What was I thinking in my alternate life?

"Otto, my man," I tell him in twenty-first-century

lingo as I climb in, "take me to Universal Worship Center."

"You got it," comes the monotonic reply.

As Otto hurtles toward the eastern mountains beyond, I gaze down at the barren, desolate landscape, the trees and grass having long ago dried to a crisp from the warming earth. In 2019, Portland was an eye-popping green. Today, it sports varying shades of browns and grays, but no supertrees. I search the Cloud for the reason. According to the historical record, it used to rain a lot here, decades ago. But the desert to our south crept north little by little, engulfing our landscape before my birth. Now it rains maybe once a month, if that. So many people have fled the Pacific Northwest for Alaska, the only place left in the United States with a temperate climate.

Not that different from the history I learned and knew. But there's no mention of supertrees, and, in this rendition of reality, no waving giant evergreens in sight. No wonder the earth is baking. In Tree 1's life, Bombardo hatched the idea. But in Tree 2's universe, nobody did.

"Tree?" An unfamiliar deep voice fills the compartment, and I jump. Oh, it's Otto talking to me. "You're quiet today."

"Uh," I stammer, awkward. "Just have a lot on my mind." He must be used to the chattier Tree 1.

A hologram of an older gentleman materializes in front of me. "Tree, are you on your way?"

A startled gasp flies out my mouth. "Who are you?"

The man's entire face frowns, and then I recognize him. Grandpop Alby, alive, well, and forty years older than his presuicide internet photos. My heart does another giant leap as if it threatens to fail me before this day ends.

He makes a knocking gesture. "Are you having technical difficulties?"

"Yeah, for a second there." I inhale a steadying breath. "I'm on my way to the funeral. I assume that's what you're referring to."

Maybe this is a dream. I pinch my arm and wince at the pain.

This is real.

Now Grandpop Alby peers at me through cyberspace, searching his image of my face. "I told you your mom was saving you a seat. Got your speech ready?"

What speech? "I'll be there in five minutes. See you." I swipe his image away with trembling fingers. I'd better have prepared a speech in my other life. Now, I just need to locate it in the next five minutes.

If only I could awaken from this nightmare. This surreal world where long-dead relatives live and breathe and talk to me as if I've known them all my life.

But I'm never going to, am I?

# 44

# Me

**July 2120**

The only vaguely familiar face I see when I arrive at Universal Worship Center is Grandpop Alby, leaning on a cane. My brain is aflame. Saving Paige's life had such far-reaching effects, and now nothing I know to be reality is true anymore. I don't know who the good guys are. I have no clue who to avoid.

Is Glim one of the good ones now? Is Grandpop no longer a murderer?

As I push my way through the crowd, I'm struck by the lack of security robots, unlike Bombardo's funeral. Grandpop beckons me over and points to the vast interior. "Your mom and dad just got here."

I long to see my parents' familiar faces, to receive their grounding hugs. To feel like me again.

I pat his shoulder. Feels appropriate. "I hope you don't mind if I pass on the speech. I've had a crazy week."

"Not a problem. Feel free to lean on Grandpop's old

311

shoulder if you need to."

"Let's catch up later, okay?" I say over the hum of voices, pausing to pray before I head toward the main entrance to find my parents. I loosen my clenched jaw and infuse my prayer with a fervent intensity. Please, God, let them be the same parents I know and love.

And what's up with this praying business that comes so naturally now? I thought I didn't believe in God.

Yet, I do. And I have a favorable opinion of Him. Deep down, I know He is a trustworthy and merciful God. But how did I come to that knowledge?

This must be how people with amnesia feel.

A second familiar person rushes inside, panting as though he's just managed to catch the autobus at the last minute.

Glim!

I freeze, then step backward onto Grandpop's foot. What is Glim doing here?

Behind him trails Helix, but something's different about him, something I can't discern.

Glim catches my eye, and his startled expression almost makes me laugh. I would laugh if I weren't so confounded— no, panicked. My mouth goes dry as he moves toward me, and my heart sets to pounding so hard my limbs break out in trembles. He narrows his eyes at me and speaks my thoughts aloud. "What are you doing here?"

I clear my throat, but my voice croaks anyway. "Uh, attending my great-grandma's funeral." I tip my head. "I-I could ask you the same thing." Great. Now I'm the one stuttering?

He glances inside, then turns a glare on me. "Emmeline Carpenter was the daughter of President Zeller-Blair's best friend. I'm here to pay my respects."

I sense movement behind me, and Grandpop steps forward, holding out his hand. "You two must be the Zeller brothers."

I do a double take. I'm starting to acclimate to Tree 2's life being full of surprises.

Glim's face transforms with a smile, they introduce themselves, and I'm invisible. Yet, Glim's words get me thinking about my friend Paige, who lived a long, full life after all, even forming a close friendship with a former president.

I need my mom. Swiveling away from Glim and Helix, I make my way down a side aisle. And there she is, sitting five rows back, looking the way I know her. With tears threatening, I jostle people's knees to get to her and give her a long, tight hug. "Mom." My voice on her shoulder is muffled. "I'm so glad to see you."

"Good to see you too, Tree."

Smiling into my face, she releases me, and I hug my dad next, who says, "I didn't think you'd be this broken up over Grandma Lena's death."

"It's just... I feel so forch to see you two. You wouldn't believe how crazy life is all of a sudden."

A furrow pops out on Mom's brow, and she frowns.

"Good crazy or bad crazy?"

I shrug and chuckle. "A little of both."

People are still filing in. We have about five minutes until start time. Mom lays her soft hand on mine. "Anything you need to talk about?"

I settle back in the chair. "Maybe someday." I can't tell them of my recent adventures. They'd send me for a mental health evaluation.

From Mom's searching gaze, she's hoping I'll open up. Instead, I ask her, "Did you know Grandma Paige well?"

"Grandma Paige?" Mom tilts her head. "Do you mean Lena?"

I white-knuckle the edge of the chair, bracing myself. "No, Paige. Lena's mother. How well did you know her?"

"Not that well. She spent the last twelve or so years of her life in a care facility."

Ah, poor Paige. "How old was she when she died?"

"It was about fifteen years ago, don't you remember? She was a hundred and ten. I've always been grateful to her for suggesting the name Katrice for you."

"She picked my name?" Had I known that in my other life?

"I told you the story many years ago, but you must have forgotten. She once had a friend named Katrice," my mom explains, "whom she liked a lot, but lost touch with, and she always wondered what happened to her. You're named in her honor."

"Wow." My brain is unraveling, overdosing on shock.

"You were the only girl born in the family for three generations," my mom goes on in her flowery-sweet voice, "and she'd been waiting for decades for a girl she could name Katrice." She patted my shoulder.

"What kind of career did she have?"

Mom gives me a bewildered glance. "Why the sudden interest in Grandma Paige?"

"I have my reasons. Humor me. Please?"

"Well, you must remember her and her husband's invention. Back when everyone had smartphones with apps. You may not know it was so successful that graduation rates increased seventy-five percent in her district. She was nominated Educator of the Year, which later led to her selection as Oregon's Director of Education. She spent her career there until the day she retired."

"Wow, really?"

Mom puts her palm on my forehead, the way she did when I was a child with a fever. "You don't remember these details?"

I shrug. "Vaguely."

"Since we're on the subject, I'll share one more quick story about Paige before we start. Before she passed away, your dad and I grabbed one last chance to see her. Remember how she clutched your hand and called you Breezy and told you that you saved her life? She'd had a stroke and wasn't in her right mind, which explains it."

"I vaguely recall." Pretending this is merely a sweet story, I smile and order my voice to stop trembling. "Who was Breezy?"

"Breezy was a nurse who administered lifesaving medication when Paige lay deathly ill during childbirth. The weird part came when the hospital couldn't figure out who Breezy was. She wasn't an employee. And she never showed up again. According to Grandma Lena, Paige was convinced Breezy was an angel sent from God."

I force a chuckle. "I'm glad, then, she chose the name Katrice instead of Breezy."

"Isn't that the name of one of your dormmates?"

"It is. So it would've been confusing if we had the same name."

"By the way, before I forget, Lena willed an autopod to you. She said it goes by Fern, and she found it hidden in the back of her property."

I take in a shaky breath. "Where'd it come from?"

"She'd heard a fanciful story from her parents about it being an alien spaceship. But they never knew for sure how it ended up on their property."

So Paige did find Fern. Paige's conclusion made sense, considering the era when she lived. But I had hoped she'd figure it out after reading my story.

"She'd like you to have it," Mom goes on. "Being the only girl in the ancestral lineage has its perks, doesn't it?"

Did she want me to have it because her mother had told her my story? Had Paige known who I was when she named me?

The room swims as Grandpop heads for the stage,

followed by Glim and Helix, who find seats further along the row from me. I pray I don't pass out from shock.

The room is full now, so many here to pay tribute to a relative I barely knew. Yet for a moment in time, her mother was one of my best friends.

Further along the row, Glim shifts, wafting a woodsy scent my way. He rests ankle on knee, staring at the platform dotted with images and memorabilia, unaware of my presence. My skin prickles as his appealing scent tickles my nose, and I force my attention away, remembering the strong attraction he held for me.

But now my stomach churns at the knowledge of who he is, what he's gotten away with. And it would do no good to have him arrested for a 120-year-old murder. I'd be laughed out of the room.

I squeeze my knees as wave after wave of frustration washes over me. Then the proceedings begin, and I get caught up in the stories of my great-grandmother's life. Before I know it, Grandpop Alby, whom Tree 1 never knew, takes the stage and soon has us all in stitches. Although he's a stranger, I feel as though I've known him for years.

He could've been a stand-up comedian, that Albert Carpenter.

But then he grows serious, looking straight at me.

"My mother Emmeline Carpenter was a wonderful person," Grandpop says. "Most of you know how close she and her twin brother, my uncle Mason, were and how they were instrumental in getting the drug culture on East

Burnside cleaned up. The two of them even got arrested years ago for proselytizing." He glances our way, toward a small man sitting in front of me, next to a lady with a gray Afro, both somehow familiar.

"We have some folks here whom Emmeline befriended all those years ago, and they want to share a few words with you today." Grandpop gestures at the row in front of me. "We'll start with Lakota Jensen."

I gasp when the lady with the Afro stands, her body bent with age, and shuffles forward, fumbling with the sound holosettings. In quavering tones, she launches into a story of how Grandma Emmeline helped her get off drugs and saved her life in the process. "She had a strong faith in God," she says, wiping her eyes with a fabritishue Grandpop hands her, "and gave credit to her mother's prayers."

Next, the short man gets to his feet and makes his way to Grandpa's side. He stands no taller than an eight-year-old child, but his deep voice seems unexpected from someone of such stature.

It's Monroe, alive and breathing, here to tell a similar story of how Mason and Emmeline invested time and resources to rescue him from a life of addiction. Yet, the last time I saw him, he was running from the scene of his own crime.

Grandpop's voice booms through the vast room. "Emmeline Carpenter was reconciled to God. I can see her walking those streets of gold she so looked forward to seeing someday. Her someday has arrived." He tugs on his shiny black bow tie. "And she would love for all of you to join her when your time comes." Even though his gaze darts here and there around the room, it always returns to me. The prickles return, but not from Glim's proximity this time.

"Are you ready to die?" Grandpop goes on, his eyes boring a hole in me. I try to look away, but it's like someone tied an invisible rope between us. "Emmeline was ready to die. By God's grace, she lived a long, full life."

All because her mother survived. A roaring in my head blocks out his next words.

But he catches my attention with a reference to a recent news feature. "A young man and his family recently lost their lives when his autopod crashed. I'm sure you all remember the tragic story. Do you think he woke up that morning thinking, 'This is going to be the day my family and I die?' Not likely. We don't know when our time is up. I am here to encourage each of you to believe there's a God we're accountable to and to put your trust in His Son, Jesus Christ, who made a way for us to be reconciled to God."

"Amen," Mom whispers beside me while I nod. Grandpop is inviting people forward who are ready to give their lives to Christ, who are ready to have their sins removed "as far as the east is from the west."

Glim lurches upward and grabs his brother's arm, who stumbles toward the altar. And now I see why Helix looks different from the images I remember from my Tree 1 life.

No longer an eager elf, his intelligent eyes and observant smile tell a different story. Either he's extremely unphotogenic, or he's matured into an appealing young man. He's almost as handsome as Glim. Yet Glim's charm doesn't reach my heart anymore.

How did altering Paige's future alter the Zeller brothers' destinies as well? I get that only God has the right to mess with destiny. Only He has the authority to redeem people's pasts. Despite technological advances, we're limited by His sovereignty. We can't play God.

What have I done? So far, the changes I've seen are either positive or neutral. But what if...

When the service ends, people are filing out, and I'm still frozen, unable to believe the things I've learned. Finally, my parents and I stand and make our way to the front. Grandpop hugs us, and I peek at Helix. He smiles at me, his eyes gleaming with something close to joy. Nice smile. As we stare, something else flickers in his eyes. Something a lot like interest.

What a strange world. Helix, Glim's "evil twin," is actually his good twin.

"Glim," Grandpop calls over the din of voices, "be sure to get your brother plugged into your church, okay?"

Glim nods at his brother, who turns his attention from me. "Bro, you'll love our church." Glim's voice drops, and I step closer. "We're registered as a book club, and so far, the proprietor hasn't caught on that the book we talk about is the Bible. We meet in my dorm's schoolroom...about twenty-five of us."

I can't keep from blurting, "Why would Gertrud care?"

Glim spins my way. "Who?"

I gulp. "I mean, your proprietor? Why would she care?"

His eyes narrow at me, and his jaw tautens, showing me in a most unmistakable way what he thinks of me. "Our proprietor is a man who hates all religion, and he heads up the ROC movement for Oregon."

"The what?"

"You know, the ROC. Repurpose Our Churches. He and his gang want to turn all church buildings into rehabilitation facilities and the like."

"Really?"

Helix eyes me, but I resist the temptation to shift my gaze.

"Really. Their slogan is 'Rehab over Religion.' So the last thing we want is to tell him what we're really doing." Glim turns away, not interested in further interaction with me. Still wrapping my brain around the idea of a churchgoing Glim, I file the info away. He pats his twin on the shoulder. "When we get back, I'll introduce you to some other believers."

With a wave to Grandpop, Glim leaves. Helix gives me a wave, even though we didn't speak a word to each other. I toss him an uncertain smile and wave back. Grandpop winks. Really? Is my interest in Helix so obvious?

Grandpop tells me he has something for me in his autopod. I follow him to the podlot where he pulls a ragged Bible—probably more than fifty years old—from a tall stack in the back of his pod. "Here's the old Bible I told you about. Since they aren't made anymore, I keep a stash on hand to give to people."

Holding a physical book again feels good. I enjoy the sensation of thumbing its brittle pages, then hug the Bible to my chest. Somehow, I'm aware that my access to the Bible all these years has been on the Cloud. A question whose answer I don't know looms—Is this a world where religion has been outlawed? "What if someone sees it?"

From his funny look, I asked the wrong question. "Tell them it's an old classic book your grandpop gave you. You could also see it as a great opportunity to tell them about the Lord."

"Would I be penalty-fined?" I hold my breath, awaiting his reaction.

The crease between his eyes deepens. "Penalty-fined? I'm not sure why you think you would be. But even if you were, Jesus said we are blessed if we are persecuted for His sake."

Good. I shrug, then open it. It smells ancient. I find my favorite verse, I Peter 5:7: "Casting all your care upon him; for he careth for you."

How did this come to be my favorite verse?

Right. Paige referred to it once or twice after she'd vented over a stressful teaching day. "Listen to me fretting," she'd say with a light chuckle. "I need to cast these cares, these wayward students, on my heavenly Father. They're in the Lord's hands." Could it be her powerful faith in God's loving care passed down through the generations and landed on me?

Nope. I can't say I thought he lived in Medford.

"You thought I what?"

"I thought you looked a lot like your brother."

Still grinning, he falls into step beside me. Unforced, natural. He's holding something in his other hand.

"What's that?"

His grin falters. "Oh, this?" He holds it up as if he doesn't recognize it. "Just a drone." His gaze finds his shuffling feet. The planes of his face stretch over angular cheekbones.

The last time I used a drone… Could it be for the same purpose? Could Helix be tracking someone?

Like me?

It could explain his sudden appearance. And his evasiveness. The thought doesn't creep me out. I'm flattered. Assuming it's true.

We pass beneath the waving branches of a massive Douglas fir. "What's the drone for?" I venture.

He studies a high branch, its needles the same deep green as the bridge above us. "I use drones for all kinds of things. But mainly to test my latest invention."

I stop, hands on hips. "Okay, you piqued my curiosity. You have to tell me about your invention."

He stops, his eyes lit like Glim's when he talks about his projects. "You can't tell anyone."

"I won't." Who would I tell?

"My brother is the only person who knows."

The truth hits me at the same time he says, "A

325

time machine."

I can't speak. My tongue is dry. Then I manage to gulp out, "That's awesome." I swallow hard. "I had a dream about traveling through time." Not untrue. Plus, a dreamlike quality still hovers over me. He'd never believe it's reality.

We continue along the path, side by side. "Will you tell me about your dream? And I'll tell you about my machine."

"You wouldn't believe the things I experienced."

"Sure I would," he says, giving the leash a light tug. "It's a dream. Anything's possible."

# THE END

# ACKNOWLEDGEMENTS

A big thank you to the brilliant editing prowess of Deirdre Lockhart, Brilliant Cut Editing. You made this story snap, crackle and pop!

If not for my pal Al M., I wouldn't have become aware of the serious truancy problems in some local schools. Children are our future, as they say, and if they aren't in school, where are they? How are their minds developing? I channeled all my concern into this story, with help from a couple of local teachers, Teresa and Tina, who let me pick their brains about some of the challenges teachers face these days. Kudos to all the teachers who deal with the same daily conflicts as Paige does, yet still persevere!

A shout out to beta readers Jennifer Lindsay and Shirley Schwartz, who honestly pointed out problems in the first and second drafts and offered helpful suggestions. It wouldn't be the same story without the two of you. And to my critique partners and fellow authors, the Awesome Critters team of Donna Hues, Shirley Schwartz, Gwendolyn Harmon, and Connie Edwards—you all are truly awesome critters!

D. K. Till

# ABOUT THE AUTHOR

*Welcome to the world of D. K. Till, where The Future and The Present collide.*

D.K. Till writes Split-Time Fiction with A Twist, a blend of the dual timeline fiction she enjoys mixed with a big helping of the sci-fi she loved as a child. The indie author from the land of microbrews and coffee snobs fell in love with reading in kindergarten when her older sister taught her to read. She used to impress her parents' friends by reading aloud the entire short story The One Hundred Hats of Bartholomew Cubbins. In first grade, she knew she wanted to write stories, too. Throughout her childhood and teens, she either had her nose in a book or was attempting to write one.

But life got in the way, marriage and children set her dreams aside for higher purposes. Today, with children grown and retirement pending, she's reopened that dream package and is now living the life she had only imagined.

The author is a huge fan of the Back to the Future trilogy, inspiring her to write time travel, too. Thus the Time Passengers series was born. A classic rock lover, she plans to name her titles after hit rock songs of the 70s. After the release of Starry Starry Night, be on the lookout for books #2 and #3, Midnight Rider and Nights in White Satin.

from You? Or did You simply allow me to mess with Your divine plan?"

So many Bible verses speak of the sovereign hand of God. The fact I know this still makes me shake my head. Job from the Bible must have felt this way. "Things too wonderful for me," he says in Job 42:3, "which I knew not." Like Job, I have to come to terms with concepts too big for my puny human brain to grasp. I may never understand how God can use any and all human intentions to fulfill His grand plan.

Bestie lunges at a russet dog, which yips back like a tiny child standing up to a bully. I pull her along away from the Chihuahua.

Someone clears his throat. "Hey," says a male voice.

I look over into the face of Helix.

He's holding the other end of the leash, grinning as if glad to see me. "Weren't you at the funeral today?"

"Y-yes," I stammer, too startled to do anything else. "Um, is this your dog?" I indicate the little creature sharing sniffs with Bestie, both dogs circling each other as if deciding whether to play nice and be friends.

"No, it belongs to one of my brothers' dormmates. She was restless, and so was I. So I did the logical thing. Got us both outside for a walk."

"Are you staying with your brother?"

His quizzical expression warns me I'm not supposed to know he's not from here. "For a little while."

Needing to save face, I blurt, "'Cuz I thought you—"

One ordinary woman's life reached so far into the future. I'm a different person because she lived. And so are many others. Children can read and religious freedom remains a national value.

Yet we still live in dormitories instead of houses, and certain elements still exist who desire to stamp out religious expression.

Anxious to get home and have a long conversation with God about all these earth-shattering discoveries, I tell Grandpa goodbye. But I'm also eager to finagle a way to see Helix again. Or was I imagining the undercurrent between us? I hop in Otto. "Take me home." How soon will I get Fern back? Will Otto be offended when he's replaced?

"Home we go," Otto intones.

In a way, I miss the previous century when machines didn't come with feelings. It made for a simpler, albeit more predictable, life. On the other hand, life was more precarious then. People were far more likely to become injured or die from car accidents than we are now from autopod malfunctions.

In a pensive mood, I grab Bestie's leash. I take her for a walk, heading to Cathedral Park and St. Johns Bridge. I kick at dirt mounds the moles generated yesterday as the lofty undergirding of Portland's most imaged bridge hangs four hundred feet above us. "God, I can't wrap my brain around this alternate universe."

He hears me, a vast chasm between Tree 2 and Tree 1. "But what does it mean? Was this alteration of my world

* 9 7 8 1 7 3 7 0 6 1 8 2 3 *